Divine Poison

AB Morgan

To Heather

Don't try this at home!

Ai Morg

✝

First published in 2017 by Bloodhound Books

www.bloodhoundbooks.com

Print ISBN 978-1-912175-86-4

Also By AB Morgan
A Justifiable Madness

Praise For AB Morgan

"I finished this book very quickly as it's an interesting and engrossing read. An excellent debut from Alison Morgan."
Mark Tilbury - Author

"This is the debut novel of Alison Morgan and I thoroughly enjoyed it. It is a psychological thriller mixed in with some real events and gives a refreshing read from an unusual place..."
Susan Hampson - Books From Dusk Till Dawn

"A fantastic read with brilliant characters."
Susan Angela Wallace - Goodreads Reviewer

"You want to know what happens and the way that this is written is superb at hooking you in and holding your attention."
Kate Noble - The Quiet Knitter

"This is a great book that will keep you gripped throughout."
Julie Lacey - Goodreads Reviewer

"This story will make you wander who is the madman and what goes on within the system...A dark little twister of a read..."
Livia Sbarbaro - Goodreads Reviewer

"This is a really well written and unique storyline."
Philomena Callan - Cheekypee Reads And Reviews

For all my hard-working friends and colleagues in the world of mental health services. Please forgive the liberties taken in the telling of this story.

Divine Poison

Chapter One

I opened the shiny, brass flap of the letterbox as far as I could from the outside before I pushed my face right up close to peer inside the front hallway. Lying on the hall carpet was a scattered pile of letters and advertising flyers, illuminated by the early autumn sun as it shone through the frosted glass panes of the front door; I sniffed.

My heart, which had been playing regular pounding drumbeats, skipped one or two as I recognised the smell of death. Not overwhelming but it was there, a sickly pungent odour. There's no other smell quite like it and stubbornly it inhabits your nose and throat for hours.

Sparkey, the cat, appeared from around the corner and rushed up to greet me with some dramatically effective purring and leg-rubbing to gain my attention, and a brief fuss.

'Bollocks,' I muttered as I stepped back in response to the clue afforded me by the letterbox.

Having rummaged around in a haphazard manner, tutting and sighing, I eventually located my mobile phone in the depths of my handbag. I contacted Kelly, our team administrator at the Lensham Community Mental Health Team – LCMHT – where I had worked for the past eight years.

'Kelly, it's me, Monica.'

'I know it's you, silly, I recognise that voice. You only left an hour ago. Got car problems?' she asked brightly.

'Nope. That would be a preferable option right now. Kelly, I went to the ward but Jan Collins hadn't made it in time for her hospital discharge meeting today. It's most unlike her. I don't suppose she's phoned this morning?'

Something wasn't right.

I had been on holiday for a week. A one-week break from the NHS treadmill, during which I stayed at home merrily tinkering in the garden and tidying the house. There's nothing better to free the soul, than de-cluttering a wardrobe full of clothes, some which would never fit again, or were rash purchases in the first place. I'd like to think I'm a bright woman, so why is it I continue to delude myself that I can fit into clothes two sizes too small or will still be able to get away with wearing a halter-neck dress? With shoulders like a Russian shot-putter, it's not an attractive look on me, and I haven't been a size twelve for years. As a result of my efforts, I managed to fill several large bags of clothing for the charity shop.

Before I left the team at work to cope without me, I allocated my caseload to the other members of the team. The only slight concern I had, as I left for the week, was for Jan Collins.

Jan was recovering in hospital from a serious manic episode that had occurred in unfortunate circumstances, resulting in us having to liaise with French health authorities to transfer her back to the UK. Numerous eyebrows were raised in the genteel streets of the small town where *les gendarmes* had eventually detained her, naked and confused.

Since her divorce, Jan had been looking for love again, and the man she had found recently turned out to be a 'Class A' con artist. According to the rumours, in the short time they were both in France on a romantic holiday for two, he persuaded her to buy a small property in Perpignan. God knows how an intelligent woman like Jan fell for that. Whatever the reason, before she made a uninhibited public appearance in a manic state, she went on a spending spree. And as soon as she ended up in a French mental hospital, the conman abandoned her. Monsieur Le Bastard.

Back in England, there was enormous pressure on psychiatric hospital beds. As soon as a patient was sent on home leave, another patient in dire need of mental health services would fill their place. Like musical beds but without the music.

On the Friday before my holiday I took a phone call from Pargiter Ward. 'What do you mean you're sending Jan home for a week's leave? Who decided that?' I was stunned.

'She's doing a lot better now, so Dr Siddiqui offered her the chance to go home and come back a week on Monday for a discharge meeting,' the staff nurse proudly announced.

I began to drum the desk with my fingers. 'But I'm on holiday next week. It's a bloody Friday afternoon and you have left me three hours to organise someone else to carry out a home visit to see Jan. Community staff don't grow on trees, you know.' I stopped short of using my favourite swear word. 'We'll phone you back to confirm arrangements. You can tell Adnan from me that I'm not impressed with his idea of discharge planning.'

Fortunately our new support worker, Steph, who had worked on the wards for a few years, already knew Jan and she offered to visit her on the Wednesday I was off. Jan readily agreed, and a time was arranged between them. It wasn't ideal but it was better than nothing.

My first appointment, on the Monday of my return to the chaos of community mental health nursing, was to attend the discharge meeting on Pargiter Ward for Jan. She was due to be seen at ten o'clock and I had planned to meet her at the ward at nine-thirty to catch up before we went into the meeting together. An attempt at a risk assessment was what I had envisaged, but there was no sign of her. Her home phone rang unanswered when I called.

It was most unlike her not to show up. Strangely, she had not been at home when Steph called to visit her as planned on the Wednesday and she hadn't responded to phone calls, or notes put through her door. Neither had she phoned the office to cancel or rearrange.

Whilst I was on the ward, I discussed the dilemma with the consultant, Dr Adnan Siddiqui, who I had known professionally for over ten years. An uneasy feeling was gnawing at me. Adnan was a good man but, buckling under the pressure for beds, he had taken to making hasty decisions at times. Frustratingly, he didn't want to know when I tried to express my niggling uncertainties about Jan. Blind eye, deaf ear, what you don't know can't hurt you. That sort of flavour.

'Monica, I'm sure you can find her at her home. You assess the situation, and we can discharge Mrs Collins in her absence, if all has gone well. She's back on injections, so you can take over with no real problem. Phone me if you have any specific concerns, but for now we'll take her off our books.'

'That was a bit contradictory, Adnan, are we discharging her in her absence? Or will you wait for me to let you know all is well?'

'Yes.'

'Yes, what?' I asked in exasperation. This was not a difficult question. Adnan was getting like the other consultants; dictatorial and inconsistent when under stress.

'Yes, we will discharge her today *in absentia*,' he confirmed. As if saying it in Latin made it more formal.

'Right, I'll see if I can track her down, then,' and I marched away, in a bit of a huff.

Chapter Two

Twenty minutes later there I was, standing outside Jan's house, sniffing a letterbox, with a cat rubbing up my legs. Her car was parked on the driveway but the windows to the house were shut, lounge curtains closed. I thought it prudent to phone Kelly again at the office, to let her know I was going snooping around at the back of Jan's house, and that I might have to call the police. I asked her to make Eddie, the team manager, aware.

'Houston, we have a problem …' I confirmed a few minutes later, and when I explained the dilemma, she put me straight through to Eddie.

*

Jan lived on a well-manicured estate, in a semi-detached, executive home. I had assumed that her divorce settlement, several years previously, was providing the money to keep her in relative luxury. A sufficient level of trust was needed before Jan would eventually share with me that she'd once been a woman of independent means, thanks to a successful career in journalism. 'What do you write about?' I'd asked out of interest.

'I'm a historian, a theological historian to be more specific. I'm not so much in demand these days, but I still write the occasional article or paper.' I recall nodding but not admitting my ignorance, and hazarding a guess at what being a theological historian actually entailed. Knowing about her past career did at least help to explain the vast library of books taking up much of the wall space in her airy, thoughtfully furnished home. My conclusion was that Jan's husband and her lucrative career had departed hand in hand, as a direct result of her unmanaged mental health difficulties.

*

The side gate to the right of the house was secured from the inside but it took no effort to slide back the bolt and make my way into her back garden. Jan and I were both tall ladies, and she had shown me how easy it was to reach over the top of the head-high gate and to unbolt it from there. 'I think it's an ingenious idea,' she'd said, with a gleam in her eye. 'I'm hoping to confound the burglars who are, in the main, short and scrawny individuals. They won't stand a chance of reaching a bolt this high up.' Her assumption may have explained why she was romantically drawn to tall, intellectual men, most of whom were uninteresting or unreliable, especially the most recent boyfriend, Liam-the-conman.

With Sparkey the cat in tow at the rear of the house, I walked to the far end, and peered through ancient patio doors, a gap in the curtains, and into the kitchen. Sparkey hopped neatly through the kitchen door cat flap a few feet further along.

'Oh God, Jan, what have you done …?'

There, on the kitchen table, were packets and packets of tablets, scattered as they had been left. A glass with an inch or so of clear liquid in it stood abandoned. I assumed the glass tumbler contained water, but it could easily have been gin or vodka.

Startled when the wind caught the gate, slamming it shut, I jumped, and as I turned to see where the noise had come from, I thought I saw a man's leg from the knee down to a plain black shoe. Someone was walking out of the gate. Whoever it was had seen me and turned to leave straight away. I shouted.

'Hello. Can I help you? Hello.' Walking swiftly, I stepped through the back gate into the front driveway but there was no one there. 'I must be seeing things,' I said, reassuring myself by talking out loud.

Trembling slightly, I contacted the police, who promised to respond urgently. *I expect they want an excuse to practice their forensic skills,* I thought.

Fair play to Eddie, my manager; with years of experience and unflappable in any given situation, he had left the office to join me at Jan's house as soon as I confirmed my worst fears to him. He arrived well before our local constabulary.

'Eddie, thanks for the support. So glad you're here. Want a quick whiff at the letter box?'

Of course he did. He nodded, confirming my hypothesis.

'Great first day back, eh, Monica? This one will be messy because of the bastard boyfriend, so I suspect it will be 'Coroner's Court here we come again'.'

I enjoyed working with Eddie: no nonsense, no false sentimentality, straight to the point.

'Nice house she's got here,' Eddie said, looking at Jan's home in admiration. 'She wasn't short of a penny, that's for sure.'

'This isn't right, Eddie. Jan wouldn't kill herself. I know her and she's not the type. I mean it. She was so happy before she went to France, but even after all that happened to her, she was determined to pick up her writing again. She said so when I saw her on the ward.' I explained to Eddie that I thought I'd seen a man follow me to the back of the house.

'What do you think?' he asked. 'Liam-the-conman?'

I shrugged.

The police arrived. A sergeant, who was very pragmatic and wonderfully masterful, took charge immediately. With him was a young, fresh-faced police officer who, although nervous, was polite and attentive. He hung on every word the sergeant was saying to Eddie and me. Details were taken later, but first the two policemen searched the house, and following the smell, found Jan upstairs in her bed. Dead.

'She's not in a good state,' the young officer reported. His face had a ghastly grey pallor to it and he looked perilously close to throwing up.

'She is dead, I take it?' I asked, somewhat confused by the declaration.

'Oh, yes.'

'Well, no one is in a good state when they're dead, young man, take my word for it.' Eddie was keen to educate the officer, who did not seem to appreciate the humour. He focussed on maintaining a professional demeanour and not embarrassing himself by losing his stomach contents.

Sergeant Masterful – I can't recall his real name – came to the rescue of his junior colleague, by setting an example. 'I'm afraid Mrs Collins, the lady of the house, is dead. She's in her bedroom upstairs. Now ... with it being quite warm weather, the heating on and the windows closed, she's in a state of decomposition. I think it would be unfair of me to ask you to identify the body. Is there a relative we could contact to do the identification later?'

Eddie looked at me for the answer to the question.

'Only an ancient aunt, as far as we know. Her best friend, Lily, lives about fifty miles away, but she'll be devastated. We couldn't ask her. There's an ex-husband somewhere but we don't have any contact details for him. Eddie and I will do it.'

Sergeant Masterful radioed in to inform his superiors. In response to my reports of an unknown man being on the premises, he sent his junior officer to search around the back of the house and in the garden for evidence of anyone trying to break in recently. I was still wrestling with the uncertainty of the circumstances in which I had found the body. Why had someone followed me?

The front door was now smashed to smithereens where Sergeant Masterful had used force to gain entry but, apart from my sighting of a man's leg, there was nothing obvious to hint at foul play.

I'd seen plenty of dead bodies in my time as a nurse and, although you do become accustomed to dealing with the practicalities, it's never easy to manage the feelings of sadness and emotional discomfort. I'd smelt death often, but only once, unforgettably, had I experienced gangrene on the living.

As a result of that particular episode, I always referred to these moments as "pineapple time". It was a welcome discovery, a few years previously, to find that fresh pineapple takes the taste of death and gangrene away from your mouth. It magically alleviates the smell stuck in your nostrils. The trick with any putrid smell, I have also found, is to breathe through your mouth.

'Eddie, it's pineapple time.'

He agreed without any form of protest. It's what we do. We take the rough with the smooth. There's a vast amount of rough to cope with, and a twisted sense of humour is required, as is pineapple on occasion, and alcohol at the end of the day.

We went upstairs, accompanied by Sergeant Masterful and an ever-increasing odour of death. Breathing through open mouths, we shakily confirmed Jan's identity for the record, although the body on the bed didn't resemble the Jan I knew. Her hair was the same and I recognised her dressing gown but she was a variety of deep purples and blues, as if she had become one giant, swollen bruise. She didn't look peaceful. She looked assaulted by life and battered by death. The overwhelming smell of putrefaction was so warmly cloying, sickly and thick, I could almost feel it on my tongue. It was no wonder the young officer downstairs had struggled to avoid vomiting.

Eddie found the thermostat, and would have turned off the unnecessary heating, but we were told to disturb nothing, so returned downstairs to await the arrival of a senior officer, medical confirmation of death, and transport for the body. Meanwhile Eddie and I helped the police sergeant to identify the tablets on the kitchen table, and estimate how many Jan had taken. There were packets of lithium, carbamazepine and olanzapine. Jan had emptied her whole medicine cupboard by the looks of things. There were plasters, throat lozenges, paracetamol, and a bottle half-full of liquid Kemadrin among the scattered debris on the kitchen table. We tried not to touch anything.

'Blast and buggeration! Look at that, Eddie, dothiepin. That would have done the job on its own.' I directed Eddie's gaze to the packet, with a point of my index finger. He agreed with me.

'It's not used much anymore. Too toxic in overdose,' he confirmed for the benefit of the officers present.

'She hadn't been prescribed a lot of these meds in years. Probably stockpiled them,' I informed Sergeant Masterful, who noted down the relevant information and took a careful record of the tablets that Jan should have been taking currently, as prescribed.

'Why would she have kept so many of these tablets if she didn't use them anymore?' he asked.

'Well, it's difficult to say. It's unlikely that she'd planned to keep them in case she decided to top herself one day. She wasn't really like that. She seemed so positive and I was under the impression that she'd been relaxed and happy before she went to France. I suppose she could be the sort of person to keep tablets just in case. Or she simply didn't get around to returning them to a pharmacy and knew better than to flush them down the sink. It's anyone's guess,' I replied.

The doors to a wall unit cupboard were wide open, and this was where Jan had kept her medication. I could see more drugs squirrelled away, still in the pharmacy bags she had taken them home in. This sight made me feel sad and inadequate. Why didn't I know this? Why had I suggested last winter that she might feel less sedated if we reduced her medication? Why had I supported her to stop taking injections?

There were to be nights of questions about Jan's death to keep me awake before we had to prepare for Coroner's Court, which could be months away.

Pending the imminent arrival of a police inspector or detective from the station, the young police officer was to be left with the deceased, Jan, while Sergeant Masterful came with Eddie and me to our office, a mile or so away. Before departing, Eddie and I spooked the young officer with a few tales of ghosts and groaning bodies and then we cruelly left him alone in the smelly house, with only Sparkey the cat for living company.

The sergeant required details of friends and nearest relatives. When making his enquiries, he appeared intrigued by our reference to a missing boyfriend. 'I'll let the investigating officer know that and he'll probably have to follow up once we get back to the station.'

There was no suspicion of anything other than suicide. No note was evident. Nevertheless it was obvious to me, from what we found inside the house, that Jan had simply made the decision to poison herself with prescribed medication. Perhaps the embarrassment of being taken for a complete ride by Liam had been too much for her to bear after all.

I phoned Consultant Psychiatrist Adnan Siddiqui.

'Adnan, it's Monica. Have you recorded Jan Collins as discharged *in absentia* yet? Why? Because if not, I suggest you hold fire. She's dead. I found her at home … suicide by massive overdose … no, the police are already dealing with the situation … Yes, I'm okay, thanks for asking. Of course, I'll update you with anything … I don't know what more you need to know. Dead is dead … No, that's okay. Bye, then.' Apart from asking the few relevant details, he had been lost for words and I had been curt. I think I was cross with him for not heeding my warning about sending Jan on home leave when I was on holiday. She had been through a terrible time and it wasn't fair to expect her to cope without a lot of support.

When we arrived back at the office it was quiet, which was in my favour. Eddie and I dealt with the sergeant's request for information, after which I had reports to write and risk incident forms to complete, and I knew for certain that I would have hundreds of questions from senior management to contend with. What a way to undo the relaxation I'd achieved in my week off.

Chapter Three

As she came back into base from her early morning appointments, I managed to catch Steph, the new support worker. I needed to clarify a couple of points with her for the reports and for my own peace of mind. She had done exactly as I had asked, and had been round to Jan's house at about one o'clock the previous Wednesday, but there had been no reply to the door.

'Were the lounge curtains open or closed, did you notice?'

Steph had a good think about this question. She worked her staccato way through her recall of arriving, parking, approaching the door, ringing the loud doorbell, waiting, waiting, and ringing the doorbell again.

'No, I can't remember. I'm not sure if I looked. The neighbour said Jan must have been out because the vicar had tried the door a few minutes before I turned up, and he'd given up too.'

'The vicar?' This was news to me. Since when had Jan joined the God Squad?

'Apparently. Must be the same one who visited her on the ward. She went a bit religious, I think, when she was high.'

'Yes, she did, didn't she? Still, I didn't know she was friendly with the vicar. Thanks, Steph, I was curious, that's all. Are you all right? It can be a bit of a shock when patients kill themselves.'

'Yeah. Though I've been thinking about whether she was already dead when I was ringing her doorbell and putting notes through her letter box.'

'If she was, you couldn't have done anything. Try not to worry.' I had to leave young Steph to her thoughts, as my phone rang.

The police had assured me they would be contacting the known relatives and Jan's best friend, Lily. Predictably, as soon as each of them was informed, they phoned the team office to speak to me as if needing confirmation. It was a long day.

Three of us shared the small office space as best we could, making use of old fashioned desks and temperamental, battered, metal filing cabinets bulging with case notes. Two irritatingly untidy social work colleagues, and me, Mrs Organised, were wedged into one pokey room. My social work colleagues were, on the whole, great company and without the mutual support we would definitely have struggled to maintain our own sanity in such a stressful working environment. Toni and Anne were well aware that I hated the mess in the office and by way of a humorous dig at me, Anne had invested in an enamelled sign, which took pride of place on the wall above her scruffy paper-strewn desk. It read; 'A tidy desk is a sign of a sick mind'. Maybe she was right.

The previous month, we had finally been given our own computers and a printer to share between us, which took up even more space. Who would have thought it was 2005? The NHS Mental Health Services, especially in Lensham, always lagged behind everyone else in terms of efficiency. For that reason alone, I still very much valued a good old-fashioned message book.

When I had glanced at my message book before heading off to ward round that Monday morning, there was a memo from Kelly regarding a name I had failed to recognise or recollect. Frank Hughes wanted me to call as he was worried about his sister. A telephone number was left for me to make use of, which I had put on my list of things to do.

He phoned again while I was mid-report writing.

'Monica, I have Frank Hughes on the phone for you. Jan Collins's brother. He's been trying to contact her all week, so I don't think he knows. Can I put him through?' I had no choice other than to take the call. I didn't even know Jan had a brother until that very moment and the police had not been in contact with him, as they were also unaware of his existence. So, instead of giving reassurance, I had to break the news to Frank that his sister was dead.

We talked for several minutes, and although on the surface he seemed upset, this related more to his negative opinion of Jan's boyfriend, and where her savings money was kept. Frank was intent on discussing with the police the possibility that this fellow had killed Jan.

'I'm sorry, Mr Hughes, but I've never met Liam. He was never at the house when I called to see Jan and I can only tell you what she told me. Liam was younger than Jan, tall, thick set, and intelligent and she enjoyed his company. I do know that Jan had careful arrangements regarding her finances but of course I don't have the details of what the exact provisions were. I'm sorry, I know that sounds unhelpful.'

'Yes it does. You don't seem to know much about your own patient, do you? Why on earth did you let her go to France in the first place? It's a bloody disgrace and I have a good mind to make a formal complaint.'

'Mr Hughes, I appreciate that you're upset to hear about your sister's death, but please be assured that she was perfectly within her rights to go on holiday with whoever she pleased, and her health was not a cause for concern before she went. She is – I mean, was, an extremely capable woman.'

'Unlike yourself ...'

I ignored the boorish attitude and ill manners, thanked Frank Hughes for his call and passed on to him the police sergeant's name and the number to call at the police station in Hollberry. I hoped that would be the last time I would have to deal with him. It wasn't.

A short while later Eddie popped his head around my office door, but as I was ending another call, he turned as if to go. Needing to update him, I beckoned with one hand, and placed the other over the mouthpiece. 'Eddie, hang on a minute.' Eddie swivelled back into the midden of an office space, where I gave him the latest on Jan's brother and his theory that Jan had been killed.

'It looks like the police are taking him seriously. They've phoned me to ask if we could go down to the station, to have fingerprints taken,' he said.

'What the fu … Why?'

'They must suspect foul play, or they're paying lip-service by doing something in response to Mr Hughes and his demands. Anyway, they need our fingerprints to distinguish them from any others they find on the property. It's a good job we did as we were told for once and didn't fiddle with anything while we were there. By the way, I've sent Kelly out to get us both some fresh pineapple. I can't get the stench out of my nostrils.'

'Me neither.' I wrinkled up my nose.

A Detective Sergeant Adams had kindly informed Eddie that matey-boy Liam-the-conman had been suspected of breaking into her house while Jan was in hospital. The offence would have occurred in the week before both she and I went on leave. Jan had reported it to police but she didn't tell me.

After a few phone calls to the inpatient psychiatric unit at Hollberry Hospital, Eddie and I uncovered that Jan had been given permission by the ward consultant to go home for one day. Ostensibly this was to check on her house and, we were told, in preparation for a trial of longer home leave. The ward had neglected to tell us, so we had no idea she'd been there. Jan, it seems, didn't tell the ward staff about her break-in either, which was most peculiar.

According to the police, Jan reported that she had a number of items stolen, but DS Adams insisted that the break-in wasn't reported as a ransacking; it was a careful removal of cash, one or two items of value, and paperwork relating to the holiday in Perpignan. Jan obviously had immediately concluded her burglar had to be boyfriend Liam, and reported him. She must have been furious when he'd abandoned her in France and even more enraged that he had returned to take advantage of her again.

Police were still looking for Liam to question him in connection with the break-in, and he was nowhere to be found. Anyway, the news of a possible burglary connected with Jan's death, and my sighting of a man's leg, resulted in Eddie and me having to make a trip to the nick in case Liam had murdered Jan.

'Oh, bloody hell. This is a real nightmare.'

'That's nothing. The sergeant rang me after that. He wants us to find a home for the cat.'

I'd forgotten about Sparkey. Although I wanted to, I couldn't take Sparkey home myself because Deefer, our Staffordshire bull terrier, would eat the poor thing. Deefer loved people, but wasn't too accepting of other dogs, let alone cats.

'Oh God. Poor Sparkey. No panic. I'll give Emma a ring, she does fostering.'

'Kids or cats?'

'Cats, you fool. She's not responsible enough to have any more kids. She has two of her own, and they're practically feral.' I contacted my old friend and fellow nurse Emma Foster, an ironic surname for one so keen to adopt animals. In actual fact, she had become Mrs Emma Frost since she married her farmer boyfriend, Jake, years earlier. She decided against a double-barrelled surname, as Foster-Frost sounded pretentious. So, like me, she kept her maiden name for professional dealings; and married name for her private life. Very handy it is too, to have a couple of names. Emma had recently landed herself a specialist nurse position at the Lensham Drug and Alcohol Service, or Len-DAS as it was known locally. She worked part-time to fit in around the children and the family farming business. Glad to have Sparkey, Emma arranged to meet me at Jan's address after work. Problem sorted.

I phoned Max, my husband, to forewarn him of my undoubted lateness home due to 'a hideous day.' I had thought he would absorb what I was trying to communicate but he seemed more intent on outdoing me with his own Monday tales of woe.

'You think that's bad? I had the bloody factory inspector round … Elf and Safety tosspot! Not the right guards on the machines apparently. The obnoxious twat was threatening me. I wagged my finger at him, and you know what that means!'

Yes, I did. Finger wagging was stage one. It usually indicated that stage two was imminent and would usually be a good whack. Fortunately, with age came a modicum of wisdom, enabling Max to control stage two. His whacking was mostly confined to the rugby pitch, or it had been. He had finally semi-retired only to be wheeled out for the odd veterans' game. These days I stood on the touchline with the car jump leads in my hands, at the ready, in case his heart could take no more. Occasionally, Max turned the most peculiar puce colour, and I became convinced a coronary was on the cards every time he played.

When I finally arrived home late, and Max demanded to know why, I realised he had failed to absorb one single word I'd said to him on the phone earlier. Great. No takeaway for dinner then. There were many Mars vs Venus communication breakdowns in our house. John N. Gray had it pegged in his book *Men are from Mars, Women are from Venus*. Max speaks and understands boy language and behaviour, because he is from Mars, and most of what I have to say seems to be misunderstood.

'I'll cook, shall I?'

'You normally do … by the way how much did you pay for that medicine cabinet thing?'

I was not really in the mood to discuss my spontaneous whim of a purchase from the local antiques auction. It was my money.

Rapidly, I caught on to the fact Max was fishing.

'I assume you're bidding on another bloody motorbike on eBay,' I challenged.

By the look on his face, I had been spot on.

He was forever trying to convince me these were investments, not boys' toys. 'Look, my lovely. Do what you will. I found one of my patients dead today, so it's hardly important in the great scheme of things how much money I spent on myself. Besides which, if you'd only realised how important passing those exams were for me, then perhaps I wouldn't have had to buy myself a present to celebrate my own achievement.'

I had passed the requirements to become a nurse prescriber, for which I would get paid no extra money nor get promotion. I was hugely proud of myself.

'Oh, someone died?'

The information had reached its final destination, at last.

'Yes. It was very smelly and sad,' I replied, keeping the information simple for Neanderthal Man. Frustratingly, he could be incredibly astute and intuitive on rare occasions. Never when it was needed, it would seem.

My reward was a hug, which caught me off guard.

'So how much did you pay?'

Chapter Four

We often sit chatting in bed, Max and I, with many of our most awkward decisions made at the end of the day. We subsequently sleep on those decisions and re-evaluate them the following morning. I couldn't escape his inquisition about my medicine cabinet. It was now in the dining room, sitting on the deep recessed corner shelf adjacent to the fireplace, but not too close to cause heat damage.

'Not as much money as a motorbike,' I offered in response, as Max continued to dig for validation of his plan to invest more hard-earned cash in future classic motorcycles.

'So, can I put in a bid for the BSA?'

'I did say I had no objection. It's your money, Max. Where are you planning to store this one? We're running out of room for these investments of yours, you know.'

'You worry too much. I'll have a shuffle about, there's always room for one more, or an extension on the garage ...'

Once I had finished telling Max about the events at the auction, he tickled me into submission, and groaning in defeat I finally confessed to the price paid for the Regency ship's doctor's medicine cabinet. He nearly fell out of bed with the shock.

'For what? A box of books, a wooden cabinet for a dwarf, and a few old bottles? Christ, Mon, they must have seen you coming!'

Showing him the catalogue helped my cause somewhat and Max begrudgingly conceded that at least I had not paid above the maximum guide price. Even so, he huffed and puffed for several days before he realised that he now had greater leeway to spend recklessly on his next bike purchase.

Exhausted by the tickling bout, I picked up the book I had been reading, but my restless mind kept diverting my thoughts elsewhere. Most recently, my interest had turned to the leather-bound journals, which had formed part of the auction lot alongside the medicine cabinet. So far, I had only turned a few pages of one or two journals, which contained complicated chemical equations and a few scribbled notes in the margin. This was disappointing, but I remained optimistic that there would be more appealing detail on other pages of these slim books. All I needed was a quiet moment to myself to delve into them and discover the life of the ship's doctor. How exciting. There were bound to have been several amputations, soothing of wounds after a sound flogging with a cat-o'-nine-tails and ... actually I wasn't sure what went on in ships of the Regency era. *I must look that up,* I thought to myself.

Truthfully, I had become completely carried away at the antiques auction. I'd never been before, although there was a well-known one in town, which often advertised pending auctions in the local paper, and it caught my eye for once. An auction of antiques and collectables was due to take place when I was to be off work for the week; the viewings were on the Friday.

I was determined not purchase a naff vase, or an item of frivolous jewellery which I would never wear. My search was for an item apt for a nurse prescriber. Especially after the hard work and endless study, and because most of the time on the course I had felt completely out of my depth.

My reward for passing the final exam, the assignments, and assessments, needed to be reflective of the hard graft, and the stress. Finally, it should repay the tears of frustration I had shed, when grappling with the bewildering concepts in the pharmacology module.

When I took myself to Yarlsmere Auctions on the Friday I spent time leafing through the catalogue, exploring the many investment possibilities. I found the items on my shortlist and weighed up the pros and cons of each against my gut feeling and emotional response to each. This was not purely a financial investment; it was also a well-earned selfish reward. By the end of the viewing, I was certain about which lot to bid on, and how much my maximum would be. Not a word to Max.

On the day of the auction my forethought and sensible preparation became redundant. I was seriously considering putting in a bid or two for a beautiful, pharmacist's glass amphora in a shade of raspberry. It was huge, and a fantastic shape with an upside-down teardrop stopper. I remembered seeing these as a child and being fascinated that such artistic objects were to be found at the chemist's.

As an auction virgin, I was a bit confused as to what I was required to do but a helpful priest turned out to be my guide for the day. He looked familiar until I realised he resembled the famous TV priest, Father Ted. As the similarity dawned on me, the priest seemed to know what I was thinking.

'I'm Father Raymond, by the way.'

His timing was impeccable, as I was about to blurt out what he had already second-guessed, but he didn't have the requisite Irish accent. This was fortunate for me because, not only do I have a habit of speaking before thinking at times, but I also love an accent, to the degree that I find myself imitating them, as the sincerest form of flattery. It's an affliction which has been with me for many a year, and one for which I blame my father. He does the exact same thing.

Father Raymond was roughly my height, around about the six-foot mark, with a shock of thick salt and pepper grey hair, and a slim build. There was nothing remarkable about his features, other than his stately dark eyebrows. He was a gentleman in his fifties, who happened to be a priest and at an auction, and apparently interested in unusual theological items.

'What sort of items would that be?' I enquired, genuinely intrigued.

This was not easy to explain, I was told. 'They may be books, or icons, but not usually larger items.' Father Raymond was confined to living in rather humble circumstances as a visiting priest to the area.

'I'm seeking a small gift for my host, Father Joseph, who is kindly accommodating me. I'm lodging with him as a temporary guest if you like.' I gathered from Father Raymond that although he was not a minister at the church, he was visiting the diocese from elsewhere, and was heavily involved in setting up street projects around the country. Locally, he helped to run guided self-help support groups. 'It's part of an interdenominational project, called "Pathways". We provide active strategies to address the needs of the vulnerable with mental health problems.'

Most honourable and commendable, I thought. This meant we had common ground on which to extend our acquaintance, and we chatted amicably for the whole morning.

'I feel rather ashamed that our services haven't been more actively involved in the work you're doing,' I finally admitted. I had heard on local radio that the churches in town had joined together to offer more than a bric-a-brac sale, but in all honesty, I hadn't been interested enough to pursue the information.

Father Raymond didn't appear to be offended in any way, and extended an open invitation; 'Drop in anytime'. He accepted that not everyone went to church these days.

'I'm one of those very people,' I confessed.

Father Raymond light-heartedly suggested that I should become his next mission in life. He smiled broadly, and said in a gently mocking tone, 'Never fear, salvation is at hand. You're never too old to be converted, Monica.'

Brushing aside the subject of faith, he divulged his own weakness. 'You know, I get a secret thrill from visiting antiques auctions,' he said. 'I often go along purely for the excitement of watching the bidding without the need to enter the fray myself. Less of a risk that way. I don't have much money to invest.'

Thou shalt not splash the cash willy-nilly, I said to myself, with an internal chuckle threatening to escape my lips. I was conscious of minding my language, not being of a particular religious persuasion; verging on the agnostic if anything. However, in the same way as I would unintentionally mimic an accent, that morning I managed to punctuate many a sentence with 'Jesus', or 'Christ' or 'God', like a form of mild Tourette's. The tension was mounting as time went on, and I was mightily relieved when the auction began so I could stop putting both my feet in my mouth with such excruciating regularity.

Father Raymond had a point. The auction was thrilling. I found myself captivated by the mastery with which the auctioneer managed proceedings and manoeuvred the bidders into taking another risk. One more bid higher than they had originally intended.

My amphora was lot number 325, but before this there were several lots with a pharmacological theme, which had caught my eye but were outside the budget I had set. One was a "Regency Period Apothecary, a small medicine cabinet possibly belonging to a ship's doctor, mahogany c1820. It stands 14 inches high, and is in a lovely condition with the finest craftsmanship visible throughout". Vials, bottles, and small boxes in drawers could be seen encased in beautiful mahogany, and with the cabinet came a number of books or journals, which seemed to be leather-bound. These were detailed in the catalogue as "containing factual information and calculations relating to the original use of the cabinet". As it was way above my budget, I could only admire it and envy the person who was soon to own this piece of history and gorgeousness.

'Ah, a thing of beauty is a joy forever,' remarked Father Raymond with a wink as the cabinet was introduced as the next lot.

I am not insinuating it was Father Raymond's fault that I was the woman who made the final bid, but I have often wondered if I would have raised my hand to bid at all, if that clichéd sentiment had not made its way from my ear to my brain via my heart strings. Father Raymond, realising that I was caught in the excitement of the bidding, tried in vain to remind me about my budget limit.

'All done now at £2,190, and sold!' said the auctioneer, as his gavel smartly met the top of the handsome wooden desk at which he stood.

'Oh, God, how am I going to explain this one to Max?' I whispered aloud, noting that I had blasphemed once more. It really is a good job I'm not Catholic, as I would undoubtedly spend half my life in the confessional if I were, and an endless queue would form outside the confessional box while I divulged blasphemy, envy, and impure thoughts by the dozen.

Strangely enough, I did not experience significant feelings of regret at my impulsive purchase. Far from it, I was delighted that for once I had made what I believed to be a sound investment in a lovely antique. That it was of historical interest was an added bonus.

I first saw the word *'Paracelsus'* and the initials *'G.C.'*, when I'd given the cabinet a thorough examination at the viewing on the day before, and dismissed it as an option, being too pricy. The name and initials were engraved on small brass plaques and looked like a more recent addition. Secretly I hoped, with childlike excitement, that the journals would reveal its full history.

Father Raymond was again my guide through the process of claiming my prize and paying for it, and he waited to help load the cabinet into the boot of my car. Before I meandered off to fetch my vehicle, I made a promise to call into St David's Church Hall in the near future, to see for myself the work of the Pathways Project.

'I'll bring along some of the leaflets we use; it's the least I can do by way of a thank you for all your help today. I would've been lost without your advice.'

'I think you actually ignored my advice, Monica.' Father Raymond nodded down towards the cabinet that he was holding in both arms. I chuckled as I juggled my handbag, car keys, and journals while heading for the car.

Responsibly, on returning home from the auction, I decided to clean and polish the medicine cabinet before it was to be housed in the dining room. The labels on the bottles and jars within the cabinet were faded, but most remained fairly legible. Soon I concluded that I would need a Latin dictionary, and hoped the Internet would reveal the answers because I hadn't the faintest idea what some of the contents were. The labels read: *Gentaine, Philo Pomanium, Ipecac, Astafetida* and many more equally mysterious names.

'Surely it wouldn't have mercury inside, would it?' I queried to myself as I picked up a small vial labelled *Mercurial.*

One or two of the jars had a chemical symbol rather than a full name, and this stumped me completely. My memory from school of the periodic table had been dragged back into use during my prescribing course, but most of the relevant information about elements and compounds had long since faded into oblivion. As well as the name *'Paracelsus'* and the initials *'G.C.'* on the outside of the cabinet, there was another carefully inscribed narrow brass plaque on the inside, which was revealed each time the doors were opened. It read *Sola dosis facit venenum.* My curiosity needed to be answered at once and I could not wait to find out what this particular Latin phrase meant.

I fired up the temperamental computer, and eventually was rewarded with my answer. Those words translated as "Only the dose makes the poison" accredited to one Paracelsus, said to be the founder of toxicology.

Two mysteries solved in one fell swoop.

Paracelsus was not the name of a boat, as I had assumed, it was a Swiss German gentleman, born in 1493, who went by the impossible but marvellous name of Philippus Aureolus Theophrastus Bombastus von Hohenheim.

Fabulous! Right up my street. It was so far up my street in fact, that I felt the adrenalin hit as it arrived like a tidal wave, making my hands sticky and my heart race.

Poisoning was my weakness, not antiques auctions, and it was a subject that I had become preoccupied with for many years. It was not so much the types of poisons used, although that was of interest to me, it was more the psychology of the act and of the poisoner, that had me enthralled. I had read books about famous poisoners, about fictional poisoners, and been absorbed by TV dramas and news items whenever they arose. I wanted to understand what made them tick. What was the catalyst to their actions?

More recently, as I became a prescribing nurse, I gained a much better knowledge of the drugs I was accountable for administrating to others. Indeed, I learnt a great deal more than I was expecting to, and my fixation with poisoning, which had been relegated to the league of hobbies and interests, was reignited and elevated to the status of obsession.

Paracelsus was absolutely correct in his assertions. It is about the dose. A small amount of paracetamol is a cure for a headache but a large dose is fatal, and so it is with everything; after all, drinking too much water can kill you.

Chapter Five

On Tuesday morning Max and I were rudely awakened by our next-door neighbours' large cock. A Buff Orpington, he was a monster of a rooster who, long before dawn, continued his attempts to crow properly. It seems he could 'cock-a,' but no matter how he tried, he couldn't 'doodle-do'. His endless efforts seemed to make him more effective as an alarm clock than a standard cockerel, while at the same time being thoroughly irritating, thus ensuring he placed himself in imminent danger of being strangled and placed in the cooking pot.

Anticipating that my second day back at work was not going to be any easier than my first, I had hoped for a restful night's sleep, which was denied me by Cocka. He was most definitely at the top of my 'should be put down' list. I run two lists, the second being 'needs a good slap'.

Sure enough, waiting for me first thing was evidence that a couple of senior managers were already ensconced with Eddie in his office, poring over the case notes for Jan Collins. These were as up to date as humanly possible, and I wasn't particularly worried about the contents or whether my risk assessments and care plans were as comprehensive as required, or not. I couldn't change them.

I checked in with our administrator, Kelly, who was always the first team member at work in the mornings. She liked to run an efficient ship and, if truth were told, she hated to miss anything that she considered exciting. Working on the basis that knowledge is power, she would ensure that she had the latest information on everyone's private lives, as well as the professional day-to-day issues of the team. It was ammunition for gossip and tittle-tattle, in my opinion.

'Does Eddie need me for anything do you know, or can I catch up with a couple of visits today?' I asked, keen to get back on track with the routine community nursing tasks and visits, which were already booked into my work diary. Also, I was determined to give the senior managers the slip before they collared me. 'I have clinic to run with Steph this morning and I can't cancel that, there's no one else to run it, what with Tania at the tribunal hearing, Bill off sick, and Wendy on leave for two weeks.'

'I'll phone him, Monica. I think you both have to go to the police station today but I don't know if a specific time has been arranged. Give me a second.' She had a brief chat with the boss, and confirmed that I was free to devise my own work schedule until the afternoon. This was a relief. I could already feel the pressure of the backlog from the day before, and needed to jiggle appointments around to meet my commitments.

Steph and I prepared for clinic.

We had use of a room at a local health centre several times a week for various clinics. On a Tuesday, it was for the long-term patients who knew the system well and who waited patiently in the reception area to be seen, one at a time, for their monthly or fortnightly injections and a brief review of their overall physical health.

'I actually find this completely soul-destroying, if I'm honest with you, Steph. You can spot the old patients a mile off in reception, dulled and zombified, shaking and unkempt. It's a disgrace in this day and age when there are better medications out there. I hope the powers that be let me use the qualification I've worked so hard for. I'd review the bloody lot and start again. Give people their quality of life back. Who's first on the list?'

'Ian Oliver.'

'Oh, he's lovely. You've not met him before, have you? He tells such an amazing story.'

Ian shuffled in, managing a broad grin when he saw me, and was delighted to see a new face. 'Who's this young lady, then?' he asked, offering to shake Steph's hand. He took advantage and kissed her on the back of her proffered hand; chuckling, he apologised, 'Sorry, I so rarely get the chance to touch and kiss a young lady. It won't happen again.' He plonked himself down on the chair. Knowing the routine so well, he confirmed what dose of injection he was expecting to receive, and that the previous month he'd had his injection in his right buttock, taking the time to explain to Steph why this was important. 'They alternate, you see, young lady. Right one month, left the next. I have a bum like a rhinoceros so it makes no difference to me. I've been having these injections for twenty years, you know.'

Steph made polite conversation while I prepared the injection for Ian. 'Why have you been on them for so long? Don't you want to try some of the newer medications? They have less side effects.' She had clearly noticed how tremulous Ian was and that his facial features seemed like a mask for most of the time, making him slur.

'I wouldn't dare change it now. I had a dreadful time. Schizophrenia can be like a living nightmare. I'd rather be fat and shuffle about.'

'Ian ran away to sea, didn't you?'

'Yes, I did. LSD did it for me, blew my mind. I had to escape from my paranoia, and somehow I talked my way onto a fishing boat in Grimsby as a deckhand and a cook's helper, and we went all the way to Icelandic waters. Guess what? The Cod Wars were in full swing.'

By the way she reacted, Steph obviously thought this was some sort of fantasy.

'It's true isn't it, Monica? The buggers were firing across our bows. It did nothing for my delusions. I was petrified. Eighteen years old and as mad as a hatter. Never been right since. Left buttock at the ready, nurse.'

As Ian left, he thanked us for the nice chat. 'I do look forward to clinic, it's so good to socialise.' Steph and I exchanged sad expressions. 'Living in the community's not all it's cracked up to be, is it?' Steph commented.

First on my list of home visits to make that day, I had a late-morning appointment after clinic to see Ben Tierney at his parents' house. Steph took all our larger equipment back to base. We'd had two no-shows, which meant that I would have to follow them up with a home visit sometime later.

Ben's injection was due that day but he'd always declined to attend any clinic where he would be seen in a public place with other mental health patients. He was not the type to avoid me when the date for his regular injection came around. 'Hi, Monica, come on in,' he welcomed me as always. 'Sorry if I look a bit of a mess today.'

Ben's marriage had floundered, finally sinking because of his alcohol problems, and lately the good-natured family man was showing signs of the damage done by the bottle. Rubbing his hands either side of his ruddy face, shaking slightly, with red eyes and dehydrated skin, he had an air of resignation about him. At the core of his problems was a sick and manipulative abuser who had preyed on him and his friends, as children. Ben had tried to keep the details of his abuse an agonising secret and he partially succeeded for many years. However, his world crumpled around him four years previously as the alcohol took hold and loosened his anger. Ben disclosed details whilst roaring drunk. He staggered the streets of Lensham claiming to have uncovered a conspiracy of silence covering up abuse by the Catholic Church across the world, and he was convinced that the Italian Mafia, US Mafia, and the Freemasons, were involved in funding the Holy Roman Church establishment. Poor man. That was enough to get him arrested and sectioned under the Mental Health Act, twice in two years. It didn't stop him. The drunken ranting pattern was repeated at least once a month and as a result, Ben's marriage disintegrated, forcing him to live with his elderly parents.

When sober, his disclosure of abuse was vague. Mostly, because Ben could hardly bring himself to use the relevant adjectives. What he did manage to reveal, left me with no doubt that he had been sexually abused, and by whom, in terms of gender, circumstances and profession; if you can call being a Catholic priest a profession.

At my insistence, Ben finally plucked up the courage to report his abuse formally to the police, but no action was taken.

'I told you there was no feckin' point,' Ben had said on his return. 'They looked at me as if I was some sort of sexual deviant. All they asked me was why I'd left it so long before reporting it as a crime. They assumed I was heading for another breakdown or I was attention seeking. Waste of time. Why do you think I've never reported it before?'

Mental health nurse training did not equip me with the skills to deal with sexual abuse disclosures, nor did it enable me to provide active interventions that could help. I had to rely on my instincts and the advice to encourage victims to report the crimes, 'with a view to preventing further acts of sexual violence from the alleged perpetrator'. What good is that when the police have written the person off as being mentally ill and nothing else? When Ben had returned from the police station angry, abusive, and ferociously bitter, I was at a loss. I could only listen as he explained, through furious tears, how he had tried to ask his parents for help, as a child.

'He promised me that if I kept our little secret, then I could be an altar boy, and "wouldn't that make your parents the proudest people in the congregation?" he said. I didn't even realise what he was doing was wrong to begin with. A touch here, a fondle there. I wasn't the only one. He would take us, both the boys and the girls, one by one into the sacristy or sometimes into his office, if we were at the rectory. He didn't keep us to himself either, he would arrange for invited guests to watch.'

'He did what?' I asked, hardly daring to believe what I was hearing.

'Yep. He invited other men, some in smart suits, to watch, and they would listen to us practise our Catechisms while he touched us in the name of God, and they touched themselves.

Sick fuckers.' Ben had tried to tell his parents but they didn't believe a word. He was punished for blaspheming.

'What exactly did you say to your parents?' I asked, hoping to understand their lack of action in response to the plea for help from their son.

'Oh, I said that I didn't like the way the holy father touched me on my private parts. I couldn't have been any clearer. I had nightmares, wet the bed, and attached myself like a limpet to my mother. I was a little boy who didn't know what sex was.' When he tried to avoid attending for confirmation classes, Ben's father beat him and dragged him along, instructing the priest to ensure he was morally punished. Which he was.

Once married, Ben had two young children of his own and a few years previously, as reports were coming in over the TV news about stories of alleged abuse in a children's home run by the Catholic Church, Ben began to lose control. 'I couldn't believe my own fucking eyes and ears. The Vatican denied it.

'I had a life, a job, a wife, and my girls. I'd done my best to get on and not be a victim, but I was right all along, so there was no way in hell the church was getting its hands on my children. I stopped them. I wouldn't let them go to church. Of course, I never went, ever. But Marie and the kids did, they used to go every Sunday, with Marie's mother, so I put a stop to that immediately. Marie argued with me for days and weeks. We were screaming and shouting at each other, and I took to drinking even more. On top of that the police kept locking me up, saying I was deluded, and social services became involved because they said my behaviour was abusive. I fucking died when they said that.' Ben was no longer allowed to see his own children, unless supervised, and the emotional pain of losing them was killing him.

Ben hovered a tad above rock bottom in terms of his mental health. Alcohol abuse and depression had veered into the psychotic, and he was prescribed injectable medication for his paranoia, as well as an antidepressant for his mood. He openly admitted that he liked the effect of the antipsychotic injections, although he was sure he didn't warrant having them. They allowed him to function in a fug of sedation where emotional pain couldn't break through so often or as acutely. It topped up the effects of the alcohol.

He had determinedly refused psychological therapy, but his avoidance was understandable. The past abuse, which was too agonising to put properly into spoken words, was equalled by the blame he laid at the feet of his parents, and yet without them he would have been consigned to the streets as a homeless, hopeless alcoholic. Drink was Ben's refuge, but the more he drank, the more the psychological damage and anger became apparent.

Somehow, I had managed to persuade Ben to begin attending Len-DAS, as an attempt at rescue from the brink of self-destruction. He had been to the first session but was contemplating whether or not to make a return visit. Ben was always willing to please, and was charming and kind-hearted when he was sober, but his lack of motivation to change his coping strategies was frustrating. He drank copious amounts of spirits, beer, and cheap wine. Consequentially his liver was showing signs of damage in recent blood tests.

In short, he was on a slow road to nowhere.

'Ah, now then, Nurse Monica, can I ask you a question today, if you don't mind?' Ben's parents, Sean and Manuela Tierney, were often at home when I visited and they were keen to talk to me that day. It was obvious how incredibly despairing they felt, watching as their son slowly slipped over the edge of a steep precipice, and they were desperately seeking more than divine intervention.

'I've been told by Father Joseph Kavanagh at St Francis', of a project running at St David's Church Hall, which helps people like Ben, and we want to know your opinion of the work they do there, and whether Ben would be suitable.'

Ben, real name Benito, had inherited the best features of both his parents. He had a Spanish mother, Manuela, and his father, Sean, was a gentle giant of an Irishman, which meant trouble for me because I always found myself sliding accidentally into mimicking his father's soft brogue whenever we spoke. Sean

Tierney was reassured that I had recently been invited to visit the project at St David's. 'I promise I'll give you my honest opinion as soon as I see for myself what's on offer,' I said, tempering this with a reminder that Ben might choose not to attend, even if the project offered a magic cure-all therapy. Ben had listened in to the conversation, and shook his despondent head at hearing his parents' insistence. He walked away.

It was a heart-breaking scene.

Before returning to the office to write up notes, send letters, and make phone calls, I had two patients to track down. Harvey often forgot what day he was on, so it was no great surprise that he had failed to attend his clinic appointment that morning. I made my way to the romantically named Heights, an area containing several high-rise blocks of flats. Apart from nuisance pigeons, drug dealers lurked on every corner, either in a blacked-out car or holding a bulldog on a hideous leather lead, collars studded with spikes. The dealers peddled their wares and mental health services picked up the pieces of the psychosis that arose in their customers. I hated them for it.

Harvey lived on the third floor of Green Heights with his elderly, German mother, who was marginally less bonkers than he was. I rang the bell outside the ground floor entrance and waited for a response. As I loitered impatiently, I looked around at my vehicle, gauging the likelihood of it being damaged by the time I emerged from the flats. A silver Audi was pulling in next to my car but the man inside didn't get out, he just sat there. I rang the entrance buzzer three times before obtaining an answer. '*Ja?*'

'It's Monica the nurse, Mrs Fields, I've come to see Harvey.' I was buzzed in, and decided to walk up the stairs rather than take the vertical toilet of a lift.

'Hello!' said Harvey brightly. 'Sorry I couldn't come to clinic, Mother was holding me hostage against my will and I had a meeting with the brigands from upstairs because the price of my blood has gone up on the black market.'

'Has it indeed.' I checked the drug chart and realised that Harvey had now declined three consecutive injections. 'Who decides on the market value of your blood these days, Harvey?' I asked.

'They do, the Australians. A pint each night they have from me, look here.' Harvey undid his belt and dropped his oversized trousers to reveal baggy underpants and a pair of skinny white legs. 'See the marks there, and there.' He pointed at the skin on his legs, which appeared perfectly intact. This confirmed my suspicions. Harvey was slipping back into his internal paranoid world.

'It must be scary having those people taking your blood every night. Shall we go ahead with trying to see if your injection will help you to feel less afraid?'

'No. No. I don't need it.'

I tried another tactic. 'I expect you must be fed up with these Australian brigands coming into your room at night. You must be losing a lot of sleep.'

'He hasn't slept for weeks now. I told Toni and she knows all about it,' Mrs Fields interjected. Toni, Harvey's social worker and my office mate, had mentioned the difficulties she was having with Harvey and that signs of relapse were becoming more prominent. But despite my usual tricks, Harvey would not be convinced that an injection was helpful. His mother supported his decision, mostly because she didn't want to upset him and make him irritable, but also because she sometimes became so convinced by his stories that she joined in the fantasies. Tricky.

'Would you take some tablets, instead?' I offered. That was a mistake. Harvey asked me to leave, in no uncertain terms, and I beat a hasty retreat to the door, promising Mrs Fields to return with Toni to negotiate a way of avoiding another trip to hospital for Harvey before matters became too risky to manage.

As I stepped from their flat door onto the landing, I looked out of the window and down to where my car was parked. The man in the silver Audi was standing, resting against the side of the Audi's bonnet, between my car and his.

I phoned Kelly, wanting advice from Eddie. There was something about the situation that made the marker on my crapometer twitch. 'The crapometer', like a milometer, or the clapometer as used on *Opportunity Knocks* to rate audience response, is a standard form of measurement. In this case, it's used by mental health practitioners only, and it rates the level of risk of soiling your own underwear in extreme or violent situations.

'Do you want me to call the police?'

'No. There's no point. He hasn't done anything. Tell Eddie, I'll keep my mobile phone in my hand and I'll phone the police if I have to.'

'Keep this call going and I'll listen in. If it gets heated *I'll* call the police,' Kelly insisted.

I approached my car, trying to look confident and professional. 'Can I help you?'

There was a pause, during which I unlocked my car and put my clinical bag into the boot. I couldn't get to the driver's door without passing within touching distance of the stranger. The man had eyes like a shark and he said nothing, but he did at least move so that I could get into my car. Saying a very curt 'thank you' I drove away without further delay. I couldn't find the other patient who had failed to turn up for clinic, so by the time I returned to the office I was in need of a rant.

'Who was he?' asked Kelly, about the man with shark's eyes.

'No, I've no idea who he is, probably the drug dealers' evil mastermind. He gave me the bloody willies, though.' I shivered.

After writing up my notes of the morning's work, and talking through with Toni what the options were for Harvey Fields, I made a quick call to St David's Church Hall to gather details about the Pathways Project groups run by Father Raymond. Once this was clarified, I checked my message book, but as nothing required my urgent attention, I had the luxury of a short lunch break. Stuffing a couple of sad sandwiches into my mouth, washed down with a cup of tea, I started to feel more human again, until Eddie nabbed me.

'Are you free for our trip to the nick?'

We arrived at the front desk in Hollberry Police Station and duly announced the reason for our attendance to the elderly desk sergeant. There was a short wait until a grey-suited DS Adams, who was of indeterminate age, eventually greeted us. I hadn't come across him in my travels before, as I tended to have more regular dealings with the local beat officer for Lensham. There was a lot of crossover between our two professions. This, however, was the first time that my personal data had been taken for the record: name, professional details, home address, and my fingerprints.

Eddie tried to make light of the situation, 'It's a fair cop, guv, it was me wot dun it ...' I humoured him with a small titter, but DS Adams wore a deadpan expression throughout. Eddie screwed up his face in acknowledgement of his own poor taste. 'Not really the time for levity, is it. Sorry.'

DS Adams expressed regret for the inconvenience of having to ask us for fingerprints, but implied that their use may not be necessary.

'I'm waiting on confirmation from the DI. Mrs Collins's house was in order, apart from the kitchen, of course, and there are no indicators for this being a suspicious death. However, Mrs Collins's brother has been insistent that his sister's death was not suicide, and he's demanding investigation into her recent boyfriend. If you can fill in any of the blanks for us that would be greatly appreciated.'

Eddie and I mentioned what we knew about Jan Collins, her family, her background, and anything else we could furnish DS Adams with regarding Jan's relationship with Liam, the conman boyfriend.

'Do you have any idea where they met? Who else Mrs Collins may have introduced him to, anything at all?' asked DS Adams, who was obviously clueless regarding Liam, other than the fact they had a surname for him: Brookes. 'I'm quite new to the area, but my colleagues know their patch well, and I'm reliably informed that Liam Brookes isn't known to the local police here. Nothing is showing as outstanding in terms of warrants or traffic violations.' DS Adams most certainly wasn't local; I had determined a background accent when he spoke, with the unmistakable vowel sounds of the Midlands giving him away.

Eddie and I were of little help as informants. We were in the dark about Liam Brookes. 'Jan had mentioned him to me in passing and as part of our general chit chat, although she hadn't been particularly expansive on the subject. She always seemed to have one or two man-friends on the go at any one time. They tended to float into her life and usually it was six months or so before they finally drifted away again, no damage done. Liam was assumed to be one of these transient boyfriends until Jan announced he was taking her on a romantic holiday to France,' I said.

'Do we know anything about his past misdemeanours?' asked DS Adams.

'No, we didn't know anything untoward had happened until our team was contacted by Jan's best friend, Lily. She was worried because Jan had stopped phoning her as regularly as she normally would.'

According to Lily, Jan and Liam had stayed in France longer than they were originally booked for, cancelling the return flights, and therefore Jan could have run out of medication; if she was taking it. After several days of silence, Lily had managed to contact Jan's mobile phone but had spoken to Liam. He gave her the news that Jan had been arrested for indecent exposure and taken to Hôpital Corbet, a French mental hospital, and he provided Lily with the contact details. That was the last time Liam was heard from.

Recounting these facts to DS Adams, I recalled in painful detail the hard work required in achieving repatriation of my patient from a French hospital. What a dreadful pickle that had been to sort out, especially as my French was not up to discussing relapse signatures, medication, and care transfer planning.

During one conversation with French Consultant Psychiatrist Dr Reynaud, I mispronounced a phrase so badly that it resembled a tasteless French expression, which made the consultant burst out laughing. The hilarity reverberated around the office she was in, as she duly informed everyone present at her end of the phone of my faux pas. I had described a scene of oral sex apparently. Mortified with embarrassment, I lost all confidence in speaking any French whatsoever.

Dr Reynaud's English was far superior, and thus after my pronunciation calamity, we continued negotiations in my mother tongue for safety's sake and that of international relations.

On arrest, Jan had been naked, highly distressed, paranoid and screaming aloud that she was burning hot, hence the need to divest herself of every item of clothing. I was only too aware that she had a history of stripping off her clothes when manic, and thus none of what was reported had surprised me.

When Jan had been extremely disturbed on arrival at the Corbet Unit, the team there assumed illicit substances were to blame; however, this was soon discounted after a negative result from the standard drug screening tests.

'We had concern that your lady was toxic from anticholinergics, you know about this?' Dr Reynaud had asked me.

'Well, I'm not an expert, but I know it's very dangerous.'

'*Oui*, very dangerous. She was hot, flushed, and very confused, making it hard to say if she was delirious or psychotic. Difficult to tell, but she did get better quickly when we treated her for ACS. Could she have taken too much Kemadrin by accident?'

'I suppose it's possible, but she only uses it if absolutely necessary and she hadn't needed to take any since she went on to olanzapine.'

'We found some hyoscine hydrobromide in her bags, delivered by her boyfriend. So, our theory is that she took the hyoscine for travel sickness and this, added to the Kemadrin, resulted in toxic poison.'

'Goodness. Thank you for being so thorough and helpful. *Merci beaucoup*,' I bravely replied. 'So, Jan – Mrs Collins – hadn't run out of her tablets then, she still had some with her?'

'Oh, *oui*. She had tablets with her. We don't know if she was taking them of course.' That was the unanswerable question. Was Jan taking her medication?

Dr Reynaud had also thrown light on the possibility that Jan had not been manic, but had instead been toxic.

Apart from toxic poisoning, the French ward team at the Hôpital Corbet had recorded that Jan had been preoccupied with the belief that her life was endangered by top-secret information known only to her and her boyfriend. Liam Brookes, the so-called boyfriend, had visited the hospital to see that Jan was safe but had only stayed long enough to deliver her belongings.

Dr Reynaud had spoken to him.

'*Oui*, he was a pleasant man and upset because he was shocked that his lady had been seen naked in the streets. He said she would be ashamed but he didn't speak with her. I think he was upset that she had smashed up their laptop. Expensive, *non*? After that, we try to telephone him but we could not find him and he didn't visit the hospital again. Very sad.'

However, Liam Brookes had left an address where he was staying, which Dr Reynaud read out to me. At the time, I wondered whether Liam had returned to the UK, leaving Jan to fend for herself. What a thoughtless bugger.

I gave DS Adams a précis of the events and of my conversations with Dr Reynaud. Other than that, I only had a vague description of him. Lily hadn't met Liam in the flesh either, and as she was my only other source of information on Jan, there was nothing of real consequence to offer DS Adams.

Our time at the police station was pretty much wasted, which was confirmed when an apology of sorts was forthcoming from DS Adams. 'The investigating team have determined that the suicide and the robbery were two separate, unconnected incidents, although one may have been the precursor for the other. Besides which, with no real evidence of foul play, we can't justify the time and expense for any investigation. We only had Mrs Collins's word that there had actually been a break-in and she is now dead. I suppose I'll be the one left to inform her brother.'

'He's a charmer, isn't he?' I said sarcastically. I was ignored. So, I tried a different tack. 'Was anything found to indicate a forced entry? I reported to your officers that I'd seen a man when I was at Jan's house.'

'We made a note that you think you saw someone leaving through the gate, but that wasn't much to go on, I'm afraid. No sign of forced entry at the back of the house but the lock had recently been replaced, it's brand new.'

Taking a business card from the baby-faced DS Charles Adams, I promised to find out what I could from Jan's friends in case there was anything else awry. In return, I was given permission to call him by his first name.

'Charlie, Chuck or Chas?' I enquired cheekily. This was met with a stern look, and I realised far too late that the detective sergeant was lacking a sense of humour. He wouldn't survive long in his job without one, I thought.

'Charles, if you don't mind.'

Out of the corner of my eye I saw Eddie grinning like an idiot at my rebuke from the humourless detective.

Chapter Six

With time unexpectedly available, I suggested to Eddie that a trip to St David's Church Hall might be in order, not only to check on the support offerings for the vulnerable by the Pathways Project, but also to catch up with Father Raymond as I had promised.

'St David's isn't Catholic,' remarked Eddie. I explained, as far as I could, about the project and their links into the homeless teams, soup kitchens, and refuges run by other church volunteer groups in the town.

Eddie, announcing how impressed he was, agreed we should check out the workshops. 'We can't be seen to recommend or refer patients if there's not a sound evidence base for what's on offer, remember, besides which, the project will be in direct competition with our own services.' Eddie seemed to be thinking out loud. 'If it turns out to be load of faith-healing mumbo jumbo or bible bashing then we have to back off,' he informed me. As if I needed reminding.

'No, you're right. There's nothing worse than being preached at, but, "each to their own", as they say,' I replied. If people wanted to go to church that was great, as was having a strong belief to guide and bring comfort. Looking back, I admitted to myself that any religious faith must have been knocked out of me as a child when forced to attend church, not once, but twice on a Sunday. I couldn't wait to escape from the clutches of the righteous.

When Eddie and I arrived at the hall, I think we were both pleasantly surprised by how organised the project appeared to be. There, on a neat colourful poster, were the timetabled current events: discussion groups, anxiety management courses, assertiveness skills training, and rolling programmes for sleep problems.

As we were nosing around in the entrance hall, I spied Father Raymond through some Georgian double doors, overseeing what looked like a creative workshop. Small groups of adults were clustered around tables with coloured pens and sticky notes, deep in serious discussion and joining in with ideas. There was a soothing hubbub of low-level chatter, which reached us as we stood peering through the rectangular glass panels.

Father Raymond recognised me immediately and beckoned to Eddie and me to enter the room. As he strolled towards us, his dog collar was the only giveaway as to his religious occupation. I introduced Eddie as my boss, and after shaking hands Father Raymond explained what the group was so busily attending to.

'This would usually be a discussion group of current events, but to be honest we've had to modify today's plan. We only found out this morning that one of the ladies, Jan, who used to come here regularly, has sadly taken her own life. Her friends here are struggling to make sense of the events leading up to her death, as are we all.'

The jungle drums work extremely fast in the mental health community and word had leaked out from Pargiter Ward. I noticed a couple of Jan's close friends and asked if I could offer my support to them directly. They had seen us and were making their way towards me with open arms and tearful, distraught faces. Noticing their response to Eddie and me, Father Raymond herded us into a small room to one side of the large main hall.

Vanessa, Karen, and Pip had known Jan for years. They had been to art groups together and at one time or another met when they were inpatients on Pargiter Ward. Since then, they had formed a cohesive self-support group nicknamed the Coffee Tuesday Comrades, for obvious reasons. The benefits had been immeasurable. Willowy, tall, and wise, Pip was like an older brother to Karen and Vanessa. He put his arms around the shoulders of his two younger comrades, as if trying to protect them from the dreadful reality of losing their mother figure. Her loss was overwhelming them. All three gushed with questions through their sobs, most of which Eddie and I had no answer for.

'But why would she kill herself, Monica?'

'Why?'

'Monica, something's not right about this. I spoke to her last Sunday and Monday,' Pip said. 'She was fine. Honestly. We talked about Liam and she said there were things we didn't understand, but that Liam had to stay in France. She'd been having dreadful trouble getting hold of him and was waiting for him to phone her back.'

Helpfully, Pip, Karen, and Vanessa spilled forth about Jan and Liam Brookes. The more I heard the more confused I became. He, apparently, had started to go along to the discussion group not long after the project first started and had taken to Jan almost immediately. She and her three friends of the Coffee Tuesday Comrades had been stalwarts of the group right from the outset. Liam, I was told, had been accepted by them as a friendly, knowledgeable individual who had a cheery disposition and showed concern for the wellbeing of the people who met regularly at St David's Church Hall. He'd also helped out with one or two of the homelessness programmes, according to Father Raymond, who had returned to see how we were faring.

'It appears he may have fooled us all. Poor Jan,' Father Raymond said with a shake of his head. While the facts about how Liam met Jan were interesting, it appeared nobody knew where Liam was from, where he lived, or what his background was. He was purporting to be a retired businessman, whose mental health had taken a negative turn when his wife had left him destitute through a nasty divorce. He had been lodging locally but no one in the group had seen him for weeks. That was it.

After making offers of further support, Eddie and I spent a short while with Father Raymond over a welcome cup of tea. By the time we left, we were reassured as to the intentions of the Pathways Project and the way it was facilitated. 'The group leaders have additional qualifications in motivational interviewing, solution focussed therapy, and one or two have a bona fide certificate of accreditation in CBT techniques,' Father Raymond announced proudly. 'And, there are plans afoot to merge services, or at least to share group work, with local drug and alcohol services.'

We walked back to Eddie's car, slowly taking in the potential consequences of what we had discovered inside the doors to St David's Church Hall. 'How on earth did we miss out on the information about this particular project, Mon?' Eddie was plainly embarrassed by the fact that we were oblivious to the sterling work the project had been doing for six months.

'Awkward, wasn't it?' I could only assume we had become so blinkered to meeting targets and running around chasing policy requirements, that we had failed to appreciate the effective mental health work happening on our very doorstep.

'We'd better start looking at the job adverts, if this keeps up,' Eddie said with a sigh of resignation, which was not like him. A wholehearted supporter of the NHS, he normally gave short shrift to any threat to our monopoly of provision for the mentally unwell. As we seemed to be working harder and going nowhere these days, I for one could see no reason not to advocate for new services. There were several patients on my caseload who would definitely benefit from what was on offer at Pathways. I thought of Ian.

With this in mind I called Sean Tierney, Ben's father, to update him on my findings. A delighted Sean thanked me for my incredibly rapid response to his enquiry. However, I would have bet my week's wages that nothing whatsoever would drag Ben to any church hall.

Selfishly I also thought that if I handled the situation carefully enough, he might, as an alternative, appease his parents by agreeing to my plan to go regularly to Len-DAS, where I could leave him in the capable hands of my friend Emma, who has a gift for achieving the impossible.

Slightly devious of me to think in this way, but it was with the best intentions.

Chapter Seven

All scheming and tactics related to work were long forgotten as soon as I arrived home. Once I had taken Deefer for a long walk, over the fields and back again, I had the house to myself for a while. Those daily dog walks helped to clear my mind and allowed me to switch my head from nurse to wife. Max had thoughtfully called to let me know he was planning to meet up with his old mate, Robbie, at the bike club, before heading home. They were sure to be plotting which motorbike investment to seek out next. What I needed them to do, was to make a decision and disappear for a day or two to a classic bike show or to John O'Groats in search of the Holy Grail of bikes and allow me a whole weekend of reading through the cabinet journals belonging to G.C. The Paracelsus riddle wasn't too difficult to solve as it turned out, I just hadn't heard of him before, but clues were missing as to the identity of G.C.

Before starting the dinner preparations, I decided to whet my appetite for history by leafing quickly through one of the journals, which had only 'G.C.' printed on the front cover. A number of the journals had a title, such as *Tinctures* or *Liniments* and these were crammed full of complicated equations and recipes. I wasn't interested in them. Not now.

The first *G.C.* journal was badly water damaged and I turned several pages before I could discern more than a line or two. When I did, I was ecstatic with what was uncovered.

... with Laudanum, there were many examples of poisoning, especially during the Victorian and Edwardian eras, when use of arsenic 'The inheritance poison', was favoured. Thallium was

ascribed the name of 'the poisoner's poison' because of its colourless and odourless nature ...

... strychnine and cyanide will be found to be anomalous at post mortem, thus alerting authorities to foul play.

Cremation, previously the poisoner's best friend, is no longer, as even the ashes will reveal secrets if asked ...

A skilful poisoner considers circumstances in which the intended victim, these days referred to as 'the mark', could conceivably have accidentally ingested, or perhaps inhaled poison. This only requires knowledge of such poisons and their individual characteristics.

Most essentially the conventions of 'the mark' are required to be known. Do they habitually stroll in the woods with their dog? Do they order a special item from the bakers? It is most advantageous if 'the mark' is in receipt of regular treatment with prescribed medication – this can be so effective in overdose – one simply requires access to information on the toxicity of the medicine and a reference list or compendium is a prerequisite.

Oh my God! This man is giving advice about poisoning. Is he a murderer?

The coincidence was not lost on me. I had, only the day before, been confronted by death from an overdose of prescribed medication. Whether Jan's death was suicide or not was still unclear, and a number of doubts had plagued me for more than twenty-four hours despite distracting myself.

A sense of urgency arose in me, galvanising me into action, making me arrange the journals in relevant and chronological order. Did I possess all the journals and how would I know if I didn't? How awful it would be to discover that I'd bought tantalisingly few of the total set.

I was shaking in anticipation.

'Wine, I need vino plonko ... and chocolate.'

Setting about the task with grim determination not to panic and not to spill any wine on the precious books, concentrating hard, I worked out that there were eight salvageable chemical recipe books and four others. Two of the journals turned out not to contain recipes, but revealed numerical coding of some sort, much of which had initials to anonymise the relevant parts, I assumed, and on each page, were running totals carried forward to the next. The totals were in pounds, shillings, and pence sterling. The dates ranged over decades from the 1940s to the 1970s and were made in two different sets of handwriting. One type of handwriting did not occur again after the 1960s, and the other, I deduced belonged to G.C. The sums of money in the running totals were considerable. Hundreds of thousands of pounds.

G.C., whoever he was, had lots of money and only two initials, which was bothering me. Some recent research had apparently proven that people with three or more initials were believed by others to be more intelligent and therefore did better in business. Richer by courtesy of their names. I thought I was the only unfortunate individual whose parents had found it too taxing to arrive at a middle name for their child, and a first-born at that. Once I had discovered my own parents' omission, I felt quite aggrieved at not being given a middle name. Why was it that G.C.'s parents had also been unable to settle upon a suitable set of names for their son? I wondered if he was adopted or perhaps orphaned and only had two names for one of those reasons. Like, Oliver Twist. *Very possible*, I thought.

Revisiting this conundrum and the unrecognisable coding in the journals would have to wait. It was too onerous a task for a simple mind like mine after a couple of problematic days at work.

Turning my attention to the remaining journals, I opened up a whole new world. Beginning another slightly water-damaged journal, picked at random, I couldn't put it down.

All through the war, I worked alongside Mr M, the pharmacist, as his assistant. I admired Mr M for his extensive knowledge of curative home remedies, which were often less financially burdensome than the manufactured tinctures and lotions to be found on the shelves. He shared his wisdom readily with the good folk of the town, who remained indebted to this generous man until the day he sadly passed away.

His son, young Mr M, had returned from the war a broken man who had then relied upon me most heavily to guide him in re-learning the requirements of the family business, almost as if he had never experienced it previously. He was a pharmacist, like his father, but Burma had deprived him of his confidence and he narrowly avoided death or insanity. I believe it was for that reason he never once spoke of the terrors he endured during his incarceration as a prisoner of war.

The hardships for the everyday people of this country continued long after the end of the conflict and yet, in contrast, the dispensary seemed to prosper. I had been certain that with the end of the war my employment would be in jeopardy, for it was the case that my mother and I had blown into the town like the wind, uninvited. Desperation drove us to seek out and to stay with relatives as evacuees from London and we never once returned there.

Neither young Mr M nor his father ever indicated that my employment with them was to be terminated once the war had finished. Conversely, Mr M senior made me a life-changing proposal, which would secure my ability to remain financially independent. As a young adult, I had an ability to adapt and to learn rapidly, soaking up knowledge and skills as if I were a sponge.

My family name was synonymous with poisoning, and for this reason, I was introvert by nature, and particular not to seek attention nor to attain friendship other than on a superficial level, fearing that disclosure of my family history would undermine acceptance by the local welcoming community.

My obsession with privacy was not borne out of pure selfishness but was for my mother's benefit. She had finally been able to evade the hounds of the press, who, for many years, had persisted in speculating as to her part in the poisoning of Father, Aunt V, and Grandmother.

What a clue. "A family name synonymous with poisoning". Who on earth could that be? I wondered. Someone who had poisoned three family members … Surname beginning with the letter C.

The authorities, the investigations, and the inquests failed to identify the guilty party, but for years afterwards society deemed my dear mother to be guilty and she suffered dreadfully until such time as we escaped London and achieved anonymity using father's middle name as our surname. Legally of course, we still retained our former surnames, and it was this secret I feared would be revealed.

Oh no, the surname doesn't begin with C.

It will be after my death that these scattered memoirs may come to light, but in spite of this I will not disclose the facts. For certain, the vultures will speculate and damage my mother's memory. My own guilt, however, is to be revealed within, as a cathartic confession of sorts.

I demanded revenge for my mother's unwarranted emotional torture and vowed to seek out the guilty party to ensure that he, for it was my own uncle, would be held to account. My wish was not to come true, for my uncle had, by design, moved to America with his wife. It was the war that robbed him of his life, not me. He boarded a ship, supposedly on business, bound for Great Britain, before the United States joined the war, but the ship was torpedoed by a German U boat and sank without a trace. Only a handful of passengers and crew survived. My uncle was not among them. His wife informed my mother of the events, who seemed saddened by the loss of yet another member of the family, although I am not convinced that she had even considered that her own brother had deliberately thrown the burden of suspicion and guilt in her direction. He died an innocent man, because his crimes were never proven. He had killed for money.

Cheated and unfairly robbed of restitution, a gaping hole was filled by a bitter appetite for revenge, which I eventually learnt to feed. This I achieved by ensuring removal from society, those who are truly evil and where justice had failed in its duty. It has been a most satisfying compromise; morally, psychologically, and financially.

Not once did it ever occur to me that my first, but unintended victim would, by default, dictate my future path in life, causing destiny to veer wildly from its predetermined course. I have little regret. It has been a lucrative career and allowed me to live in comfort, some would argue, luxury. Living in obscurity, abstaining from both marriage and children were the prices paid.

I recall in the late 1950s, Mr Adatti, long since deceased, with no offspring or relatives in this country (I am therefore at liberty to use his name), regularly gave his custom to the dispensary. He was a victim of his wife's tongue and of her fists. On at least one occasion that the Messrs M were aware of, Mr Adatti was assaulted with a deadly weapon at the hands of his spouse. Once, almost certainly, she had used an iron poker and on a later occasion had caused considerable damage to his person with a skillet. Mr Adatti managed to manufacture a variety of implausible explanations for the injuries with which he presented for assistance. Our local doctor shared our considerable concerns for the man, but could not persuade Mr Adatti to confess to his hellish matrimonial existence. The doctor therefore took a fresh perspective. Treating the perpetrator, to save the victim, he decided to prescribe the new antidepressant medication imipramine to Mrs Adatti in an attempt to alleviate her most foul temperament.

The powerful combination of knowledge, fear, and desperation must have given Mr Adatti the impetus to act. When he called at the dispensary to collect the first prescription for his wife, I enlightened him to the fact that imipramine had been found to be fatally toxic in overdose, and in order to avoid such a catastrophe, he should ensure that his wife was made aware of this and not encouraged to take more than the prescribed daily dose. It was a whispered suggestion on my part and not intended as anything other than helpful guidance.

Never have I seen such a relieved and unburdened man at a funeral. In an unexpected twist of fate, Mrs Adatti had come into a sizeable inheritance the year before, which she had appeared unwilling to share with her long-suffering husband. He inherited every penny.

I am certain that Mr Adatti would have danced upon her grave, if it were not for the certain knowledge that this would have aroused suspicion. He could have done, because no one questioned her death. It was simply an accidental overdose.

Mr Adatti made a private donation to Mr M and to the local doctor by way of a gift of thanks for aid in his darkest hours. It was a tidy sum, from which I too benefitted.

That single opportune moment, when I imparted knowledge to Mr Adatti, which then gave rise to his freedom and to retribution for years of wretched suffering, gave respite from my unrequited need for personal vengeance. Such liberating emotions meant that I would forever seek more of those sweet moments, like a gambler or an opium addict, or in the same way in which an actor seeks adulation for a performance.

Mr M had long been a purveyor of fine poisons, all legal and above board, carefully accounted for. Yet, despite working alongside him for many years, I had initially failed to realise what additional services he offered, for a fee of course. I was soon to become privy to the alternative business, which enabled prosperity for both Mr M and for myself.

In a cavernous laboratory within the building, referred to as 'the Apothecary' there was the most comprehensive collection of chemicals, compounds, tinctures, and tonics outside of that owned by Merlin himself, I would imagine. As well as cures for boils, syphilis, and other unfortunate ailments, abortions were available, although never named as such. Income was also derived from the local convalescent homes, cottage hospitals, isolation hospitals, and asylums, who all required assistance with enabling their residents to 'pass peacefully' and it was Mr M who provided invaluable solutions for these demands, using the same humane approach taken by veterinary medicine.

Mr M was a marvel. He provided a postal service for home remedies to be sent to those who lived out of the local area and for whom a journey into town would have been far too taxing. Regrettably, it became apparent to Mr M senior, that his son, through no fault of his own, was unable to grasp the intricacies of the 'recipes' for these herbal specialities. Fine, exact measurements were required, as well as distillation processes, infusions, and centrifugal separations.

Another apprentice was required by the Master and I had the aptitude for the task.

I grasped with both hands the offer made by Mr M to become his apprentice.

Now, it is not beyond the wit of the everyday man in the street to understand why he offered me this, but the level of risk he was taking in exposing his own unlawful practices had to be ameliorated, if not offset altogether.

That risk was indeed cleverly countered by Mr M who had taken the trouble to confirm my true identity and that of my mother. He had assistance from a number of valued 'customers' within the Civil Service, shall we say. He knew I was trustworthy enough to keep secrets. For one so young, I held many better than a vault at the Bank of England. Thus, the binding contract was made and I had seven years of learning ahead of me.

Mr M was a thoughtful master. He gave me a special gift in recognition of my acceptance of his tutelage. A fine antique polished medicine cabinet, which had once belonged to a ship's doctor. He had a small brass plaque made with my initials engraved on it. My false initials, G.C. Within, there were a variety of bottles, glass vials, earthenware storage jars, a small pestle and mortar, minuscule silver spoons, and dainty pillboxes in crafted drawers. It was thing of beauty to me, and remains so as I gaze at it now.

That had solved another part of the puzzle. The engraved plaques had been added much later in the cabinet's life. How brilliant it was to have such detailed provenance with my antique. I was going to stop what I was doing and return to the usual household chores and routines that awaited me, but I couldn't prevent myself from reading on.

This form of education is never completed, and so it was that for twenty years, I worked alongside Mr M senior. His son took on my previous role, and, being a qualified pharmacist, he could dispense prescriptions as the honest face of the business. Meanwhile, behind the scenes, much cash was being generated by less lawful means in exchange for unusual remedies, and in absolute secrecy. This business plan made perfect sense.

The business thrived, leaving less time for Mr M and myself to take on special assignments of our own and out of necessity we became discerning as to which contracts we chose.

Mr M wholeheartedly approved of my moral approach to justice and the pair of us would keep a close eye on the news, on court reports, on inquests, and especially the verdicts from the Coroner's Court. Specifically, we were keeping our beady eyes open for cases where justice was seen not to have been done, or where there had been a technicality preventing a sound verdict, despite irrefutable evidence of guilt. We targeted rapists, sex offenders, murderers, and serial killers, some of whom were unprincipled poisoners. They were unlike ourselves in every respect.

Mr M and I performed a most valuable service to society. We were the new Resistance. We were vigilantes in the true sense of the word. Vigilant for the personification of evil.

This required a strict code of conduct, thorough vetting procedures, impeccable planning and execution. Mr M had learnt valuable lessons over the years. Mistakes that I was keen not to repeat.

There are key areas for consideration in the tools used by a poisoning mercenary, for that is what we were, in essence.

The overriding question as you read this will be, why poison?

Why would I, as the daughter of a woman falsely accused of poisoning become a poisoner?

The answer is more straightforward than you would care to imagine.

Chapter Eight

'Oh my God! G.C. is a woman!!' I shouted out loud. Deefer, who was sitting expectantly waiting for his dinner, jumped as if startled by my sudden outburst. 'She's a woman,' I repeated breathlessly. Deefer pricked up his ears at such an amazing revelation. Picking up the journal from where I had dropped it, I read the whole thing again from the start to the point of my discovery that G.C. was female.

'Bloody effing Nora!' I exclaimed, using one of my best friend's alternative swear phrases. Holding G.C.'s secrets in my hands was superbly thrilling. I had experienced the odd coincidence in life, who hasn't? But this was astounding by anyone's standards. Had the cabinet found *me* at the auction? Were all the journals in my possession? I needed to know for certain because I did not want to miss one word of what G.C. had to share with me. The only way to tell was to read them word for word.

'Shit.'

I had let time run away with me and Max would be home soon, with no dinner awaiting him. This would be viewed as a failure in my wifely duties and an infringement of the unwritten rules of our marriage. He would know that I had distracted myself again and he had not yet forgiven me for spending so much time on my academic studies over the last year.

Max knows how to twist the thumbscrews of guilt when necessary.

Dashing into the kitchen with Deefer at my heels, I racked my brains to arrive at a quick supper recipe. I stood flapping my arms at the contents of the fridge, seeking inspiration. Irritatingly, I was horribly distracted from the task in hand because I was desperate to know who G.C. was. She had already given me enough clues, but I strained my memory banks trying to recall a case of three family members being poisoned; a father, an aunt, and a grandmother. I had read about this. I knew this case.

My memory bank is more of a memory library. I always thought everyone had one. My memory library can be a little slow in revealing its hidden facts, but as I stood at the fridge, with the door open, nothing was forthcoming. As I hurriedly prepared my cheat's version of pasta al forno for dinner, I searched it once more for information about who G.C. might be.

At last, it came to me. 'Gotcha!'

When Max arrived home, I played the dutiful wife as required, prioritising his needs for a while, by deliberately cosseting him. 'Hard day at work again?' Kiss. 'You'll feel better after a hot shower. Dinner's nearly ready.'

Once he had eaten his fill and parked himself sprawled in front of the television, it was not long before he drifted off into a cosy sleep alongside Deefer on the settee.

Free to finish the duties of the scullery maid, I washed up and tidied the kitchen, before commencing my mission to find the story of a well-known poisoning, which I was sure happened around the 1930s. I had read it in a book. All I had to do was to find that book in my extensive collection. When I did, it was such an immense relief to unearth exactly what I had been looking for that I sat down on the spare bed, clutching the book as if it were a precious artefact.

'You're Grace's daughter ... are you a Grace too? Or a Georgina? I don't know anything about you,' I whispered to the book. A slightly dog-eared paperback written in the 1970s, which had detailed documentation of the poisonings and inquests into three deaths, held the information I needed. Late 1920s was the era. This must mean that the prime suspect, Grace, could not be G.C., as she would have been in her early thirties at the time. She could not have been a young adult during the Second World War. Her daughter would have been. The young G.C. had been less than ten years old at the time the deaths in her family had occurred. She was barely mentioned anywhere in records of the inquests and yet they must have had a profound impact on her life.

I could easily imagine the young G.C. becoming protective of her mother and desperately seeking an answer as to who the real culprit was. She would never have considered her mother to be guilty, and it appeared, by what she had written, that she believed that her uncle was to blame. How frustrating that nothing was ever proved.

G.C. and I had much in common, and I anticipated she would have a lot to teach me about poisoning through her writings. I assumed she too was named Grace, and that was how I referred to her from then on. Such a tingling ran up my spine when I read her words about understanding the habits of intended victims, and leading others to believe suicide was the cause of death. How apt. For my dreadful discovery of Jan's body had appeared to be just that. Suicide.

Was it? Could Liam Brookes have been sitting opposite her at her kitchen table, forcing her to swallow tablets? Unlikely. Did she really have good reason to kill herself? Was Liam really in France or had he returned and taken Jan's money? Had he fooled her and everyone else, like Father Raymond said? Was it Liam's leg I had seen as he headed out of her back gate?

Without a doubt, if I had taken the journals upstairs for bedtime reading I would have been awake all night, and Max would have been furious. So I decided to ration my doses of excitement to the evenings after work. I had so much on my plate already that a good night's sleep was a priority.

Max woke up from his doze on the settee in good time to go straight to bed, where he lay wide awake. Irritatingly he chose this time of day to reflect on matters financial, work, and bike related. As we sat in bed I pretended to listen as he chatted but never once did he ask about my day. He was more interested in what I had planned for the next evening as far as food was concerned.

'I have no bloody idea. I'll rustle something up, don't worry, you won't starve.'

'I tell you what, I'll cook tomorrow,' he offered. 'Chinese, a kebab, pizza, or curry?'

We agreed on curry for the following night, and eventually Max drifted into a deep sleep, again. The only sounds he made, apart from his sonorous breathing, were the ones of tuneless windy trumpeting as he flatulently deflated.

Although fatigued, I was awake for much of the night mulling over my new discovery; G.C.'s true identity. The anticipation of what else I would find contained in those journals almost tempted me out of bed, but I stuck to my rigid self-imposed restrictions, as spare energy for work was required. When I did eventually fall asleep, I was plagued by pictures of Jan, battered and bruised, lying on her deathbed, followed by scenes of her running naked down cobbled streets escaping from tiny pixies with swords. There was even a slight smell of death in my dreams, although on reflection, it could just as easily have been Max farting again.

Chapter Nine

On my arrival at work, I had a letter waiting in my correspondence tray from Lily, who had promised to furnish me with a photo of Liam Brookes. Jan had sent her one before they went to France, which had been taken of the group who attended the Pathways Project. There were cheerful and familiar faces in the photo, including those of the diminutive, anxiety-ridden Vanessa with her curly blonde hair, Karen sporting her best Dr Marten boots, and Pip standing protectively behind them, next to Jan. There were a few other faces I recognised but I couldn't immediately bring their names to mind. Standing next to Father Raymond, two other clergymen and one female vicar, distinguishable by dog collars, was a tall, solidly built man in dark-rimmed glasses. He had a thick head of dark auburn hair, was clean-shaven, and stood tall and proud with his shoulders back as a confident man does. I think it was the details that made him stand out and not necessarily the arrow that Jan had drawn on the photo to help Lily identify the new man in her life. Although in casual clothing, he was neat, thoughtfully dressed, shiny-clean, and well kempt. Liam Brookes looked like a man who was in the wrong place. Most odd.

I picked up the phone and gave Lily a quick call to thank her for taking the time and trouble to send the photo. She was pleased to have a chance to talk about Jan, I think. She was struggling with the loss of her life-long friend and the sadness could be heard in her voice.

'You can keep the photo if you like, Monica. I have dozens of better ones and I don't want to keep a reminder of that monstrous man, thank you very much. Have the police found him yet, do you know?'

I had no news for her, as Liam seemed to have vanished, but as we spoke we both concluded he must have gone back to France, perhaps trying to take ownership of the flat bought with Jan's money. Lily promised to let me know of the funeral arrangements once she had been in touch with Jan's brother, which led me to confess my shame at not knowing he existed until Jan's death.

'That's hardly surprising. He wasn't even on Jan's Christmas card list,' Lily said, easing my discomfort. 'They didn't get on, especially not as young children. He was a dreadful bully and she couldn't wait for him to leave home. So, after university she never returned, got a top civil service job, married Jeff, and lived happily ever after. Well, until the first signs of the menopause, then woof. She went bonkers.'

'The menopause, are you sure? She must have been very young for the menopause.'

'Poor Jan. She had really bad hormonal problems for years. I can't remember what it's called, fibroids, endometricals or something like that. She and Jeff couldn't have children, but when things got worse in the downstairs department, she had to have a hysterical-ectomy and it was after that she had the first bonkers spectacular.' I didn't laugh even though I had always called it a hysterical-ectomy too. 'I can't imagine how sad they were not to have children,' Lily added. I could.

Jan's first manic episode took its place in mental health history when she'd brought the M1 motorway to a standstill for several hours. The local and national press reported her naked dash along the carriageway, weaving between the lanes, 'dicing with death'. Reports had detailed how she ran down a grass bank and, 'like superwoman, lifted a manhole cover before disappearing down into the main sewer'. There were stories of roadblocks, police, fire crews, farmers with tractors and ropes, all attempting to extricate Jan from the manhole while she ranted at the world, covered in human excrement.

The whole extraordinary scene made the television news headlines. Luckily it was before the days of mobile phones with cameras otherwise her suicide could easily have come at a much earlier time in her life. Never did she forget the embarrassment, and even though her memory of that day was not perfect, it was the likely catalyst to the eventual end of her career.

For many reasons, that was not the last of the reckless events which peppered Jan's life, and she had her fair share of depression to deal with after each manic high.

Jan had written a small piece for a leading mental health charity entitled: 'Living with Bipolar Disorder is a Life of Ups and Downs'. In it, she described how being high or hypomanic provides a sense of euphoria, is exhilarating and can be magical. She wrote, 'Those who experience such levels of activity are privileged to have an unexpected increase in abilities. One young lady I came across in hospital said she learnt a new language on each occasion she became hypomanic. She helped me to understand the power of hypomania. Colours appear brighter, sounds more acute, the brain fires on all cylinders at once with increased and improved vocabulary, and even mathematical skills become newly available to those who never previously possessed them.

'But with this level of enlightenment comes a dark and dangerous power. Full-blown mania. It can be deadly. The brain races as thoughts become increasingly complex and confused. Sleep is impossible, and the number of tasks taken on can never hope to be completed. The need to eat and drink, to wash and dress can be overridden by this force, and such acute psychotic beliefs arise that the sufferer is lost to reality. The unfortunate consequence to this rollercoaster is the intense pleasure derived from the hypomanic state. It draws people back, and they will, like any good alcoholic, convince themselves they can avoid the manic phase. Some never learn and others do. The hard way."

Jan tried to manage her life without recourse to medication but the consequential repeating pattern of mania and depression forced her to accept it as a necessary evil. Unfortunately, by that time, she had lost the dedication and love of her husband, who had been drained of empathy and exhausted by her mania. She had spent too many weeks of her fifth decade under a Section of the Mental Health Act and he never reconciled himself with the fact that the medication treatment had all but extinguished Jan's lively spark. It had been snuffed out. Her eccentric creativity had been suppressed by antipsychotic injections.

When I first met her, Sparkey had become her only daily companion. Her life was a series of groups, coffee mornings with friends and trips on coaches to National Trust sites, to break up the monotony. When she met Liam, things changed, and he seemed to reignite her curiosity about life and a wish to travel abroad again. How sad to have ended in loss of trust, in tears, and in tragedy.

My brief telephone conversation with Lily somehow nudged my memory and prompted me into pulling together information leaflets for the Pathways Project team. At the LCMHT offices we always kept a stock of the leaflets produced by MIND and Rethink and a few other resources about medication which I had agreed with Eddie to provide free of charge to the project. I was passing by St David's Church Hall on my rounds, and it was no great hardship to pop in and drop these off. I did just that.

On my way there, I deliberately drove past Jan Collins's house. Her car was still outside and a silver saloon was parked beside it on the driveway. A man in a dark suit was examining the boarded-up front door and seemed to be trying the door handle. I stopped my car across the driveway entrance and shouted to him as I approached, unwisely leaving the relative safety of my vehicle. 'Can I help you?'

'I doubt it. Unless you know who I speak to about gaining access to this property.' The man turned to speak to me and he was not in a good frame of mind, judging from his fearsome expression. Then I saw the shark eyes.

'That depends on who you are, I suppose.'

'What business is it of yours?'

'I'm a friend of the owner, in a professional capacity.' I thought that the man with the shark eyes had failed to recognise me, but I was wrong.

'I know full well who you are.' He made his way towards my car to confront me, a key in his hand attached to a simple fob. His voice and abrupt manner gave me an excellent clue as to who I was speaking to.

'Are you Mr Frank Hughes, by any chance?' That stopped him in his tracks. 'We've spoken on the phone,' I said offering my hand to shake. He ignored it and began a furious and whispered tirade of accusations. 'Why would you be watching me? Why are you always snooping about here, there and everywhere? Can't you mind your own bloody business? She's dead and you have no right to be here.'

'Now hang on there, Mr Hughes, I'm parked on a public road. I had no idea who you were and you looked like you were trying to break in.'

A murderous look from shark eyes, an aggressive stance, and Frank Hughes suddenly became a threat. 'How dare you make such a fucking outrageous accusation, you conniving bitch! I have a key to the front door.'

I had moved backwards in reaction to his outburst and yet he strode towards me to poke me in the chest with the key, reversing me into my own car door. His anger had taken me by surprise.

'Mr Hughes, I'm not shouting at you and I'm not swearing at you. I am asking you to back off, so that I can get into my car and leave.' Fortunately, this tried and tested strategy worked in the street every bit as well as it did on the acute psychiatric wards. I safely made a hasty retreat.

Phoning the office from the car park at St David's Church Hall, I alerted Kelly to my confrontation with Frank Hughes. 'What an appalling man. You should report him to the police. Zero tolerance for abuse of NHS staff, Monica,' she reminded me.

'I am a bit shaken, I have to admit. What a complete arsehole. He's already threatened to make a formal complaint against me and I haven't done anything wrong.'

As I let myself in through the front doors of the hall I asked an elderly lady, who seemed to be acting as an unofficial receptionist, where I should deposit the leaflets. People were leaving at the end of the morning sessions and heading off for lunch. Meanwhile, I was politely directed to place the leaflets on a large oak table in the entrance hall to the main building where I set the box down, grateful to unburden my aching arms. I headed for the toilets, taking much needed advantage of the clean facilities. The adrenalin surge created by my run-in with Frank Hughes had caused havoc with my bladder.

As I sat there, privately cocooned in a cubicle, a couple of familiar voices could be heard as they talked about Jan Collins. The conversation echoed as the sound bounced from the porcelain sinks and bare walls.

'I wonder where Father Raymond got the impression Jan had paid for the holiday to France? She didn't. It wasn't a hotel holiday, was it …? They went to Liam's flat there.'

'Yeah. Weird. He keeps telling everyone the same story. She gave a load of her money to that shit of a brother of hers anyway, to bail him out of another failed business opportunity; so she couldn't have paid.'

'No, she couldn't. Did you speak to Liam?'

'I've tried loads of times but his phone's dead. He's vanished.'

Remaining silently perched on the loo, with my legs becoming numb, I struggled to piece together the puzzle about Jan and Liam. However, the information about Jan's brother was very interesting and I wondered how much money Jan did have stashed away and how much he was still after.

I waited until the voices outside the toilet door had gone before I left the cubicle, washed my hands and stepped into the entrance hall in time to see Karen and Vanessa walking across the car park together, deep in conversation.

Amongst the remaining small crowd exiting the main hall were Sean and Manuela Tierney, Ben's parents. They were talking animatedly with a lady vicar who had been showing them around and they didn't notice me as they passed by. They had failed to shut the front door behind them, so I walked over to do the dutiful thing, but as I was about to pull the door towards me, I saw Father Raymond. He was approaching from the opposite direction and crossed paths with Sean, Manuela, and the vicar. I heard them both being introduced to Father Raymond, and he took their hands in his as they appeared to explain their son's plight, and how Father Joseph had recommended the Pathways Project. I couldn't hear everything being said, but Father Raymond welcomed their interest in the project and then continued towards me, thankfully looking at his feet, deep in thought with hand on chin.

This gave me enough time to backtrack to the table and resume arranging the leaflets. I could have chosen to stay at the door and have a conversation with Father Raymond about what I had just witnessed, but there had been tell-tale signs in his body language that made me instinctively pretend I had not been a witness to the meeting.

'Oh, hello, Monica, I see my plan to convert you is beginning to work,' he joked as he approached the table to scan the leaflets I had donated. He nodded appreciatively and asked me briefly about my recent purchase at the auction.

'The lovely cabinet is in pride of place in my dining room, and I have to say that I'm getting enormous pleasure from what I've read so far in the journals. They're pretty badly damaged but what I have managed to read seems to be intriguing.' I was deliberately vague, not having the time to spend chatting. Father Raymond appeared to have his own agenda and rapidly changed the subject by asking for my advice.

'Some of the group, who are friends of Jan Collins, want to do something meaningful in her memory. I'm not sure exactly what they're intending but I suspect it's not about planting a tree. They want to make a statement or have a project dedicated to her. Can you chat to them and give your guidance? They would appreciate it.'

'I suspect, Father, this is a trick on your part to get me to come back …' I quipped, smiling at him. 'Yes of course, no problem.

I'll be back to join everyone for a vol-au-vent after the funeral so I'll do what you ask as a special favour to Jan, to them and to you, but not necessarily to God. The jury is still out on that one'.

I made my excuses and left, hoping to catch up with Ben's parents before they disappeared, but I was out of luck. There was no sign of them, which was probably for the best, as Sean could talk for England, as well as for Ireland. I had to make another phone call to DS Charles Adams. Earlier I had left him a message to contact me; I was keen to update him on the information given to me by Jan's friends regarding Frank and Liam. At first, I didn't think I would bother, as I was certain the police enquiries must have revealed everything that I had found out. Nevertheless, I had promised.

DS Adams was in and out of the station all day long and we played telephone ping pong that morning, missing each other by minutes and leaving messages. Mobile phone to my ear, I sat in my car, on hold for a few minutes while he was located and because Charles Adams was such a cold fish of a man, I wasn't looking forward to the conversation. To be honest, I struggled with people who didn't possess a sense of humour, evidenced by the fact I had taken to referring to him as 'DS Dynamic', knowing it would have insulted him were he ever to find out, and because my nicknames for people amused Kelly at the office.

'Hello, Monica, sorry, we keep missing each other,' came the monotone voice of DS Adams, as dull as ever. 'I take it you have news on Mr Liam Brookes?'

'I do, I also want to ask about Jan's brother, Frank Hughes, but I'm not sure how useful any of this will be to you.'

'You'd be surprised.'

'So far, I've found out that Liam Brookes was a regular at the new Pathways Project running at St David's Church Hall, and he befriended a number of the people there. It seems that's where he met Jan. Her friends tell me he put a lot of effort into being accepted and in befriending everyone and they quite liked the man. He volunteered at a couple of the homeless shelters too. But he didn't talk about himself a lot and very little about his private life is known.'

'Always the way, I'm afraid.'

'I do, however, have a recent photo of him, courtesy of Jan's best friend.'

'Now that will be useful ... can you scan it and email it through to us at the station? The email address should be on the card I gave you.'

'If I had a scanner, I could.'

With the usual lack of NHS technology available, a plan was made for me to take the photo to the station and for DS Adams to personally make a scanned copy. Lucky me. More time to spend with DS Dynamic, the grey-suited man, and he wasn't even physically attractive. So far, the bloke had no redeeming features other than taking his job seriously.

DS Adams was as good as his word and he efficiently scanned the photo, handing me back the original and making a few comments about Liam, much along the lines of my own thoughts.

'I really shouldn't say this, but he looks out of place. Too clean.'

'My thoughts exactly,' I confirmed with a nod at the photo. 'Jan's friends think he may have skedaddled back to France, is that a possibility?'

'Yes, I would say so. He's free to do just that. He hasn't been charged with any crime and we have no evidence to indicate one has been committed. That's about all I can tell you at this point. Sorry.'

Was he was playing his cards close to his chest? Or were the police not bothering to follow up on Liam Brookes? Either way, I felt justified in having contacted the police with what little information I had gathered. DS Adams asked me for the names of Jan's friends at the Pathways group as he thought they might have useful information worth pursuing. However it looked as if Jan's death was suicide and the only possible crime was in relation to financial abuse. Jan was a vulnerable lonely woman. Nothing more than a sad story.

'Well, I think Jan's friends at the project may have a different perspective on Liam Brookes from the one we have accepted as being the truth,' I ventured, confessing to my eavesdropping moment in the ladies' toilets at St David's.

DS Adams appeared more interested in Jan's brother.

'The rude gentleman who was so insistent ...I remember him well enough.' A thoughtful look crossed Charles's face.

'He was at Jan's house today trying unsuccessfully to open the front door with a key. I assume the lock had been changed. Well, I stopped because he looked like he was someone trying to break in, and challenged him. He's a nasty piece of work. You'll probably get a call from him, yelling again.'

'Thanks for the tip-off. I'll let the desk sergeant know.' I was asked to keep my ears open for any other useful titbits, particularly regarding Jan's brother. Charles seemed to have lost interest in Liam Brookes.

Chapter Ten

A week later, the funeral was held. It was a sobering event. Jan's Coffee Comrades stood together for comfort, joined by other friends that Jan had made over the last few years. Lily and her husband Jim were there, as expected, and Lily waved as she recognised me, despite us only having met a couple of times in person. She indicated for me to sit next to her, for which I was grateful. Otherwise I would have hovered at the back on my own, looking lost and unloved.

One or two spare vicars and a priest turned up from the Pathways Project, as if on standby in case the one at the crematorium wasn't up to the job.

Jan's ex-husband was introduced by a whisper from Lily, he sat on the other side of her and Jim, with a fine looking woman, who I assumed was his second wife. Jan's brother, who wore a sour expression for much of the time, ended up at the front with an elderly lady who was confirmed as being Jan's ancient Aunt Clarissa. I shuddered slightly when I saw Frank Hughes again. Apart from family, there were about a dozen other mourners in total, none of whom were recognised by Lily or me.

As we made our way out of the church at the end of the short service, and mostly due to bad timing on my part, I stepped from the pew into the direct path of Frank, who gave me such a withering look that I stepped back again and trod on Lily's toes.

'Goodness, he doesn't seem to like you much either,' she said. 'I thought he only reserved those evil eyes for me.'

'Really? What have you done to upset him so much?'

'He's always hated me. I got in the way of his ability to manipulate his sister into lending him money. What did *you* do?'

'I got the blame for allowing his sister to die, and for not preventing her boyfriend from spending her money for her.'

'Money. It's always about money with Frank. As soon as he knew Jan was dead, he came around to see me and demanded my key to her house. Unfeeling monster. Still, I suppose he inherits the lot, so he won't have to worry now, will he? If I was Aunt Clarissa I'd be careful though. She's loaded and he knows it. Look how he guards her.' At Lily's words, I turned around to face her, making sure that she had spoken in playful jest, but realising soon enough that she hadn't.

After the plain, simple, gloomy service, there was an offer of tea and cake at the church hall. Father Raymond had sidled up to me immediately after the service to make sure I was planning on joining Jan's friends as promised and, if I hadn't known better, I would have thought it was yet another effort on his part to get me to a church more regularly.

'Anyway,' I asked, out of mild curiosity, 'are you allowed in to a non-Catholic funeral?'

'Why, are Catholics not allowed?'

'I've no idea, Father, I'm afraid my knowledge of the Catholic Church is a smidgen above not a lot.' Which was true. 'But while I have your attention, I have an idea I'd like to run past you. It's irrelevant what denomination you are for this, but what do you think of a medication amnesty as a project in memory of Jan Collins?'

Father Raymond raised his magnificent eyebrows and grinned. 'You're going to have to explain what you mean exactly, please, Monica.'

This idea had come to me in the shower where I am often inspired, and I thought it was a brilliant plan that should have been thought of years ago. I had in mind to advertise far and wide that an amnesty was being held for anyone who had stocks or stores of unused medication in their homes. Many people didn't know what to do with old tablets or where to take them for safe disposal. Some people kept hold of medicines, and despite not taking them, would regularly collect the prescriptions as a pretence, so as not to offend the doctor or upset their family members. Whatever the reason, the fewer tablets and medicines available to an individual, the less chance of successful suicide. That was the idea behind the plan.

'A suicide reduction initiative if you like, or perhaps a risk reduction strategy would be more accurate, but you get my drift.'

Father Raymond was beaming at me. 'Monica, that's perfect!'

Over tea and delicious cake at St David's, the idea was put to Jan's friends who, without exception, wanted to run with the initiative, especially Lily, who desperately wanted to join in with the organisation. She was absorbed, without hesitation, by the group of friends from the Pathways Project, and the Coffee Tuesday Comrades made her most welcome.

There were several areas of planning for a medication amnesty which required careful consideration and I offered, out of a sense of loyalty to Jan and her close friends, to help in organising the collection, storage, and disposal practicalities. The enthusiastic Pathways team were keen to create posters and to push the idea through local radio and newspapers. So, despite the sad circumstances of the day there were smiles exchanged across coffee and walnut cake, lemon drizzle, and vol-au-vents.

Frank Hughes glared at me every so often, when he thought other people weren't looking, and I began to wonder what evil thoughts were going through his mind and why he was targeting me.

'Why is it you can only get vol-au-vents at buffet occasions?' I asked Vanessa, who was handing out food on large metal platters.

'I know, that's why I love weddings, birthdays, and anniversaries,' she replied, a brave smile hiding her heartache.

The chicken and mushroom vol-au-vents had tasted unusually good and thanks to Vanessa, I had eaten too many before the end of the afternoon. Every time she passed by, she would update me on the ideas she and Karen had come up with for the medicines amnesty. On one occasion, she caught Frank giving me one of his death stares. 'You know who he is, don't you?'

'Yes, Vanessa, although I find it hard to believe, he is apparently Jan's brother.'

'Stepbrother. He's the nastiest piece of filth that walks the streets.' I was shocked at what Vanessa had said; she was usually so unassuming. 'He calls himself a businessman, and talks about business dealings and new ventures as if he's legitimate.'

'Isn't he?' I asked in a whisper.

'I thought you were streetwise. No. He's into supplying the drug dealers for miles around, and the rumour is, he's upset his competitors, owes money, and has his own expensive cocaine habit.'

I had been right. He was the drug dealer boss. That explained a lot.

The Jan Collins Memorial Project Team held our first official meeting a week after Jan's funeral. In that short amount of time, I'd had my work cut out to liaise with the hospital pharmacy, clinical waste services, and the NHS Trust to ensure the project could run smoothly, efficiently, and above all, safely.

It occurred to me that the local drug addicts and dealers would be looking for an opportunity to take advantage of lots of pharmaceuticals being in the same place at the same time, so we would have to carefully manage the drop-off sites.

My lightbulb moment in the bathroom seemed to be taking shape very quickly, and when the Hollberry NHS Trust directors heard about it, they were all over it like a rash. I had given them the gift of positive marketing to make them look good and put them in the running for the "NHS Trust of the Year Initiative Prize".

I wasn't interested in self-aggrandisement but it made the amnesty planning one hell of a lot easier. I asked and then received. Magic.

Posters were ordered based on the designs from the Pathways team, who had come up trumps within a few days. The hospital pharmacy arranged for large capacity clinical waste bins to be provided, and for daily collections from St David's, which was to be one of the non-NHS amnesty points, along with the walk-in day centre for the homeless in the town centre. It was a breeze. The start date for the amnesty was to be three weeks from Jan's funeral and would have two weeks to run at the non-NHS sites for safety reasons.

Before the big launch day, all I had left to do was to confirm the security arrangements at the walk-in centre and St David's and to arrange interviews with the local radio station, which I was handing over to Jan's friends. They were now working on their script and had come up with a catchy strap line:

"Too many pills, kills."

This initiative was for them really and the energy created by their enthusiasm was gratifying. I watched as Pip helped Karen prepare for her radio interview like a proud parent, and it was plain to see her confidence increasing on an hourly basis. She decided to dye her hair electric blue for the occasion, which Vanessa found hilarious. 'You're going on the radio!' she reminded her friend, who nodded and smiled. 'I know but I still want to look my best. I might get a slot on breakfast telly.'

Karen, Pip, and Vanessa would lead the media coverage but the NHS would still smell of roses as a result, and thus everyone was a winner. Including me. I was simply intrigued by what people may have hiding in their cupboards.

One unforeseen outcome of the project happened quite early on in proceedings. I had a call from Lily, who was in tears. She had just received news that she was to be the sole beneficiary of Jan's will. Frank had been on the phone making threats, refusing to hand back the house key still in his possession and she wanted to warn me of his fury. Also, since she had spent a lot of time with Jan's other friends as part of the project planning team, her faith in her best friend had unravelled. Jan had confided in her that it was Father Raymond who had raised the possibility that Liam had stolen money from her and was a confidence trickster, and encouraged Jan to report him to the police.

What Jan's other friends revealed was a very different side to Liam. They described a kind, considerate man, who had invited Jan to stay at his holiday home. She hadn't paid a penny.

'I wonder why Jan would say Liam was making her invest in a property in Perpignan when he already had one of his own, and plenty of money?' Lily queried.

I had wondered this too.

'And why would a priest undermine the good name of another man without obvious reason? Why would Jan hide the fact her own brother had bullied her into lending him money and then pretend Liam had swindled her out of it?' questioned the sniffing Lily from the end of the phone line.

Poor Lily had more questions than answers and I tried, unsuccessfully, to ease her distress with pathetic placatory remarks.

'I'm sure she had her reasons, or perhaps it was part of her illness.' Which it could have been.

Lily continued to say that she had offered to collect Jan from Hollberry hospital on the Friday she was going home for the week. 'Jan said she already had a lift from Father Raymond who had organised a taxi for her and he was going to help her with her luggage.' This was news to me. 'She found him so comforting and helpful,' added Lily.

Had Father Raymond been the last person to see Jan alive?

Was he the vicar who had been seen by the neighbours on the Wednesday when Steph had tried to visit Jan at home? If so, why hadn't he mentioned this?

'He even fed Sparkey while she was away,' Lily mentioned without thinking what this implied.

Father Raymond had keys to Jan's house.

I phoned the police control desk and left another message for DS Dynamic, suggesting he make sure to include Father Raymond in his questioning of Jan's friends at the Pathways Project and to ask about feeding the cat.

Chapter Eleven

Every evening since the auction, I had indulged in meticulous investigation of Grace's journals. I was still not wholly convinced that I had the full set in my possession and had contacted the auctioneers who had sold me the cabinet. Explaining my dilemma to a helpful man on the phone, I was given enough information to aid me in my quest, and Yarlsmere's were happy to send out another copy of the catalogue, as I had lost mine to Max, who had taken it to work for some inexplicable reason. In addition, I was given the name of the solicitors who had organised the sale of a variety of pharmaceutical items, auctioned as part of probate arrangements. Only the solicitors, Aitken, Brown and Partners, would hold the details, I was informed. I hadn't noticed at the time of the auction quite how many items relating to pharmaceuticals and chemistry were in the sale catalogue, although at the time I weighed up the options of bidding on a number of them. What I was hoping for was clarification as to whether other journals existed and had been sold as part of different lots. If not, I would have to assume I had the entire set.

My instruction through G.C. about the art and science of poisoning had been a revelation so far. Mr M seemed to have been a dedicated teacher and he ensured Grace had received a solid foundation in the history of the apothecary, as well as in the finer details of acting as one. This was wise of him. I was learning something new every time I turned a page.

…and I had long thought that it was the war that had obliged me with an opportunity that most women would never have imagined. However, under the tutelage of Mr M, I became a willing historian as

well as a chemist and learnt that I was far from being unique as the only female apothecary in history, I was but one of many.

Apothecaries were in direct competition with the physicians of the time. Despite a conflict and professional jealousies, one could not exist without the other, because without apothecaries, physicians would be without 'materia medica' with which to perform their medical practice.

Poisoning was rife in the 1600's it seems, and in Italy, the Italian clergy were obliged to advise the Pope himself, of the extraordinary number of confessions by young wives purporting to have murdered, by poisoning, their own husbands. This led to an unusual abundance of young widows in Rome.

The motives, as ever, appear to have been either infidelity or money. Poison was readily available through numerous vendors in a position to make themselves a tidy sum of money. One such poison vendor was a woman by the name of Giulia Tofana, who became so famous in Rome for selling poison to women with murder on their minds, that she had a poison named after her, 'Aqua Tofana'. The historians indicate that Giulia spent time with apothecaries and had learnt the art of poison making. It ended in tragedy when a customer finally disclosed to the authorities at the Vatican the extent of the poisonings, and Giulia, despite having taken refuge in a church, was hunted down, arrested, tortured, and executed alongside her daughter and three helpers in 1659 following confession to over 600 poisonings.

Mr M was wise to ensure my knowledge of these historical events as it teaches many valuable lessons of modesty, humility, and the value of remaining unobtrusive to name but a few. Giulia Tofana was far too well known by her extensive customer base to remain unnoticed by the authorities.

The need to remain inconspicuous was not heeded by many historical poisoners, which is why the words 'notorious' and 'poisoner' always appear together. The 'notorious poisoners' are ones who have been careless in the main, and seemed most determined to obtain notoriety leaving a trail in their wake. It is said that an effective burglar is one who is never caught, and so it is with poisoning.

What is it that leads a healer such as a chemist, or indeed a doctor, to become a poisoner? Is there a sense of duty to reduce suffering in others that may justify the first steps across that moral line? Or are there circumstances in which chance presents options for redressing an injustice or drives us to seek revenge?

Why poison if that is the case?

There is no doubt that it has its advantages over alternative means of depriving another of life, of killing, of assassination, and of murder, call it what you will. These are worth exploring and examining as they may be more suited to the task in hand.

Poisoning has advantages above other methods. For example, if suffering is required, there are endless options to ensure the intended victim writhes in pain and vomits torturously before death releases them. A delay between administration of the poison and its impact, can ensure that the assailant is miles away and has a cast iron alibi at the time of the victim's actual death and some poisons leave barely a trace of their action, leaving the coroner with a mysterious, unexplained death.

There are risks of course, and like any weapon, the utmost care must be taken to avoid accidental self-poisoning in the delivery method.

For both Mr M and me, the art of poisoning and our services for specific requirements was a well-thought-out side-line to what was otherwise a legitimate business. These days it would be seen as filling a much-needed gap in the market. We remained undetectable in the 'Apothecary' room, which was well hidden from any inspection that may take place in the dispensary, and it was never seen by anyone other than by Mr M, his son and myself. Not even Bridget, the cleaner, entered our inner sanctum.

There were simple rules that we observed for our personal services:

1. *Ensure, above all else, that the intended victim deserves or benefits from death.*
2. *Never leave orphans as a result.*
3. *Double-check the identity of the intended victim before acting. (Beware twins).*

4. *Research your intended victim thoroughly.*
5. *Never disclose one's true identity.*
6. *Never kill more than one member of any one family.*
7. *Never choose a method by which others may inadvertently be poisoned.*
8. *Take delivery, timing, and contingency options into account in each case.*
9. *Vary methods to avoid a pattern being established.*
10. *If in any doubt, abort the plan.*

These were our Ten Commandments and they were developed by Mr M after a series of unfortunate events. Commandment seven was a case in point.

One dark, winter evening, early on in my apprenticeship, Mr M sat with a warming cup of tea and recounted the wretched tale of the misdirected pie.

He had decided to deliver a tasty arsenic pie to a man of despicable reputation, who, despite committing several heinous crimes of torture, extortion, and murder for money, had escaped the long arm of the law, leaving broken and devastated lives in his wake. The man was a social pariah and would not be missed. No family were known of and therefore no children or wife would be disadvantaged as a result. He was a man of enormous girth with a voracious appetite to whom the baker would deliver a basket of bread, pies, and buns, direct to his door at the break of dawn every day, collecting the previous day's empty basket at the same time. This happened six days a week, with double pie and bread being left on a Saturday. With no one else living at the address, Mr M had a straightforward plan to replace one of the baker's pies with his own; steak, ale, and cyanide.

There were no difficulties with the delivery of the pie on the Saturday, it was a plain switch, resulting in Mr M having pie for lunch courtesy of the baker. But in a frightening unexpected twist, news broke the very next day via gossip at the local church, which indicated that the intended victim had found his housekeeper dead. The housekeeper was an elderly cleaning lady who was employed out of necessity but whom the man in question only paid to work a few hours on a Saturday morning and he begrudged the money.

Mr M admitted to the failures that were to lead to the commandments being enshrined in his future practice. He had overlooked the existence of a housekeeper by not being thorough enough in his research and he had chosen a delivery method that was risky, inasmuch as it was not target-specific in nature. We do indeed live and learn.

Well, what an education I was getting here! The way Grace wrote was so matter-of-fact that it was disarming. Smiling to myself as I read through her memories of her apprenticeship and the factual pros and cons of chosen methods for assassins, I began to wonder if these journals were a device of an elaborate hoax or perhaps a work of fiction. Once I had reached the part about the Ten Commandments, I finally convinced myself that I had probably become completely carried away with the whole idea being based in fact. Ridiculous. I still kept on reading for the enjoyment of the story as it was highly entertaining. So much so that it was tempting to convert Grace's writing into a publishable work.

Other people should read this, I concluded, and that night I read aloud to Max excerpts of what Grace had written about poisoning as a weapon of choice for assassins. This resulted in us having a lively debate about what method we would choose were we to have a change of career and become travelling hit men.

'I'd definitely go for a long-distance sniper approach, like *Day of the Jackal.* Clean, efficient, and I could make a getaway over the rooftops and onto my Triumph, racing through the streets of Rome.'

'Being a sniper in Rome, that's predictable for you. It wasn't Rome by the way, it was Paris in *Day of the Jackal.* I think I could do rifles with silencers, but I couldn't do knives, too up-close and personal and you'd get covered in blood. The police always catch the knife killers because of the blood. If you think about it, you'd need to be physically strong to use a knife if you had to grapple with the victim, and I don't fancy a death embrace with someone I don't know very well. They might have smelly breath,' I said as Max turned to me with a quizzical expression.

'What are you talking about, you idiot woman? You're only going to kill people you know?'

'No, I mean knives wouldn't be my weapon of choice if I were an assassin. I think I would be a sneaky killer. Locking someone in a sauna until they cooked, and making it look like an accident with a faulty door handle mechanism. Tampering with their brakes, that sort of thing.'

'Give over, you wouldn't have a clue where to start with brake fluid levels.'

Our conversation was fun and took my mind away from the work I had to catch up on. I had missed several hours of caseload work time by taking on Jan's memorial medication amnesty, which was to launch in two days' time, and I was not sleeping well.

The Jan Collins Memorial Project Team had done a sterling job and had gone down a storm on local radio. To such an extent that the morning DJ, Danny Wakeman, who had the most apt name for a breakfast radio show host, was offering to run reminders each day for a fortnight. A much better outcome than we could have hoped for. Karen, Vanessa, and Pip were bursting with excited chatter when I met with them after the radio interview.

'You sounded so calm and professional. The facts were accurate and I don't think you could have done a better job. I certainly couldn't have come across so well. Fantastic effort, guys,' I said as the three started to relive the whole experience.

'Danny said we were representing the responsible face of the good people of Lensham and Hollberry. Did you hear him describing us? That was funny.'

'Yeah, he really loved my hair,' Karen said, sparkling with the stimulation of temporary fame. She had taken the lead in the interview and she had exceeded her own expectations, and mine.

DJ Danny Wakeman 'time to wake, man' kept the local population abreast of any exciting developments, and during

Karen's interview, gave credit to Jan's friends for doing something positive in her memory, as well as trying to address suicide risk. He appeared to revel in the drama of Jan's suicide and was trying to delve much deeper into her personal life than was necessary. Karen had fended off his personal questions about her friend.

'Jan was a private person, I don't think she would want me to go into that sort of detail.'

One unpredicted effect of Danny's obsession with the dramatic was his plan to dedicate a whole section of one show to a phone-in. We didn't know that was his intention.

'I know many of you out there will want to share your own stories of how you have lost friends and relatives to suicide. We know, don't we, that the impact on families can be devastating, but what did you do to cope with the aftermath? Do you think what Jan Collins's friends are doing is the right thing? Or is it an insult to her memory to focus on the means of her death? Phone in, let's talk about this.' I'm sure he thought his efforts to be very laudable, but to me, he sounded insincere and egotistical.

Inevitably the story of Jan's mental illness and her disappearing boyfriend came out in the local papers and this spun off into calls to Danny's show from individuals who had been duped into parting with money by dubious partners.

'Good morning. We have Sylvia on the line. G'morning to you, Sylvia. Now you say you had an affair with a man who you trusted, but how did he repay that trust, Sylvia?' Sylvia, who sounded like she smoked forty fags a day, growled her way through a sad tale of treachery and betrayal. The older woman, younger man, widow with lots of money, love-rat story. I switched over to BBC Radio Two.

As well as local radio and newspaper articles written by Pip and Vanessa, posters were placed in inventive venues such as public toilets, nightclub bars, village halls, sports centres, colleges, and the hospital itself. The awareness raising campaign was off to a flying start, in fact there were drop-offs being made at the hospital pharmacy well before the official launch day, which was really encouraging for the willing volunteers to hear.

The police were delighted with the media efforts highlighting their interest in locating Liam, and DS Adams secured himself a spot on Danny's 'time to wake, man' breakfast show the day after Karen's appearance. I had to tune in for that one. He appealed to the public for support in 'seeking this man in connection with an ongoing police enquiry'. His voice lacked any inflection and far from waking the listeners up during their morning commute, DS Adams was sending them to sleep with his dull, expressionless appeal.

'God save us. Is it me, or do all Brummies sound depressed? Come on, Eeyore, liven up! You should be reading *The Book at Bedtime*, even I would fall asleep to that boring voice,' I shouted at the car radio as I drove to work.

The media coverage had a snowball effect. At the church hall on the day of the medication amnesty launch, we were inundated with bags of old medication in various forms. In the first wave of enthusiastic depositors was Sean Tierney.

'Well now, Nurse Monica, what a fine idea you've had, God bless you. The wife and I have emptied out a whole cupboard.' He then leant in to whisper to me, 'We're glad to be getting shot of this lot. Manuela is scared to death that Benito will one day be so drunk, he'll accidentally kill himself.' He shook my hand, pumping my whole arm vigorously as he spoke, and my shoulder was aching by the time he let me go. He had held up the queue behind him.

Luckily, I had managed to railroad Emma Foster into helping me with the initial influx on day one. I had tempted her with the promise of tea and cake. She was a superstar as usual and immediately organised separation of tablets from liquids. What an oversight on my part, I honestly didn't think people would deposit their old cough mixtures, and ancient liniments for aching joints, let alone liquids that, quite frankly, could kill a horse.

Emma updated me with news that Sparkey was settling in well at the farm, being a hit with the children especially. 'The girls love him. He's absolutely bonkers.' I made a mental note to pass this on to Father Raymond. He hadn't mentioned Sparkey, but if he had been feeding him when Jan was away then he must have wondered what happened to him, surely?

'Mon, do you want cream for haemorrhoids in the liquid, or solid department?'

'Oh God, do we need a bloody creams and lotions section as well?'

'Not necessarily. But we do need a swearing and blaspheming box,' Emma scolded, suggesting that I was on the verge of full-blown Tourette's in a place of religion. She rarely swore these days because of having young children in the house but she used to eff and jeff with the best of them.

'Oh shit, sorry.'

'Monica!'

'Sorry ...'

We rapidly filled the clinical waste boxes and by the end of the first day, they were bursting. Anticipating this difficulty, I made arrangements with the hospital to make an exchange of full ones for empties, plus a few extra, well before four o'clock. We could not risk leaving such vast quantities of medicines in a church hall overnight. The bottled items had to stand in cardboard boxes and milk crates that we had purloined from a storeroom at the hall. When I phoned them for advice, I was reminded by one of the pharmacists at the hospital that, 'You can't pour any old liquid medication down the sink without a risk to public health.'

'No, indeed, we might create mutant crocodiles in the sewers,' I added with a laugh. This was not reciprocated. Apparently, pharmacists are serious folk.

'Any Viagra amongst this lot?' Emma asked with a cheeky grin.

'Why on earth would you ask that question?' She and Jake were not having bedroom difficulties at their age, were they?

'Apparently it works well for women if they take it …' Emma hadn't really changed that much when she became a mum, she still had the naughty imp about her. Thank God.

The Pathways Project team had turned the medication amnesty launch into an opportunity to advertise their good work. There was tea, cake, and information for all, just about. With the realisation that the turnout was twice the number anticipated, cakes were re-cut to half the original portion sizes, but nobody noticed. Throughout the day there was a gently positive atmosphere in the hall and many willing hands were available to help load up my car before four o'clock. I declined a marvellously kind offer from an ancient lady churchwarden to "ride shotgun" with me. I recognised her face.

'You should be careful, dear, you could be mugged by druggies and other unsavoury types.' I took her advice, paid careful attention to my rear-view mirror in the event that I was being followed, and headed straight to the pharmacy delivery bay at the back of the hospital.

Emma had left earlier to pick up her children and I was relying on a couple of other helpers to wait for me to return with the empty clinical waste bins before locking up. The door to the hall was to be closed at four o'clock sharp as advertised. When I returned, there was a box of medicines dumped outside the church hall entrance, and no one was there to let me back in with the replacement clinical containers. Typical. I put the box of dumped medicines in my car rather than leave it outside.

This was another issue I had failed to anticipate. What if others were tempted to do the same? I rustled up a handwritten sign for the door, which requested that medication was not to be left outside and reminding people that it may fall into the wrong hands or be eaten by animals.

There was only one other car in the car park, a silver saloon beneath the trees. I could see someone sitting in the driver's seat but couldn't make out his or her features. Convinced that it was Frank Hughes, I kept the car in my sight. I had been expecting him to confront me by turning up at the office, but now I was wondering whether he had something else in mind. I added to the handwritten sign 'No drugs are left on the premises overnight'.

I made it home in one piece. No druggies and no psychopathic Frank Hughes put in an appearance.

Chapter Twelve

The next amnesty day was almost as manic as the first, and whilst doing my rounds of the drop-off points to ensure that the systems were working as planned, I finally caught up with Father Raymond. Popping into St David's Church Hall first thing with the replacement clinical containers I was handed a welcome cup of tea by Vanessa, who winked at me.

The police hadn't spoken to her or Karen and Pip about Liam Brookes yet, although Jan had died four weeks ago. 'They're probably dealing with the information coming in from the public as a result of DS Adams' appeal on the radio,' Pip suggested. 'I'm a bit cross about how they made it sound like he was a villain, but at least someone is looking for him. We can't get hold of him and we don't know where to try next.' Pip saying he was 'a bit cross' made me smile to myself. He didn't possess the ability to be furious or angry. Mildly irritated was the worst I'd ever seen from Pip.

'I liked Liam,' Vanessa said wistfully, as she offered me a biscuit. We were about to have a conversation regarding the mysterious disappearing Liam, when Father Raymond appeared with an elderly and doddery Father Joseph, who he was showing around the medication amnesty set up. I apologised to Vanessa for cutting her short, and took my opportunity to update Father Raymond on Sparkey's welfare.

'Father, you're a modest man. Lily tells me that you looked after Sparkey for Jan when she was in hospital, and when she was in France of course.'

'Yes, I did. But I think he ran away. I went back several times after I heard about Jan's death but the neighbours said they hadn't seen him. God bless the little thing.'

'Oh no, he's fine,' I reassured the doleful priest.

There had clearly been an oversight on my part. I should have at least let the neighbours know where we had moved the cat to. Mind you, as I had no idea that Father Raymond existed in Jan's life until after her death, I couldn't have known to inform *him* until now. All I had done was to put a short note through to Jan's next-door neighbours to assure them that I was taking responsibility for rehoming Sparkey. They would usually have been the ones to feed him whenever Jan was away, and sometimes when she wasn't.

Father Raymond seemed genuinely relieved to hear how well Sparkey had settled with his new family.

'Looking after cats. All part of the work of a street priest, Miss Monica,' interjected Father Joseph.

This was when the difference between the two priests became clearer, thanks to a succinct explanation from Father Joseph who, because of deafness, shouted at me, 'I minister in the local Catholic Church to a congregation and Father Raymond here works with community projects. He's often moved after a few months to set up projects elsewhere. The resident parish priest always hosts him, you see, wherever he lands.' Father Joseph then turned to talk to Vanessa with the ultimate goal of helping himself to more biscuits. 'How long have you been the priest at St Francis'?' I heard Vanessa ask.

'I've been twice in total, young lady. I was here about twenty years ago, and then I was asked to return four years ago this November. It's lovely to be back.'

'Another biscuit, Father?' Father Joseph happily chatted to Vanessa for as long as the supply of biscuits lasted.

'I like the nomadic life, really.' Father Raymond nodded sagely.

'It sounds as if you rarely have chance to put down any roots,' I said, quickly adding, 'On a slightly different note, and with your street priest shoes on; have you heard anything to help the police find Liam Brookes? You must have known him fairly well?'

'Yes,' agreed Father Raymond, with a direct and steady gaze. 'He seemed, on the surface, a decent enough chap, but it is a sad fact that the vulnerable can be so easily hoodwinked by those with less than honourable intentions.' Father Raymond shuffled his feet and stepped towards Father Joseph, putting his hand into the small of the elderly priest's back as if to guide him further away. I was under the distinct impression that Liam Brookes was a subject that Father Raymond did not wish to discuss with me. Undeterred, I prodded a little further.

'Did you know that Liam Brookes paid for Jan's holiday to France and went to see her in hospital when she was there?'

Father Raymond fidgeted more noticeably and suggested that, 'We should arrange to meet and talk these important matters through in private, in case discussing such unpleasantries should upset Jan's close friends.'

'Of course, I wasn't thinking. Good idea. I'll give you my number at work.'

As I scribbled down the office number on a scrap piece of paper my mobile rang.

'Oh, speak of the devil,' I answered the call with an apologetic glance. 'Sorry …' I muttered as I took the call. 'Kelly, how can I help? Shit, really? Okay, I'll call her … soon as. Thanks.'

As I ended the call, I looked up and was met by disapproving stares from the two priests, and several smirks from Vanessa and Karen. Yes, I had said 'shit', and I had mentioned the devil and capped it off with …

'Oh God, sorry. Got to go.' My version of Tourette's was winning.

I trotted swiftly to my car, which often doubled as a mobile confidential office space, to call Emma as requested. She was having a bad day at work. Benito Tierney had turned up at Len-DAS that morning, which I thought was good news until Emma explained that he had been 'as drunk as a skunk' and was flinging accusations around, calling people 'paedos' and 'nonces' and alleging they raped him in his sleep.

'He used some very fruity language, let me tell you,' Emma announced.

Ben had made it as far as the waiting room. The doors inside were secured and could only be opened by use of a door release button under the reception desk.

The police, although called straight away, had been slow in their response, during which time much damage had been done to the fabric of the waiting room and to a number of people in a Wild West punch up. The result, Emma explained, was that Ben 'had his face well and truly battered by a massive bloke who was waiting to be seen for therapy.' Ben had then run off in the direction of the market, still splattered in blood, leaving the place in chaos.

Emma was her usual good-humoured self, and the morning's mayhem hardly registered on the 'crapometer'. A few years as a staff nurse on acute psychiatric wards has that effect.

'All in a day's work, Sherlock. Are you still coming over, later? Only I have a mystery I need help with solving.'

'Excellent.' I love a mystery, and I love going over to Emma's farm. Max disappears with Jake to look at farm machinery and old cars, and I spend time with Emma and the kids, being naughty and reading them bedtime stories.

'Oh yes. Most definitely. I'll see if I can find Ben, do my checks on the meds amnesty stuff, then Max and I will be with you by seven at the latest, I should think. We'll bring pizza, as it's Max's turn to cook!'

I found Ben without too much trouble. He was trying to gain access to his local pub by standing on the pavement remonstrating with the thin-lipped landlady of the Green Man, who was having none of it.

'Ben Tierney. Go on. Fuck off. Come back when you're sober.'

Ben had the greatest respect for the landlady at the Green Man, as it was the last remaining proper pub in the town able to tolerate him, for now. That was only because the regulars and the formidable landlady were from solid Irish stock and they respected his parents.

I tooted my car horn and Ben staggered across to huff a cloud of noxious alcohol and tobacco fumes in my direction through the small gap in the passenger side window. I parked up thinking that we could sit on a bench across the road from the pub. In actual fact, I sat on the bench, while Ben walked unsteadily up and down the pavement, ranting at the top of his voice. He was furious, bitter and enraged to the point where veins in his forehead were threatening to explode from his temples. It took a fair while for him to calm down enough to give me a slurred version of the events that had led to this superb drunken bender.

These explanations were, in the main, difficult to follow, but the upshot was that his parents had spoken about attending the Pathways Project and they had mentioned Father Joseph's name. Ben confirmed that he began a colourful rage in response.

'He fucked me up.' As he said this, Ben turned to face the lamppost that was steadying him at the time. He began to head-butt it with such force that I had to leap up to stop him knocking himself unconscious. More blood was being sprayed from his recent wounds, and although not keen on being covered in it, I had no choice other than to try to restrain him by placing my hands on his elbows and pulling him back towards me. Small raindrop-sized particles of blood were flying in every direction.

As I tried to prevent Ben from knocking himself out, I realised through the screams that after all these years Ben's abuser was still here in the town, a priest in the Roman Catholic Church. A holy man, above suspicion.

Father Joseph.

'You can't say no to God!' Ben yelled. 'I couldn't say no to God. He fucked me up. The one true Jesuit will take revenge and kill the Masons and save God. They are all sinners! They sit in church and know that the priest fucks little children.'

Completely out of the blue, Ben talked about Liam Brookes. He had heard on the radio that the police were searching for him because of Jan's death and missing money.

'He didn't need any money. They paid him.'

'Who paid him?'

'The familieshhh ...'

I didn't understand what Ben was trying to explain. He was slurring and jumping around from topic to conspiracy theory and from swearword to expletive.

What I did glean was confirmation that Liam had tracked Ben down and had talked to him about his abuse. He wanted Ben to give details towards building a case against Father Joseph.

'Had Liam been abused by him, too?'

'No. By another. Another fucking buggering sodomiser priest! You stupid fucking cow!'

My questions were not helping. So, I shut up and let him rant a bit more before suggesting that he went to A&E to have his wounds checked out and have a once-over for possible concussion. Ben declined, in no uncertain effing terms, and he staggered towards the town centre, no doubt looking for more alcohol to deaden the pain. I now had a definitive explanation for his more recent increase in consumption.

Later that evening, I found irrefutable proof that what Ben had said was nearer the truth than I imagined.

As I turned to get back into my car, I spied a silver Audi parked some way behind me, with a man sitting in it, watching. This time I remembered to take the registration number. I was now pretty certain that Frank Hughes was stalking me, but I had no idea why. One more incidence of him following me and I would be looking to make a formal complaint of my own, to the police.

Having returned to my car, I was about to call 999 and then the office to let Kelly know that I was in one piece, when the boys in blue turned up. They had been diverted from Len-DAS to the Green Man. The pub landlady had given them a call and had been watching Ben and me on the CCTV camera installed on the corner of the building. There was nothing much to tell them, other than in which direction I had seen Ben stagger, and I could only surmise that he was going to spend time in the cells. *That would be the safest outcome for him,* or so I thought at the time.

Making a conscious decision to visit Sean and Manuela Tierney, I drove straight to their home. I didn't go in. Through the enormous front window, I could see directly into their living room. Father Raymond was standing there with a comforting arm around Manuela, who was sobbing into his shoulder. Sean was in front of him shaking his hand and nodding as he did so. The scene was one of gratitude. They didn't need me.

Chapter Thirteen

I didn't have much time to worry about Frank Hughes or Ben for the rest of the day and was grateful for the diversion of a trip to Emma and Jake's farm for the evening. We never stayed too long, as we all had busy lives and early starts, but it was good to catch up. If it had been a weekend, we would have taken Deefer with us, as Emma's children loved to play with him, and he was so affectionate towards them. He was endlessly forgiving of their insistence at playing dressing-up games, putting him in their clothes and pretending he was another child. There were working collies at the farm, but they lived outside and didn't have the same character and nature as Deefer, who created a unique sparkle in the hearts of the children.

As it was a weekday and a short trip was anticipated, we left Deefer at home watching BBC One. Taking a pile of boxed pizzas with us, we arrived in good time at Folly Farm to be greeted excitedly by Sophie and Thea, aged eight and six respectively. They would normally have been much further ahead in their bedtime routine by that time of the evening, but Emma had let slip that we were due to visit. The children stubbornly refused to believe that Deefer had not come along with us. I, of course, felt guilty that we had caused such disappointment and caved in to making a promise to bring him to see them at the weekend. Then I settled onto the side of Sophie's bed to read them a story of their choosing. Lying curled up at the foot of Thea's bed was Sparkey, content and at home.

Before the rascals had been snuggled in for the night, Jake and Max had headed to a barn to discuss matters of machinery, and it was not long before the hum and rumble of engines could be heard from the house. They had known each other for years and had an easy friendship with many things in common. Jake, who was even taller than Max, was a quiet reliable farmer with a dry wit and ready smile, in contrast to Max who filled a room with his enthusiasm and opinion.

Once we were on our own, Emma wasted no time in explaining her dilemma.

'Our lodger has completely disappeared,' she informed me.

'The man who rents the Lodge House?'

'Yes, not a sign of him. His mobile phone is dead and although his rent has been paid by direct debit, he's been gone for weeks. The trouble is, Mon, he's very private and I've no details for friends, relatives, or anyone really. I'm not sure why I should be so concerned, but he always gives me the dates when he's going away, and when he is due back, and he's worryingly overdue.'

'Tell me what you do know; we'll start from there.'

'Right you are, Sherlock. His name is Nick Shafer, and he's rented from us for a couple of years now. He's single, self-employed as a freelance journalist and he works from here and a base abroad in the south of France; he splits himself between the two. He's about early forties I would say: well-built but not fat, taller than you by a good few inches, green eyes, thick dark hair worn longish touching his shoulders, but not unruly or scruffy. He was usually neat and clean, never saw him in a suit, he was well spoken and good mannered. As I said, a private man and an ideal tenant. He was going out almost every day, I assume on the trail of a story or researching his latest article. I'm not exactly sure. I didn't like to pry.'

'I think we should pry now,' I said emphatically. 'Get the keys and let's go and see what we can find.'

'Good. That's exactly what I'd hoped you'd say.'

Emma didn't need persuading further. We told Jake's mother, Grandma Frost, where we were going so that she could listen out for the children. She still lived in the rambling family farmhouse where Jake had grown up, and she, like her son, was unassuming and gentle, and managed her independence within the home without having to stamp any authority on Emma and Jake. Somehow, they seemed to naturally maintain a sense of family harmony.

As we passed by the new barn, Emma and I told the men where we were heading and I relied on Jake to absorb this information, as Max was too absorbed in a defective classic car engine to be distracted by women speaking to him. He nodded in recognition of words being spoken, but I knew the vague look meant that no facts were being taken in.

The Lodge House was a small but attractive red brick lodge at the entrance to the farm, well away from the farmhouse. It was bordered to the right by a picket fence and there were parking spaces to the left-hand side of the house, on which stood a motorbike beneath a cover of grey, black, and white waterproof material. There was no garden to speak of but there were a number of pots and planters around the porch entrance to make it attractive.

'He goes everywhere on that motorbike, rain or shine.'

'Why did he leave it this time then?'

'Oh, he usually does if he's going abroad. Saves the cost at the station. He gets a taxi which allows him more luggage, I suppose.'

'Well done, Watson, of course, silly me.'

Emma took the keys to open the heavy wooden front door, which led into a small hallway filled with shoes, boots, coats, and biker gear. It was easy to get a sense of the size of Nick Shafer by his bike leathers, which were carefully hung on a solid wooden hanger. I judged him to be about the same size as Max. We made our way into the lounge, which was partially filled by a large desk and office area, leaving only a comfy chair with footstool and a telly in one corner, for relaxation. There was a small wood-burning stove, unused for some time judging by the ashes inside. A basket of logs was strategically placed to the left of the fireplace.

We had worked together for so many years that Emma and I rarely had to give each other verbal instructions, and thus we moved in unison through to the kitchen, taking in the personal details of Nick Shafer's presence in each room. There was little in the way of food in the fridge, which made sense. Everywhere was left reasonably tidy and clean, including the bathroom and bedroom. Clothes were hung on the back of a bedroom chair, awaiting the return of their owner. It wasn't a Spartan existence on show, but it was purely functional. Male.

We returned to the centre of operations, the office in the lounge, and most importantly, the desk, which, judging by the oblong shape in the dust on its surface, was missing a laptop computer. We gave a cursory glance over an enormous pin board on the wall facing the desk, but there were no helpful photos or obvious emails or reservation details for France that we could see. Emma settled herself in the well-worn, leather swivel chair, poised for a closer look at the pin board and a rummage through the desk drawers. I took up position on the footstool, taking with me a wire tray full of correspondence and a wooden box of interesting dimensions potentially containing vital documentation.

'Right. I have an address in France,' Emma announced with some satisfaction. 'Rue de la something or other, Per-pig-nan, wherever that is.'

'Great. Your French is as good as mine by the sounds of it. I think that's pronounced Perpeenyon.' We smiled at each other.

I had picked up a few of the letters from the correspondence tray and been stunned momentarily by coincidence. The letter in my hand was from the exact same solicitors that I was planning to contact about the auction purchase of my cabinet and journals. Aitken, Brown and Partners of Martington, Lancashire.

I read the details of the letter, which seemed to indicate that Nick Shafer was employed by a person or group of persons referred to as 'our clients' who would only deal with affairs of his contract through the senior partner, Thomas Aitken. A benefactor was referred to. It was somewhat unclear at first reading.

Emma, meanwhile, was trawling through notebooks and making the odd comment or two when she came across an interesting fact.

'He has a membership card belonging to … Oh shit. Mon, look at this.'

The tone of her voice demanded an immediate reaction, which had me bouncing up from the stool and appearing at her side in seconds. We both looked at a photo ID card, the plastic type affixed to a lanyard. This one was for a volunteer support worker by the name of Liam Brookes, and there, sure enough, was a photograph of Liam Brookes staring back at me.

'What was he doing with Liam Brookes's ID card?' I asked out loud, rhetorically.

'That's Nick Shafer,' announced Emma without any hesitation, 'only with glasses on.'

'What? You are kidding! The man has been in the news and in the papers and you have only this second realised that Liam Brookes is your lodger Nick Shafer. Is your name Lois Lane? The sole difference between the two is a pair of glasses.' I was flabbergasted.

'I don't spend much time reading newspapers or watching the telly, actually,' replied an affronted Emma. 'I don't know what bloody Liam Brookes looks like. I never met him.'

We both stopped short of an argument and laughed instead.

'Superman and Clark Kent … who'd have thought?' I murmured as I phoned the police station and asked for DS Adams, not thinking for a moment that he would be on duty, but he was.

'Charles, it's Monica Morris. I think I may have some interesting information regarding Liam Brookes.' I explained what had that very moment been discovered and I was smiling at Emma, thinking what a couple of excellent detectives we would make, when the grin was wiped smartly from my face.

'Thanks all the same for the information but we are no longer looking for this gentleman. The case is firmly closed as no crime has been committed that we can identify. Instructions from the DI himself.'

'Really? But he has a false identity and he's still missing.'

'Sorry, Monica, as I said, there has been no obvious crime committed and DI Lynch has given clear instructions to give our thanks to anyone who comes forward with information, but there will be no investigation until there is evidence to the contrary. There's no crime in having two identities.'

'Oh. Okay. Thanks for listening, anyway.' There was nothing else to say to the man. His monotonous response had been clear enough, leaving me deflated and puzzled. There was no need to repeat DS Adams's words to Emma as she had picked up from my side of the conversation that the police were disinterested. Far from being disappointed, Emma became quite animated, 'Right, that settles it. We'll have to investigate for ourselves, Holmes. What do you say?'

At that she produced her flashy new Nokia mobile phone and took a few photos of Nick Shafer's pin board, the layout of the desk, the ID card, and the framed photos that hung on the walls. Her eagerness was a joy to watch and I delved back enthusiastically into the paperwork and letters in the wire tray, chortling at the ludicrousness of the situation as I sat back down on the stool.

Emma hit upon a more sensible plan.

'Shall we split this up between us? We could be here all night. You take what you've got. I'll go through the notebooks at home tonight and pop back here tomorrow. In the meantime, we'll leave Nick a note to explain why we've been through his belongings, just in case he rocks up tonight.'

'Bonzer idea, my dear Watson.'

That's what we did. I piled the box and the tray of letters into my car and as I placed them into the boot I saw, to my horror, another box, which I had completely forgotten about. The one from the drugs amnesty that I had carelessly taken because the church hall was closed. The one someone had left there without thinking of the consequences. It had remained in the far corner of my car boot, forgotten about entirely.

'Christ.' I shut the boot quickly, in shame. Emma had gone inside the farmhouse to check on the children and put the kettle on, so while the coast was clear, I reopened the boot and checked the box of medicines that I had fully intended to dispose of properly. I was praying hard and silently as I lifted the lid on the small square cardboard box and was rewarded for my efforts. 'Bloody effing Nora,' I sighed. Three sticky bottles of old cough mixture, two battered boxes of antihistamines, two half-filled jars of vitamin tablets and a box of paracetamol. Thank God for that. No controlled drugs. No prescription drugs.

I gave myself a well overdue telling off for complacency, poor concentration, and for being distracted by nonsense stories about a conman, who turned out to be a journalist. Liam, or Nick, the poor bugger was probably doing a story about the unwashed people of Hollberry and Lensham who had to resort to drugs and alcohol because services were not there to support their psychological or psychiatric needs following their abuse as children. Ben Tierney had been one of the people Liam, or should that be Nick, had interviewed. It was starting to make sense at last.

After a lovely cup of tea I extricated Max from Jake, from the repaired and sweetly running engine, and from the barn. Max and I headed home.

Our house appeared to be in darkness, worsened by the fact that we had neglected to put the outside light on before we left. Deefer had been watching BBC One, but where was the flickering light from the TV? We entered the front door and turned the lights on in the hall, took off our shoes and padded through to the lounge. No noise came from the TV or from the dog who we initially thought had taken himself to bed. He usually made a special effort to meet and greet us whenever we'd been out, but he didn't put in an appearance even after we put on the lounge lights.

'Oh God …!'

We both stood immobilised, surveying the mess.

'I'll call the police …'

'Deefer. Where is Deefer?'

The call to the police was delayed while we searched frantically for our beloved dog.

Chapter Fourteen

P anic set in once we had finished searching the whole house in vain, and we went outside to try the garage and garden shed as a last resort. I heard him squeaking and whimpering before we got there. Tears of joy rolled freely down my face, and loud sobs escaped as Max pulled open the shed door to reveal Deefer. Our dog was wagging his tail and grinning at us, as if we had successfully completed the latest game of hide and seek. Max sank to his knees and hugged the great musclebound ugliness that is our irreplaceable Deefer.

'You poxy, useless guard dog,' sniffled Max, trying desperately hard to maintain masculine pride. I had no such hang-ups, and blubbed uncontrollably in response to the overwhelming relief at finding Deefer fit and well.

It is a known fact that Staffies are useless guard dogs. They look bold and beefy, as if they represent the canine equivalent of nightclub bouncers or evil debt collectors, but in reality, they are people pleasers and loyal friends. Clearly, Deefer had befriended the burglars and they had decided to spare him by locking him in the shed. He's so soppy that he didn't bother barking, even when he heard us arrive home.

With our four-legged dog-child safe and sound, we called the police.

I don't know why we bothered. They were not interested and said they would not be in a position to send any officers to investigate. With no hint that significant harm had befallen a person, nor valuable items stolen, they suggested that we make a note of any missing items, and gave us a crime reference number for use in an insurance claim.

'Is that it? You assume that druggies or other scum-of-the-earth types have broken into our home to take our belongings and possessions, to sell for drugs, and you are not sufficiently manned to investigate because this happens so often? Is that what you are telling me?' Max was infuriated, and as a result of the additional blood circulating to his brain, he was articulate for once. He slammed the phone down. 'What do we pay bastard Council Tax for?'

Resigned to the fact that the police were not involving themselves in burglaries anymore, we took photos and set about tidying up. The TV had gone, as had the CD player, and a few pieces of inexpensive jewellery, which was hardly surprising given that I didn't possess any expensive stuff. My gold was on my fingers and a chain around my neck. Everything else was silver or cheap costume jewellery.

A moment of major alarm threatened, sending Max to the garage to check on the motorbikes. Deefer was in hot pursuit.

'No, it's okay; they're here,' came the shout from Max with added relief to its usual tone. He then went next door to make enquiries and rang round friends and neighbours in the village. He phoned the local pubs, which were a reliable source of information but all gave a negative response. No one else had been broken into that evening.

'That does not make any bloody sense,' he remarked as he walked back into the house, having checked the shed again, confirming that it contained its usual complement of tools.

My investment, the antique cabinet, was still in the dining room, drawers and doors open but undamaged. However, the journals that had been laid out on the dining table had gone.

Diving under the table, I scrabbled around on the floor for several minutes looking for them, with the belief that they had been scattered along with the placemats and empty vase that had been on the table when I was last in that room. They were nowhere to be seen.

Max found me sitting in a heap on the carpet and he recognised the expression I was wearing. Even though there was no risk of violence and no immediate danger, there was enough evidence for me to raise the marker on the crapometer. I instinctively knew there was something to fear about what had happened in our home.

'Is this one of your nutters?' accused Max.

I despaired of ever achieving a balanced and unprejudiced view from my husband about my job and the people I worked with. His clouded opinion was that everyone I had ever come across in my career was a raving psychopath or plain mad. Whilst this may have applied to most of the staff, I have found patients and their families to be, on the whole, a pleasure to help.

Needless to say, as I sat on the floor of my dining room, house in disarray, I did have a high-speed internal review of my current caseload. I briefly toyed with the idea that Ben Tierney had found where I lived and trashed the place in a drunken rampage. That thought was dismissed as readily as it had come to mind. There were bottles of booze untouched for a start, and whoever broke in had not damaged the door or the dog. Frank Hughes was the most likely, but whoever it was wanted the journals, and I couldn't see any connection between Mr Shark Eyes and the journals. He was such an angry individual that much more damage would have been done if it were him. Inevitably I became convinced that the mess in the house was made deliberately and the items stolen were done so for show.

'Druggies, my arse …'

I jumped up with a jolt, startling Max, and ran upstairs. Next to my bed had been one of the journals that I was reading to Max the night before. Miraculously it was still there, but had wedged itself between the bed and the bedside table where it must have fallen when I dozed off. Feeling overwhelmingly sad at the loss of the other journals, I slowly realised that I had built a strange relationship with Grace through her journals and she had been stolen, without me unearthing the big secret that she was withholding.

'Mon, what is in the rest of those journals?' Max asked very gently. I shrugged.

With reluctant acceptance of the situation, we set about righting the furniture and putting each room back to its previous level of arrangement. We found a total of £4.28 in the two settees, which was a small bonus. As was the fact that the vacuum cleaner was reintroduced to parts of the carpet that it hadn't seen for a while. Several fruitless minutes were spent searching for and finding the television remote control.

'Aha! Look what I've found!'

Max burst my bubble by reminding me that the TV had been stolen.

'Yes, well, they can't use it, can they, the bastards, because we have the remote.'

I was defiant in mood by then.

The result of our efforts in the lounge was the return to a tidy and welcoming cottage, but I could not shake a creeping sense that the whole of our home had been invaded and defiled. As I allowed myself a few tears several times while we completed the same process in each room, we catalogued what we noticed as missing.

The kitchen was another challenge altogether. Drawers had been opened and tipped out on the floor, cupboards emptied. Not every single one of them but enough to make a good show of rice and pasta over the worktops, everywhere. The worst mess was from the RSD. Every household has at least one. The RSD is the drawer where the small items of importance and general use live. It is home for the things we need to have close at hand or which 'may be useful you never know' such as the multi-head screwdriver, a radiator key, paperclips, electrical tape, spare phone charger cable and the rest of the odds and sods. We refer to ours as the RSD, or Random Shit Drawer. Random shit had been strewn deliberately across my kitchen. It was a soul-destroying task to find and rehome the items, but looking on the bright side, the RSD was more organised and less cluttered as a consequence.

Upstairs was a similar picture, although a bemused Max was pleasantly shocked to find that his secret stash of cash was still in the sock where it usually lay, badly hidden. The drawers had been emptied, but it appeared that the burglars had failed to carry out a search. They had lifted cheap jewellery items and left silver. This discovery only served to add weight to our hypothesis that this was a staged burglary. But why?

When we finally finished rearranging our home, a little after midnight, we consoled ourselves with a steaming shower and a nightcap. A hot chocolate with a dash of brandy, in my case. We were physically tired but unsurprisingly failed to sleep well.

Neither Max nor I had need for assistance from Cocka the cockerel in the morning, as we were awoken before first light by the doorbell ringing insistently. Deefer declined to get up and merely lifted his head to look at me when I passed by his bed on the way downstairs.

I was taken aback at who I found standing on our doorstep looking exhausted and dishevelled, and I said so.

'Crikey, you look dreadful. You'd better come in.'

'Thanks, you don't look so hot yourself.'

I pulled my dressing gown around me a little tighter and pushed wisps of stray hair behind my ears, realising in my dopey half-awake state that I was not at my best that morning. Max appeared beside me, and I went through the formalities of introducing him to DS Charles Adams as they shook hands.

'Taking us seriously, now?' enquired Max as we made our way through to the kitchen for some coffee. I could tell by Charles's blank expression that he had not come to see us about our burglary. He was in fact surprised to hear news of a break-in, and amazed to see that we had tidied up.

'We gave up on your lot. No one was remotely interested that we had been broken into.' Max showed DS Adams the pictures on his phone as proof. DS Dynamic apologised but continued to appear perplexed, although not qualifying this with an explanation at the time.

I had to ask Max to hold his thoughts about inefficiencies in the police force for a while, as I realised Charles had other priorities, which meant trouble for me no doubt.

'I'm actually not supposed to be here, so I'd be grateful if you wouldn't mention my visit to anyone. Not a single soul please. I'm on my way home from one hell of a night shift, and I'm going to have to trust you because ... well, because.

'There have been two incidents during the night. One of your patients, Ben Tierney was arrested and charged with public order offences in the early hours.'

I was not shocked at this information.

'In my opinion, formal charges should have waited until later this morning as your man was still as drunk as a lord. He should have been sobered up and had an appropriate adult with him before being questioned because of his mental health history.'

Charles looked at Max. 'That is confidential, you understand? Everything I have to tell you is confidential.'

'Understood,' replied Max, who was peculiarly quiet.

'Sorry I can't wrap that up in more helpful words, I'm too tired to think straight. While we had him in the cells, under arrest, he was also questioned in connection with an unexplained death.'

'Oh God ...' My hand went straight to my mouth, and Max thoughtfully put his arm around me.

'Father Joseph Kavanagh from St Francis' Church was found dead by his lodger, a Father Raymond, who I think you know. It appears to have been food poisoning as there was vomit everywhere, but we'll have to wait for the post mortem for confirmation on cause.'

'Lots of carrots and tomato skins?' Max queried. He has a strange fascination with such revolting details.

'Carrots yes, tomato skins yes, and a fair few kidney beans in the mix as it happens. Chilli con carne.'

'A classic food poisoning error. Someone forgot to use tinned kidney beans,' Max announced with great authority.

'You could well be right. There have been numerous food poisoning incidents since chilli con carne became fashionable in the 1970s, and a couple of deaths attributed directly to incorrect use of kidney beans, if I'm not mistaken. Obviously, you know that if you use dried kidney beans and don't soak and boil them for long enough they can cause vomiting.' We both nodded. 'But did you also know that if a slow cooker is used, the poison becomes five times more toxic? Therefore, chilli con carne is potentially fatal. The chilli con carne doesn't reach boiling point you see.'

Between them Max and Charles Adams had solved the case.

If only life were that simple.

'Whatever the actual cause, the DI wanted Benito Tierney questioned because of numerous complaints and reports, that yesterday, he'd been making drunken allegations around town about sexual abuse. As usual he'd accused Father Joseph of sexual assault and had implicated him in an organised church paedophile ring. I blame Dan Brown and that book. They're all at it, Illuminati this, Freemasons that. The usual conspiracy crap.'

'Hmmm, so I heard.'

'Father Raymond, his deputy, had also reported that earlier yesterday, Ben had been seen ranting like a madman outside the Rectory, so he had to be questioned, given such a strong motive to harm Father Joseph.'

Max shrugged and opened his hands out indicating that he was not privy to details about Ben.

After a short awkward pause, I had to ask again why DS Charles Adams had appeared on our doorstep in the early morning telling us confidential information.

'I came to apologise. When you called me yesterday with information about Liam Brookes, I was with DI Lynch, the man who has ordered there to be no detailed investigation into the death of your patient, Mrs Janet Collins. Or rather no investigation of her connection with Liam Brookes. That's why we didn't need to use your fingerprints and why I had to politely thank you and report that we no longer require information.'

'Right. I get that.'

'But there should be …' announced Charles taking a seat and gratefully accepting a strong coffee from Max. 'French police have found your man Nick Shafer, aka Liam Brookes, dead in his flat in Perpignan, and foul play is very much indicated. Carbon monoxide poisoning with a flue deliberately blocked from the outside by person or persons unknown.'

With this unwelcome news, I was visibly shaking and urged my sleepy brain to work out the complexities, but it refused to cooperate and was switched to standby mode. Therefore, for the time being, it only remained for me to become a listener, and not to contribute anything. Max didn't have any idea what Emma and I had found the previous evening at the Lodge House, and Charles was only aware that we had identified a man called Nick Shafer also known as Liam Brookes.

'How did you get the information about him being found dead?' I eventually asked, when a small neuron in my brain sparked into life.

'I speak French, and no one else at the station could take the information over the phone. The police in France had picked up on the media interest in finding our man Liam but when I gave details to the DI, I was told not to document it until he had confirmation by email. I'm still waiting.'

'Shit.'

'Yes, shit. Look, both of you … there has to be a connection between these deaths and I think you may be inadvertently involved, somehow.' DS Charles Adams looked at both Max and me alternately. 'I have to trust you because I may have to assume there is a cover-up within the police force. I need proof but I also need to blow the whistle if the cover-up is organisational. If people are being killed then it's really big.'

'Can I have time to think this through?' I asked quietly. 'Don't worry, we won't breathe a word. We may be able to help because we believe our break-in was staged, but we have to be able to trust you too and I'm so tired I need some time …'

'I didn't know about your break-in.'

DS Adams confirmed that he too required sleep to stand any chance of figuring out the best course of action. Charles was due some time off and would be available at the weekend, he told us. In an unexpected move towards being amicable, he asked us both to call him Charlie and left us his personal mobile details.

That was a major breakthrough.

'He's not as stuffy as you said he was,' commented Max when Charlie left to finally go home to bed. 'Seems like a straightforward fella.'

'Yes, but why was he really here, and why now?'

Chapter Fifteen

During the clean-up operation of our once secure sanctuary, I resolved to take a few hours off work the next day. The team would understand that I'd been a victim of a crime, I thought.

When I called the office first thing to negotiate this, Kelly was pretending to be sympathetic to the news of our burglary but was actually dismissive. I could hear it in her voice when she asked a couple of superficial questions out of pretend politeness.

'Yeah, well, I expect you were followed home by a couple of lowlifes needing drug money.' All she wanted to know was when would I be showing my face at the office.

'I'll let you know as soon as I've sorted myself out. It's not a pleasant feeling knowing that someone has been rummaging around in your smalls, uninvited.'

'No, I quite understand.' Her attempt at empathy didn't sound convincing.

When I finally managed to speak to Emma, she was between farmyard duties and childcare responsibilities. Initially, she was fairly laid back in her response to the news of our break-in and as usual was pragmatic, with her sense of humour firmly intact.

'Blimey, that's at least two mysteries for us to solve and we haven't even set up our private investigator business yet. You'll have to go part-time, Mon. I have to say; I'm a bit shocked by the news that Nick is dead. I thought he might have been in an accident or been taken seriously ill, but not dead. How sad.'

Even though she was joking about setting up as private investigators, Emma had spent a few more hours the previous evening leafing through Nick Shafer's notebooks. The name of

Aitken, Brown and Partners, which had caught my attention the previous evening, appeared intermittently in amongst other written details that were forming the signposts and patterns to evidence of Nick Shafer's life as Liam Brookes. Emma was thrilled to hear of the link to the stolen journals. At least, that was what we were assuming at the time.

'I suggest that we continue our independent research as planned, gather the relevant information, and meet at the weekend to get our heads together,' I said. Three days to get through and as Nick Shafer would not be returning we could use the Lodge House as the HQ for our investigations.

'Good plan, Sherlock.'

Within fifteen minutes, Emma had phoned me back. 'What the fuck is going on?' Emma swearing again, as she used to before she had the children, was a serious matter. 'We've called the police. Some bastard has broken into the Lodge House and trashed the place. It's a bloody mess. The motorbike is still there, as is pretty much everything of value but the desk area has been thoroughly wrecked. I'm not sure exactly what they were looking for but the pin board seems to have gone.'

'Bollocks, Emma, this is getting a bit scary. Whatever they're looking for, we have had it or have it in our possession. They were definitely after the journals at my place and I think the journals are connected with Nick Shafer and his solicitors. Are the police coming out to see you? They haven't bothered with us and just gave us a crime reference number as if we didn't count.'

'I don't think we're on their list of priorities either. Nothing of value stolen, so no need to bother. Jake is furious. He thinks the only reason the burglars didn't call on us is the two collies and the geese in the yard.'

'Yes, well, Deefer was a dead loss as a guard dog, so he's possibly right with that guess.' My work mobile was ringing, demanding my attention, cutting short the conversation with Emma.

'I've another call coming in, I'll have to phone you back later.'

It was Kelly again. The police station was requesting my presence to see Ben Tierney. The officers had realised their error and needed an appropriate adult under the requirements of the Police and Criminal Evidence Act, in order to question him properly and formally charge him with a number of offences. The solicitor allocated to Ben had been adamant in this request. Good for him.

Kelly informed me, rather brusquely, that I also had a message from Father Raymond, asking me to contact him to arrange a meeting. To ensure I was in no doubt as to her irritation, she then took great pleasure in informing me that a formal request had been made from the Coroner's Office for a report on Jan Collins. I had a fortnight to complete it and the full hearing would be in six weeks' time.

'You're not expected to be called to give evidence at the hearing but the Coroner's Office have laid out exactly what they're expecting in a report, if you can spare the time, of course.'

I heaved a steadying breath before answering her as politely as I could through slightly gritted teeth, choosing my words carefully. 'Kelly, I realise that the team are under pressure because of the medication amnesty, but I do really have a lot on my plate, so bear with me. I *will* go to the police station today as requested, I *will* write the report for the coroner as and when I can, and if you have a number for Father Raymond, I *will* call him back.'

It was plain that I was unpopular at the moment with almost every single one of my colleagues, none of whom had contacted me to enquire after my welfare. They would all know about the burglary because Kelly would have been delighted to tell them. Kelly was usually a reliable barometer as to the mood in the camp. Current mood: disgruntled.

The NHS Trust board of directors had requested that I concentrate on ensuring the smooth marketing of the medication amnesty. My hard-working, downtrodden teammates had been given no option but to share my caseload between them. As far as I was concerned, it was a godsend. However, Eddie spoke to me in private to let me know that the team were royally pissed off and they saw me as some sort of self-serving NHS puppet.

Much more of this and I would become an outcast.

I pinged a brief text message to DS Charlie Adams to let him know that I had been requested to attend the station. I didn't want to find myself in the awkward situation of being seen by him there without any forewarning. He may assume I was breaching confidence about his visit to our house that very morning. This was going to be a tricky enough trip to the nick as it was. After all, I was not supposed to know that Father Joseph was dead nor that Liam Brookes, aka Nick Shafer, was also dead.

In a pokey, square interview room, I sat with Ben, waiting for the police and the solicitor to organise carrying out a formal interview under caution. As indicators for his overall physical state, Ben was unshaven and unwashed, with filthy fingernails. The faint whiff of stale vomit paled into insignificance when Ben spoke and almost floored me with the foul, rancid stench of his breath. He looked absolutely dreadful, indicating that further vomiting was highly likely, thus explaining the need for the bucket placed on the floor to his immediate left. He had been dressed in a plain, pale green tunic and trousers, and wrapped in a blanket as he was shivering from a stupendous hangover. That was my best guess. He was trembling as he took a gulp or two from the glass of water placed in front of him and managed a weak grin in my direction.

'I've fucked up this time all right, Monica.' As if I needed telling. 'Can't remember most of it though, so I don't know if I've done the things they said.'

All I could usefully do was to advise Ben to listen to what his solicitor offered. The police doctor had deemed him fit to be questioned that morning and had not requested an assessment under the Mental Health Act, so Ben was in the hands of the criminal justice system. I was there because he was a vulnerable adult, not to assess or to provide treatment. I had to make sure I was seen to be acting in his best interests.

I wasn't sure what to do when DS Adams, still looking exhausted, strode into the interview room. In my uncertainty, I said, 'Good afternoon, officer.' Then I stopped and stared at him.

Thankfully, Charlie reached across and officiously shook my hand. 'Nice to see you again, Monica. Thanks for stepping in. It's so much easier for all concerned to have an appropriate adult that knows the individual. Ben, we are waiting for Mr Dorman, your solicitor, to finish an urgent phone call before we can begin. This will be a recorded interview, so I'll get set up. Monica, I'll need to ask you to confirm your name for the recording and to say in what capacity you are present, although you've probably done this before.'

'Yes, a fair few times.'

'Ben. How are you doing? The doctor has said that you're fit for interview. I have to say that you look a bit peaky to me, so don't forget to use that bucket if you have to. I don't want to have clear up and disinfect an interview room. Understand?'

So, this was DS Charles Adams at work. Calm and authoritative, with an air of efficient determination about him that I, for one, would not question.

A uniformed officer stuck his head around the door beckoning to DS Adams. 'Sorry, sir ...'

Charlie stepped outside the door and when he re-entered a matter of minutes later, a diminutive, slim, bird-faced man in a pinstriped suit followed him. This tiny man looked every inch the archetypal lawyer but one who had been washed on a boil cycle and who had shrunk as a result. The contrast between me, as a woman of Amazonian proportions and the pint-sized Mr Dorman, was comical. It was purely the seriousness of the situation that prevented my mouth from announcing my thoughts out loud. Mr Dormouse.

Tiny dormouse solicitor introduced himself to Ben. He had been allocated the case, and had never met Ben, or me, in his life before. I would have remembered if he had.

'It must be your lucky day, Ben.' Charlie had a face like thunder, and I was convinced that Ben was in for a rough time.

'You are not going to be questioned in regard to specific threats against a Father Joseph Kavanagh. These allegations, although serious in nature, have been dropped. However, we will proceed with allegations of common assault, of public nuisance, and a number of public order offences.'

Christ, now what? I tried to catch Charlie's eye but his face remained expressionless as he began the process of ensuring Ben was aware of his rights and then whisking through details of the evidence and the charges. Why had the charges relating to threats against Father Joseph been dropped, I wondered?

Mr Dorman made no objections other than to voice his concern that Ben had been unfairly treated during the early hours, and to announce that a complaint would be filed to that effect with the IPCC.

Two more surprises awaited me as I was leaving the station. Sean and Manuela Tierney were both standing in the corridor that led from the main front desk. Uniformed officers were at their sides, thanking them for their time. The Tierneys were wide-eyed and anxious. Sean shifted from one leg to the other, holding his wife's hand firmly in his own. I stood back against a wall to prevent them from seeing me. As I listened to them confirming that they were agreeing to help with enquiries in relation to the unexplained death of Father Joseph Kavanagh, I was holding my breath. I thought they had come to see Ben.

'We haven't done anything, Manuela, so don't worry. The officers have to ask us questions to find out how Father Joseph died, and we may have been the last people to see him alive.' Sean looked ashen as they were taken into separate rooms.

Charlie arrived beside me, and, hand on my elbow, firmly bundled me along the corridor, escorting me to the exit, while expressing his gratitude for my assistance. He buzzed me through to the front desk and from there the duty sergeant allowed my escape.

I took in the air outside the station doors. It was town flavoured, not refreshing, but a preferable alternative to the rank smell of

Ben's nervous sweat, and of vomit. Watching from the steps of the police station, I stood frozen to the spot as the police vehicle directly in front of me disgorged a furious-looking, handcuffed Frank Hughes. Despite being escorted by two uniformed officers, the sight of me enraged him, and he let rip. 'If this is down to you, you cunning, vindictive bitch, I'll find you! I *will* find you! And when I do, you'll wish you were dead.' I glanced behind me in the belief that Frank Hughes and his shark eyes were aiming his threats at someone else, but I stood alone.

'That's enough,' one of the officers sternly ordered. 'It wasn't anything to do with this lady. It was to do with you breaking the law. Several laws in fact, so if you don't hold your tongue we'll do you for threats and harassment.' The officer then motioned for me to leave and to make way for his obstreperous prisoner to be marched, unceremoniously, into the station, which gave me enough courage to make a quaking but hasty escape. I wasn't even sure what it was I had done to upset the vile, repellent git-of-a-man, but whatever he thought I'd done had created bitter violent anger.

Even though I was persona non grata, I returned to the sanctuary of the office base, and fortunately, putting aside her unfavourable opinion of me, Kelly recognised my fragile mental state as I walked in.

'Looks like a cup of strong, sweet tea is in order,' she said. I agreed, and made us both one. No hard feelings.

Hiding at my desk, I managed to produce a first draft of a chronology on which to base the report for the Coroner's Office. Two weeks was not long to complete a comprehensive report and to have it scrutinised by Eddie. As I wrote it, I sensed that I had missed some factual information, or that what I had written did not fit with the rest of the detail. There was a contradiction, an anomaly, which I couldn't identify. Not to do with timings or dates, but reasons behind actions that Jan had taken. It was so frustrating not to have my brain in full working order. I really could have done with a good night's sleep.

Having achieved at least the bare bones of a report, I phoned the number for Father Raymond, which I had stored in my mobile phone. A task on my list of things to do. I debated whether or not this was wise. He had found Father Joseph dead the night before and he was sure to be having a terrible time. And yet, I told myself, I could lend him a sympathetic ear.

'Thanks for calling, Monica. I appreciate you getting back to me so rapidly.'

I stopped myself at the very last second. Shit. I had almost revealed that I already knew of Father Joseph's death. 'No problem. Have I called at a convenient time to discuss my concerns about Liam Brookes?'

'Well, in truth, this is a difficult day. I have the police here at the moment. I'm not even certain that I can tell you why that is … but I'm sure it won't be too long before the press gets hold of the story, so you'll find out soon enough.'

'Oh dear … I'll call another day, shall I? Or better still, I'll wait for you to call me back.' Due to bad acting skills I didn't sound convincingly surprised that the police were with Father Raymond. What an idiot.

'That's a good idea. Thanks.'

Chapter Sixteen

I unloaded my car boot when I made it home, and staggered into the hallway, depositing the box and wire tray taken from the Lodge House onto the hall table. There was no Deefer wagging his tail and bouncing around excitedly at my arrival. No Deefer to take for a walk to freshen my resolve for sorting through the paperwork from the Lodge House.

Max had taken him to work. 'I'm worried about him. It must have been horrible to be shut in the shed in the dark all alone.' I couldn't believe what I had heard. Max never worried about *my* mental state, which I suspected was not as solid and dependable as it used to be, so I went for a walk without the dog. A very peculiar feeling it was too, walking without Deefer; nevertheless it allowed thinking space for a review of the previous twenty-four hours.

Why did the thief choose that day and time to search for the journals? He or she would have had to know that Max and I were going out. Why not turn up when we were both at work? Did they only go to the Lodge House at Emma's farm because they didn't find what they were looking for in my house? How did they get both of these addresses?

I started with the first question. Who knew that Max and I were going out that night? I think I mentioned it to Vanessa over a cup of tea at St David's Church Hall. Did I?

I couldn't have been heard talking to Emma on the phone confirming arrangements, as I was in my car. Was the car window open? I couldn't remember. I was tired and muddled. Was it Frank Hughes, had he followed me?

This would probably come back to me in the middle of the night when all my temporary memory losses seemed to correct themselves. *Is it an age thing, or stress?* I questioned.

The dining room was the ideal place to spread the paperwork out, so I divided the correspondence contained in the wire tray into letters or emails to aid my fact-finding. Nick Shafer had printed a number of emails from and to Aitken, Brown and Partners. But it was one of the letters that had me reaching for my mobile phone.

The letter was in an unopened white envelope, foolscap size, which Emma and I had picked up from the doormat of the Lodge House. Contained within were several sheets of paper, and my married name and address appeared amongst a list of others on the top page. This list was of people who had purchased items at Yarlsmere's auction on the day that I bought my cabinet. Against our names were listed the items we had bought, and a description of each one of us, as well as anyone we were with or standing next to. I was described as *'female, late thirties/early forties, shoulder-length dark hair, medium build, tall, approx. 6ft. Roman nose.'*

Harsh. My nose is aquiline, not Roman. Some people argue that both words mean the same thing, but aquiline sounds much more attractive. At least they didn't describe my nose as "hooked". Once I had recovered from the stark description of myself, I soon realised that someone at the auction had carefully watched me, and that someone, whoever they were, had taken photographs. I pulled the colour photos from the envelope. There were a number of shots of me, and each one included the familiar form of Father Raymond.

Someone, with the full knowledge of Aitken, Brown and Partners, had been at the auction watching every sale. Had that someone been sent to retrieve this information from the Lodge House?

These creeping realisations made me feel uneasy, cold, and vulnerable. The house was too quiet; unnerved, I went through to the kitchen to put on the radio for company. As I passed by, I checked that the front door was securely locked. The crapometer readings were rising rapidly again.

'Max, are you on your way home? You're where? What for? Blimey.'

My husband was more perturbed by our break-in than I had appreciated. When I phoned him, he had been at a local DIY superstore buying bolts and motion sensor lights and I had disturbed him in the aisle containing CCTV security systems.

It was a welcome relief to see him when he marched through the house with his purchases, heading for the garage, albeit that I had misunderstood his intent. I had stupidly assumed the additional security would be for the house. Wrong. It was for his precious sodding motorbikes.

After a hastily cobbled-together dinner at the kitchen table, we held a family security meeting in the dining room. My head was whirring with the probabilities and possibilities of who was after what and why, but I had yet to decide how best to break the news to Max about me being under surveillance.

'What?' I asked Max, who was giving me a very grave stare. 'Why are you looking at me like that?'

'I think you'd better start trying to explain just what it is that we've got ourselves into here. Is this down to some rampaging psychopath? No. That much is obvious. The break-in was designed to look like a burglary, but those bloody journals were the actual prize. Who knew you had them? And more importantly, Mon, what was in them that was so vital?'

Max fixed me with his most serious expression. He tapped his fingers impatiently on the table-top.

'I know you want me to have an answer but I can only hazard a guess in both cases. I haven't a clue what could be so important about the journals; I only read parts of them. What I do know is that I was being watched when I was at the auction.'

'Rubbish, you're being paranoid now. Frank Hughes is a drug dealer and a psychopath, granted, but he's not clever enough to be involved in stealing journals and making it look like a burglary.

Unless of course the journals contain recipes for drugs that can be sold on the street for a profit.' He knew Frank by reputation. 'How can you possibly know that you're being watched? Mon, it's not a spy story. Get a grip.' Max was being unnecessarily sarcastic again.

'I mean it. Look at this …' That was one way to break the bad news, I suppose. I handed Max the envelope with the evidence and waited for the explosion. This arrived shortly after his eyebrows shot skyward.

'What the bloody hell is this? Who the hell is following you? Hang on. All the people on the list here bought items at the auction that were being sold by Aitken and Who-jah-ma-flip. Why would a firm of solicitors go to such lengths to identify each of you?'

'Should we just phone them and ask?'

'Sleep deprivation is making you stupid, woman. Why would that be a good idea? No, I think we need to contact your detective friend, early-morning-Charlie. But I'm too knackered to think straight, so instead I suggest that we have a good sleep, and call him tomorrow when we've calmed down a bit.'

Clean sheets and a hot shower made the whole idea of bed a welcome delight. People often describe dropping off to sleep before their heads touch the pillow and I wish that could happen to me, but it never does. As soon as I had settled down and wriggled about a bit, my memory library alerted me to a missing piece of recall. Not the one I was looking for, but a picture flashed into my mind of the kitchen in Jan Collins's house the day we discovered her body. I distinctly envisaged four chairs around the kitchen table but only two had remained tucked under as good manners dictated. Two were left as if their recent occupiers had risen and moved away, completely forgetting what their mothers had taught them. Why on earth was that significant? Too dopey to care, I settled down again, only to have another intrusive image flash across my visual memory screen.

It was the kitchen table again, with the contents of her medicine cabinet scattered upon it. There at the front of my image was a box of plasters, behind that some throat lozenges, a bottle of cough mixture, and a bottle containing some liquid Kemadrin. There was the answer to my frustrations. If I were to be brave enough to take my own life, I wouldn't have bothered with these items when I knew for certain that I had paracetamol and dothiepin to choose from. I wouldn't have considered getting plasters or cough mixture out of the cupboard, let alone put them in front of me as I sat there, swallowing tablets to kill myself.

Max was commencing his snoring repertoire. This began with heavy breathing and blowhole noises, before progressing to piggy snorts and whoopee cushion exhalations. I didn't want to disturb him, and I couldn't think what else to do other than to get out of bed and scribble these two scenes down on a small notepad. I kept one to hand on my dressing table for early morning ideas or to remember items of shopping. Max was very disgruntled. 'Mon, Jesus, please just shut up and go to sleep.' I thought I'd been as silent as a ninja. Clearly not.

It is amazing what a few hours of restful, restorative sleep can achieve. I had developed a plan while I was in that semi-dreamlike state between sleep and wakefulness. I realised that the coroner asked for report chronologies because of their practical use. What was the chain of events leading to Jan Collins's death, Nick Shafer's demise, and now Father Joseph's unexplained departure from the mortal world? Was there more than a grain of truth in what Ben Tierney had always asserted when psychotic or drunk? If there was a conspiracy to silence those who disclosed or revealed evidence of organised child abuse, then this implicated the Catholic Church, and the police.

I sent an urgent text to Emma. *'Watson, we can't wait until the weekend, we have to meet today. Call me!'*

Deciding to show my face at the church hall to ensure that the amnesty was running to plan, I drove there first, totally bypassing the office. Deefer was in the car with me as I was too afraid to leave him home alone, and I was certain that his presence would be unacceptable at work. All was well with the medication amnesty in the safe hands of the volunteers, and I was reassured that I could leave them to manage without my direct input. Fortunately, the initial rush of enthusiasm had dwindled to a trickle of people popping in to dispose of the out of date contents of their medicine cupboards. I left the willing helpers to cope.

When my phone rang as I returned to my car, I assumed that it was Emma.

'Watson. My place or yours?'

'Monica? It's Father Raymond here, at the Rectory,' came the man's voice from my phone. I was embarrassed and tried to cover up my foolish error. Fancy not looking to see who was calling me before answering.

'Oh, sorry, I thought you were someone else.' It was true.

'Monica, I know we agreed to meet up for a chat, but I have to delay this for a day or so. Sadly, Father Joseph has passed away unexpectedly and I must attend to the necessary arrangements with the bishop.'

Remembering to sound stunned, I gave a small gasp. 'Oh, no. That's terrible news. Is there anything I can do?' It's the sort of thing we all say. I had no idea what would be useful for a mental health nurse to do in such circumstances, but it was a genuine offer of help.

'Could you make yourself available for the people who use the Pathways Project? A lot of them attend St Francis' Church and they'll be shocked to hear the news.'

'Of course, I'd be glad to. Was Father Joseph unwell?' I ventured.

'No, not particularly, but it seems he may have had a delicate heart. Father Joseph had food poisoning, and this appears to have caused cardiac failure. He was an old man, and perhaps he couldn't tolerate being sick.'

'That's very likely. Look, don't worry about our chat. We'll catch up soon. You have other priorities now,' I said, grateful for a delay. I needed to be armed with more facts before questioning

Father Raymond about Jan, and Nick Shafer, but I couldn't resist one final question.

'Before you go, out of interest, what did he eat that made him so unwell?'

'I'm not certain exactly. The Tierneys called to see him late that afternoon and they had a casserole with them, as a gift for both of us. It smelt delicious, but was definitely a meat dish of some kind. I'm vegetarian, so I didn't eat any. I didn't even realise the poor man was ill until I heard a crash as he fell.'

'Oh dear … I expect the ambulance turned up fairly smartish, though?'

'I called them straight away but he was dead by the time they arrived. He must have been struggling to breathe because of his heart. It was a desperate situation, to be honest with you. I'm probably only telling you because you're a nurse. It's the Tierneys I feel so sorry for. How on earth are they going to react if they find out Father Joseph died after eating their gift of food?'

'Oh, you're right. Perhaps we should keep this information to ourselves. I won't breathe a word to anyone. Sean and Manuela will be distraught if they find out. I'm not sure they can take much more.' I had to pretend I didn't know Sean and Manuela were implicated and had already been answering questions from the police. What a tangled web.

'Listen, please don't leave it too long before calling me, Father. It sounds as if you could do with talking these things through, otherwise you'll end up replaying events, endlessly wondering if there was more you could have done.'

'I already am.'

Noting the sincerity in Father Raymond's words, I began to doubt my suspicions. Was he a good man? Or was he clever at pretending to be kind natured and caring? Was he implicated in a cover-up of Father Joseph's abuse of children? Had *he* killed Father Joseph? Had he killed Jan?

I made my excuses and was about to end the conversation when Father Raymond suddenly cut me off. I looked at the screen on the mobile to confirm the call had ended, and as I did so a man ran past the end of the road. He was looking over his shoulder as he sprinted by. In that brief moment, I recognised Benito. 'He's in a hurry to get to the pub before it even opens,' I commented to Deefer. About to follow Ben out of concern, I had my hand on the ignition when my mobile phone rang. I checked it to see who was calling me. It was Emma.

'Thank God. Can we meet up? My crapometer readings are increasing,' I said.

'Mine too. Look, Mon, I'm at work until three. Can you come over to the farm after you finish? Bring everything with you and ask Max to meet us there. No one else. That is vital. No one else at all.'

'Can I bring Deefer? I daren't leave him alone again.'

'Yes, of course. He's a dog, not a person, you nellie. Are you keeping him with you today? In the car?'

'Yes. I know. I know. It's pathetic. I'll see you later.' Sitting in my car in stunned silence, I stared through the windscreen at nothing in particular, which allowed imaginary memory librarian to come up trumps. My car passenger side window was open slightly to ensure Deefer had fresh air, and this reminded me that my car window *had* been open the day of our break-in. I'd called to Ben Tierney through the open window on the passenger's side. He had huffed his foul alcohol fumes at me through the gap. This, in effect, meant that anyone passing by earlier that day outside St David's Church Hall could have heard my arrangements with Emma to visit the farm at seven o'clock that evening. Who passed by?

Chapter Seventeen

S haking myself alert, I started the engine and drove out of the car park to look for Ben, but he was nowhere to be seen on the streets. I stopped briefly to phone Max on my personal mobile, and arranged to meet him at Folly Farm after work. He seemed to listen for once.

Having done that, I required an escape from the overstimulation of town noise, to the peace of the open countryside, to ease the pressure building up inside my mind. I knew I should have taken some time off work instead of pretending to be functioning, but I wasn't really sick. Exhausted, bewildered, disturbed, but not exactly ill; so I carried on with the pretence of coping.

My rounds were taking me to the tiny village of Swandale to see a patient who was doing remarkably well. Eleanor Jones had been a star pupil and had returned to work some weeks previously after a brief psychotic episode, possibly caused by a mountain of personal stress. We all have our breaking points.

Three weeks before, I had been asked for help when her medication had started causing her to feel sedated during the day, whereas before this she had found it helpful.

'I can't believe you worked it out so quickly,' she said as we sat down to talk. It hadn't taken me long to deduce that her GP had changed the prescription to the cheaper, twice-a-day option. 'Well, it took me longer to make a phone call, write a letter of explanation and do some diplomatic manoeuvring, than it did to identify the real problem,' I said. 'Anyway, I've finally secured a promise from your GP to ensure you're prescribed the modified release version. So, the question is, have we solved the problem?'

'Yes. I can't thank you enough. I'm back to sleeping at night and functioning at work during the day. What a relief. I thought I was going to lose my job, but now I'm nearly back to full-time hours.'

The satisfaction of that positive result lifted my mood.

Deefer, who had been patiently sitting in the car, deserved a moment of freedom and I knew exactly how to reward his tolerance. The country park in Swandale was a favourite of his, and he bounded from the back seat immediately, recognising the autumn smells of the lake and woods. Quickly I stuffed a dog poo bag into my pocket, and deliberately switched off both my mobile phones before heading in an anticlockwise direction around the lake, giving myself a break for half an hour.

'Morning.'

'Morning …' I replied to a woman I recognised. Her name escaped me for a while, which only led to me convincing myself that I was heading for senility more rapidly than expected. I'd always had a good memory, but lately it was becoming unreliable, and by default, so was I.

On a bench, ahead of me, were two elderly people caught in a passionate embrace. *Blimey, there's hope for Max and me yet,* I thought, but as I neared the bench my heart sank. This was not passion being demonstrated; it was heartbreak. The couple were sobbing into each other's shoulders. Pure anguish and desolation. The man looked up. It was Sean Tierney.

'Oh no, Sean, Manuela, what on earth has happened?' The question caught in my throat. The emotion of the scene had undermined my usual professional approach to such situations. I felt tears stinging my eyes and Deefer had stopped to look up at me, worried by my tone of voice.

Sean managed to speak. 'We came looking for Ben. We bring the grandchildren sometimes. He's not allowed to have them on his own, you see, so we bring them to the playground and wildlife pond. We thought he might have come here.' Ben hadn't been seen by his parents since before his arrest.

'Don't worry, I've only just seen him. He was running towards town along Bushmead. I was parked in St David's Road.'

Having eased much of their worry, I sat with them both for a time, while between snivels and sniffs, crying and shuddering, they recounted their visit to the police station the previous day.

'The officer thought that Ben might have been telling the truth for all these years.'

'What do you mean?' I asked, hoping that I was wrong in my thinking.

'The officer asked me if Ben could have been abused when he was a child. He thought that was why our Benito said those dreadful things about Father Joseph. The police think he wanted to kill Father Joseph, and they kept asking if he could have had a chance to poison the chilli we made to take to the Rectory.'

'Good God, did they really tell you that?'

'Not exactly, no. They asked us what time we made the chilli, who cooked it, what was in it, where Ben was at the time we made the chilli … you see, don't cha?'

That sounded to me more like an interrogation than an opportunity to help police with enquiries. Manuela sobbed and squawked, 'It could be us. We could have poisoned the Father. We killed a holy man of God. They think I killed him …'

Sean stepped in, clasping his wife's head to his chest. 'The shame is almost unbearable, you see. Our son tells such lies about the Church that we are being punished for his blasphemous accusations. The officer said that either we believe our son when he says he was sexually assaulted and that we have killed Father Joseph in revenge, or that we are covering for our son. Ben would never kill anyone, and neither would we.'

'Have you been charged with anything?' I asked with disbelief heavily weighing down my ability to think rationally. How could the police be so thoughtless? Didn't they realise that Ben's parents had no acceptance of his abuse accusations?

'No. Nothing. Ben was released yesterday on bail. He's supposed to be at home, but we can't find him. We don't know what to say to him. Could he have killed Father Joseph, like the officer said?'

'I doubt it. Wasn't Ben in custody when you took the chilli to the two Fathers?'

'We don't know. We saw Father Raymond and Father Joseph at about six o'clock. Ben had been out drinking all day.'

'Well, there you are then. Ben couldn't be accused of anything. He wasn't at home to poison the chilli. If he was, he would have been too drunk to manage a poisoning.' I hoped my sound reasoning would help matters, but I hadn't accounted for Manuela's assumption that she must be the guilty party.

She wailed.

'Now calm down a bit, Manuela. You've made chilli con carne hundreds of times, so it can't be you either. Did you boil the kidney beans?' I asked.

'No, never.'

Oh, shit.

'I use the tinned ones. It's safer. I only had a small tin in stock, so I was embarrassed because it wasn't as good as my normal standard. Sean told me to stop fussing about how many beans were in the sauce.'

Phew.

'Well then, it can't be you either. So perhaps poor old Father Joseph had a heart attack or something similar. Besides, Father Raymond is fit and well. I spoke to him earlier today.' This was a fine piece of quick thinking on my part. Neither Sean nor Manuela were to know that Father Raymond didn't eat meat, and had not even tasted the chilli.

Having worked my magic, through a white lie, I saw that Sean and Manuela appeared less burdened. They could concentrate on finding their son.

'Shall I ring the Green Man? The landlady may be able to shed some light on where Ben is now.' The exhausted pair nodded gratefully.

The landlady at the Green Man pub confirmed the inevitable. 'He was here … last night, plastered. Haven't seen him today. I'll tell him you're looking for him, shall I?'

'His parents are the ones he needs to call. They're worried sick.'

'I don't doubt it! Poor folks.'

Switching both my phones on as I walked along, I made my way straight back to the car, and a tolerant Deefer had to cope with the shortest walk in his living memory. Messages beeped, and missed calls beeped, and answerphone messages beeped. 'Oh dear, something's up.'

An understatement, as it turned out.

Kelly at the office was furious when I reported in. 'Where the hell have you been?' she snarled. 'Eddie called in to St David's Church Hall. You weren't there. You haven't called in to report your plans for the day. I sent text messages, left voice mails, which you can't be bothered to reply to. It makes you look like you're too good for us mere mortals who are doing your work for you!' She had made her views abundantly clear. I had no excuses to give.

'You're quite right. I'm all over the place since the break-in and I have no excuse whatsoever. I've been with Benito Tierney's parents. They're in a really bad way.'

'Oh, I'm sorry. I didn't think they had been told yet.'

'About what bit? Father Joseph being dead, or Ben being a suspect?' I asked.

'No, Monica, about Ben being dead.'

Chapter Eighteen

The image on the screen, although grainy, was clear enough for me to see Benito Tierney stumbling along next to the train tracks away from Lensham Station in the direction of Hollberry. His arms were flailing around as if he were trying to swat away several wasps. Some way behind him, it was possible to make out the shapes of two men running to catch up, and they then launched themselves onto a steep bank away from the trackside. The express train appeared from the right of the screen, instantly obscuring the view of Ben. When it had passed by at tremendous speed, all that remained were scattered shreds of clothing with two legs protruding at an impossible angle. One had a shoeless foot still attached to it.

'Where did the rest of him go?' I asked Charlie as the screen was paused. We had silently watched a few minutes' worth of CCTV footage, which had led up to this catastrophic accident.

'Well, I'm afraid he was sucked towards the train as it passed, and the rest of him was a lot further back towards the main station. You didn't have to watch that part, you know,' Charlie said, trying to be reassuring. In truth, nothing much could have prepared me for what I had seen.

'I wanted to see for myself, but I wish I hadn't. That's a sick way to die.'

'Doesn't look like he deliberately threw himself under a train, does it?'

'No. Was he pissed that early in the day? He looked out of his tree.'

Charlie was hopeful that the forensic post mortem report would shed some light on Ben's erratic behaviour. 'The toxicology report will give us a much better idea, if they can successfully complete one. Monica, did you recognise either of those two men chasing Ben? Do you want to see that part again?' he asked.

'Yes, that bit. But can you stop the film before the train comes along? I don't think my stomach can take seeing that one more time.' I tried to smile and keep focussed but I was overwhelmingly nauseous. 'Can I take a break first?'

Reports had reached the police that Benito Tierney was being chased by two men onto the railway line immediately before he was killed by the passing express train to Nottingham. Deefer and I had been driven by Charlie to Lensham Railway Station extremely swiftly to try to help with the identification of Ben and, if possible, either of the two men who might have been implicated in his demise. The whole place was awash with ambulance crews, fire service, and police personnel.

*

Earlier, I had followed behind Sean and Manuela's car as they had driven home from the country park.

'God, Deefer, they're never going to cope with this.' I was glad to have the dog in the car with me. He was a strong calming presence when I needed it most. I knew what was to happen next. Sean and Manuela did not.

On arrival at their house, the Tierneys were met by DS Charlie Adams. He had been sent to break the news to Ben's parents that a tragic accident had occurred less than an hour previously. He then radioed for an ambulance as Sean collapsed with what looked like a heart attack. Manuela was also an appalling pale colour and the ambulance crew responded magnificently, treating her for shock, rushing her and her broken husband to A&E.

Charlie and I were both having a bad day at the office again.

There had been a few moments that morning when I thought I would be heading for a breakdown myself. How many more deaths? Two dead patients, one dead investigative journalist, and a deceased priest. Never had there been so much death in such a short span throughout my career.

*

I was useless at recognising either of the two shadowy figures who were seen pursuing Ben along the rail tracks. However, there were more camera angles and film to be watched. Information was coming in from police at the station itself, and from officers who were retracing Ben's hasty and erratic steps.

'I saw him running down Bushmead Road myself,' I had said to Charlie before we settled down to watch the CCTV footage.

'What time was that?'

This was where my memory was not clever enough to give a spontaneous reply. 'Crikey, let me think. I'd just finished talking to Father Raymond, on my mobile phone. I was parked outside the church hall in St David's Road. Well before nine, I would think.'

'Let's have a look on your mobile,' Charlie demanded, then rapidly scrolled through the phone menu and took down the details of the time I had received a call from "Fat Ray".

'It's not meant to be rude. It's shorthand code,' I said by way of explanation.

'So I see ...'

'I was going to follow Ben towards town in my car, but I had a call on my personal mobile from my friend, and I couldn't find him after that.'

'Did anyone chase after Ben at the time you saw him run past?'

'I didn't notice. I was talking to Emma for a couple of minutes.'

'Ah well, never mind. We'll see if anything else shows on the CCTV cameras. One of the team is checking the tapes at the Green Man, too.'

Charlie Adams didn't sound disappointed that I had failed to recognise the two men. 'Never mind, it was worth a shot. We'll try some of the other tapes. Standard police work ...' The door opened behind us and was filled by an enormous, imposing man. DI Lynch had popped in to see how we were progressing and to ask if he could adopt Deefer, who he spotted sitting by my feet. Deefer wagged at the large man.

'I love Staffies. A much-maligned breed. Totally undeserving of the negative press. No such thing as a bad Staffie, only a bad owner. Mrs Davis, you have a lovely dog and are a credit to him.' His booming voice filled the small room. 'No luck? Never mind. Mystery solved anyway. The two gentlemen we are looking for are here at the station. They seem to be suffering from the shock of today's events, but they've made our officers aware of the circumstances leading to their actions. They knew the young man. Lucky they didn't get killed.'

He frowned at me. 'You look shattered, why don't you take your dog home and take a break from work for a few days. I'm sure they can manage without you. We'll call you if we think you can help.'

'Thanks,' was my feeble reply.

'Hardly surprising, sir,' added Charlie. 'Monica here has been having a rough time of it lately. This is your second patient death this month, isn't it?'

I didn't need reminding.

'Keep an eye on Mrs Davis, Detective Sergeant Adams, one more and it becomes a pattern …' DI Lynch was making his whole body wobble by laughing at his own joke. I wanted to find it funny, but my recent emotional turmoil had left me flat and drained. I didn't even register that DI Lynch was calling me by my married name.

'Right, Detective Sergeant Adams, let's scrape the rest of the unlucky sod from the tracks and get the railways running again, shall we? Update me with any significant findings, but there's nothing untoward apparent. Yet another death of a mental patient.' DI Lynch's voice and thoughtless words could be heard echoing as I left the station through a staff entrance, and walked back to my car, which had been abandoned outside the Tierneys' house. I was grateful for a moment alone with Deefer. He appreciated the walk, too.

I don't usually do as I'm told by strangers, but DI Lynch had given sound advice. I called Kelly, absented myself formally from work, and went home where I locked the door securely behind me. Lying on the bed fully clothed, I cuddled Deefer and sipped at a cup of tea. I didn't want to sleep. Every time I closed my eyes with the intention of relaxing, I saw the mangled bottom half of Ben. A tortured soul. Crushed and bloodied.

Sliding from the bed I knelt on the floor, pulling towards me the only remaining G.C. journal, which I had hidden again underneath my bedside cabinet. Was it a work of fiction? Why would someone want to steal the journals in my possession? Did they know this one was missing? 'Oh, shut up, head,' I shouted at myself. 'Just read the bloody thing.'

I settled back onto neatly arranged pillows, journal in one hand, mug of tea in the other. Skimming over *The Ten Commandments* for poisoners, I reminded myself of the sad story of the accidental killing by Mr M, of the lady housekeeper. 'A bit like the chilli con carne ...' I said aloud, without conscious thought. As soon as the words left my lips I sat upright with such a jolt that I spilt my tea. Holy crap! What if the chilli *had* been poisoned but it was meant for Father Raymond and not Father Joseph? Or it had been meant for both of them? If it wasn't poisoned by Sean, Manuela, or Ben, then it had to be Father Raymond who poisoned the chilli after it had been delivered.

'Read on. Read on,' I told myself sternly. The answer had to be in the journals. I flipped pages back and forth reading a few lines here and there, trying to find a key phrase that would alert me to the core clue.

There it was. Four words: ...*Catholic boys' home deaths*. I grabbed my notebook and a pen and trawled back through the italicised writing until I came to the beginning of that section.

Mr M and I had never been asked to undertake a commission for the church and neither of us had predicted that such a request would ever arise. In 1978 however, I began researching and planning a non-commissioned work to remove four members of the Catholic Church. It was never carried out at my hand.

Our GP, Dr K, had been called to the local Catholic boys' home, St Ignatius' Home for Boys, (this is a pseudonym to protect the innocent), where three unexplained deaths had occurred. These were young boys, aged about twelve, who had been found dead after eating what were thought to be wild mushrooms. The coroner's investigation into the tragic incident reached an open verdict. It could not be determined whether the fungi had been accidentally or deliberately ingested.

Dr K held wider suspicions. He had never been asked to attend to any illness in the home, and none of the boys or staff had registered with his surgery. The health and welfare of the children was undertaken wholly by the church, it seemed. When Dr K had been asked to confirm the deaths of the boys, he witnessed the interactions between a number of the children and the priest who ran the home. Whatever he saw led Dr K to make special arrangements to speak to a number of the boys during a school day, when they were routinely examined by the school nurse, Nitty Nora. There was no Catholic school for fifty miles and this resulted in the boys from the home having to attend a local secondary school. Usually, the children from the boys' home were excluded from the annual school nurse inspection of backs for straightness, feet for corns, bunions or verrucae, and hair for lice; but on this occasion an exception was made by the headmistress. She was Dr K's wife.

Dr K was an old and trusted friend of Mr M, who was then approaching his eightieth birthday. Dr K was in a state of despair when they met. Before he left the school gates Dr K had phoned social services asking for them to take the children of St Ignatius Catholic Home for Boys into safe care and he called for the police.

According to Mr M, who sat with Dr K the evening after he had made his reports to the authorities, Dr K had taken the right moral action. The boys spoken to by Dr K had revealed, independently of each other, that the priests at the home had routinely forced the children into sexual acts in the name of God. Dr K had the names of the priests involved and had told the police the shameful truth. Dr K had come to ask Mr M about the toxicity of the mushrooms and details about how the three boys who had died may have found this particular type. He was highly suspicious about the way in which the three boys had died. His suspicions were well founded.

Dr K had written to the coroner to advise that the particular mushrooms identified could not have be picked by them unless they were under supervision, as the death cap would usually be found in deciduous woodland, whereas the report from the press indicated that they had been picking field mushrooms. Dr K questioned why the priests at the home failed to seek medical attention for the boys who would have had severe vomiting and although they may have given the impression of recovery after a couple of days, had then died of kidney and liver failure. Yet no ambulance was called.

Dr K never had the chance to see the results of his brave stand against the Catholic Church. The police and social services did investigate abuse at the home, but by the time they took any action, there had been a miraculous change of staff. Dr K was damned in the press for making unfounded malicious and litigious accusations against the Catholic Church. They blamed the fact that he was Jewish. His wife lost her post at the school on the grounds of mismanagement of child welfare. The school nurse was cross-questioned about Dr K's interviewing of the children regarding abuse, and doubt was thrown on his motives. In the end Dr K was portrayed as a sensation-seeking sex-fiend. He and his wife took their lives in what was reported to be a suicide pact. Neither Mr M nor I believed that to be a true fact.

Mr M had the names of the priests that Dr K had given him and we set about finding these men. We could not trace them at first, but what we found was an endless web of hidden abuse and financial misappropriation. There is evidence that the Catholic Church and its allies will go to any length to preserve their reputation. A whole religious authority and its protectors stood between us and the truth.

'Oh no, I can't read the rest, it's all smudged and stained,' I moan. 'What happened to the boys?' Deefer pricked his ears up and tilted his head to one side.

The Jesuits were formed as soldiers of the Catholic Church ... a small glimmer of hope ... one true Jesuit ...

'Crap. Double crap. What about the bloody Jesuits? What have they got to do with the price of sliced bread?' There was a hole in the page and then a final couple of lines written in Grace's familiar hand.

Two boys from the home have carried on the work I could not finish. Whoever is reading this, please help them.

Chapter Nineteen

I remained ambivalent about the story in the journal. It couldn't be a memoir. I wasn't even sure what had possessed me to think that it held vital information, other than the fact that some mysterious person had ransacked our home and taken every single one of the others.

'Time for your tea, Deefer, and then we shall give Sophie and Thea a treat. They can play dressing up with you.' Deefer sighed loudly. 'Give over, you love it really,' I teased.

Emma was in a determined mood when Deefer and I found her in the warmth of the kitchen at Folly Farm. The two farm collies had ignored us. They were familiar with our smell and recognised us, saving them the bother of rounding us up. The geese were in the yard and these creatures had other ideas.

'The damn things frighten me to death,' I exclaimed to Emma.

'That's the general idea, dopey. Poor Deefer, don't look so worried, they won't eat you.' I knew Emma had meant to give my dog reassurances about the geese, but at that moment, a couple of squealing miniature Emmas pranced in through the internal door. Two giggling girls swamped Deefer in hugs and cuddles. They took his lead from me without a word of welcome, and marched purposefully towards their bedroom where their grandmother was waiting to read them a favourite story. I smiled at the innocence and sheer delight on their faces. Suddenly, however, there was a dreadful screeching noise followed by screams. Emma and I turned to run towards the children when Sparkey flew past, fur puffed up on his back. He shot out of the small kitchen window, which had become his new cat flap.

'Oops, we forgot about Sparkey,' I said, as Emma checked upstairs with the girls who were now laughing. Grandma Frost confirmed that all was well and no harm done.

Recovering quickly, Emma and I set up HQ on the vast farmhouse table that stood centre stage in her kitchen. She collected a large blackboard from the adjoining room and perched it neatly onto an easel. Next to this she placed a flipchart board stocked with a new pad of paper and fat felt pens.

'I feel like I'm at a training session, or a personal seminar. You've excelled yourself again, my dear Watson.'

'You ain't seen nothin' yet, my dear Holmes,' Emma said, producing half a dozen plastic figures.

'What the hell are they? They look like mini hedgehog people.'

'No getting anything past you, is there, Holmes? That's exactly what they are. These, Sherlock old bean, are Sylvanian tree-family people, courtesy of Sophie and Thea. Each one of these small toys represents a victim, and these are the potential suspects,' she said, producing from a box a further selection of small white plastic mice-people, in frocks.

'What planet am I on?'

'There's no need to be so dismissive. I've taped together some blank flipchart paper to make our timeline with, so if we use pencil and plastic Sylvanian people we can move things around easily.' Emma smiled, full of satisfaction at her ingenuity.

'You do know there is probably a way of doing this on a computer or a spreadsheet thing?'

'Yes, but they can be hacked. This can't. End of.'

'You are without doubt the best and cleverest person I know.' She is. Her mad preparations had cheered me up so much that I had shrugged off the horrors of the day within minutes of walking through the door. Unfortunately, I still had to update her with the gory guts and blood details of Ben's death.

'Shall we start with that and work backwards or do we start with Jan's death and work forwards?' Emma asked.

'I think we actually have to start with Jan's death but work backwards if we can, to when she met Liam Brookes. If you think about it, she must have known at some point that he was Nick Shafer. They went abroad together, so unless he had two passports, she would have had to know his real name and therefore his real occupation.'

Emma nodded vigorously. 'Better than that, I'm pretty certain she was working with him. Look at this.' Emma produced a short email from Thomas Aitken of Aitken, Brown and Partners, which read: *'Please thank Mrs C for producing such excellent pots of honey. These have been decorated and will be on offer as planned. It's a shame you will have to be away, however, we anticipate a successful outcome, as the honey will be irresistible. I will write to you with the results and the letter will be waiting for you on your return.'*

'Blimey, that's very cryptic.'

'Mmm. What if the pots of honey were your journals? Make sense now?' Emma asked with a twinkle.

'I knew they weren't real … shall we start the timeline with that? Journals created by Mrs C, then offered for auction with other similar items at Yarlsmere's. A trap for whom?'

'We don't know. But it backfired somehow, because both Nick Shafer and Jan are dead.' Emma paused and took a deep breath. I could feel the heat from her brain as it worked out the variables. 'Do you have anything to indicate that Jan should have died at the same time as Nick Shafer?' she asked.

Jake appeared, ducking through the door to avoid hitting his head, and having just removed his wellies, he apologised for his smelly feet. He padded across the kitchen, announcing that he would return once he had showered. His welcome arrival gave me time to marshal my thoughts.

'Yes, I bloody do,' I said and quickly apologised to Emma for swearing as she gestured to the ceiling, reminding me of the young ears upstairs.

Emma took a small sticky label, which she wrapped around a cocktail stick to make a flag. She wrote '*Jan*' on the label and stabbed a Sylvanian hedgehog-person in the head with it. She did the same for '*Liam*' writing '*Nick*' on the other side of the label for accuracy. 'That's the first two victims. Nick died first so he can go at the beginning of the line until we can work out when. Now then, was the attempt to kill Jan carried out at the same time Nick was killed and in the same way?'

'No. Jan was lucky. The French consultant, Dr Reynaud, assessed that Jan had ACS, which can be fatal, but you would have to take a whopping dose of an anticholinergic for that to happen. If they hadn't treated her she could have died. Nick Shafer made the mistake of putting hyoscine hydrobromide in with her other medication which he took to the hospital for her, but she's never been prescribed it. She used to have the occasional dose of procyclidine when she was on injections, but she was taking olanzapine tablets when she was in France and her old supply of liquid procyclidine was at home. The killer didn't do their homework very well.'

'Could she have escaped from the flat and broken the laptop before running into the streets stripping off her clothes?' Emma suggested.

'It would make sense. There's a saying to recognise ACS. "Blind as a bat, mad as a hatter, red as a beet, hot as a hare, dry as a bone, the bowels and bladder will lose their tone, and the heart runs alone". It's a mnemonic. You see, I did learn something.'

'Is it that dangerous?' asked Emma.

'Hyoscine is the same as scopolamine, I think. It kills, basically, by shutting down the nervous system so you stop breathing before you lose consciousness. Poisoners use it on people diagnosed with mental health problems because the side effects can mimic psychosis. Hence, "Mad as a hatter". The poison gets missed as a cause until it's too late. So, Jan was fortunate.'

'You are a worry.' Emma was giving me a strange look. 'Sir Arthur Conan Doyle has had a bad influence on you, I reckon.' She laughed. 'Let's do one of those police diagrams.'

'Okay. I'll write what we know about each person on a separate sheet of flipchart paper and we should be able to piece together the connections, with any luck.'

This plan paid dividends a few minutes later. Having reviewed what I knew about Jan Collins's medical history, I decided to make a call to the French mental health unit in the hope that someone there spoke English and could find the answer to my question.

'*Bonsoir, Je m'appelle Monica Morris. Je suis une infirmiere psychiatrique d'Angleterre.*' I was trembling with nerves as I spoke, fearful that I was about to commit a dreadful language cock-up again. '*Je ne parle pas Français très bien.*'

By divine intervention a confident reply in faultless English emanated from the phone. I had the good fortune to be speaking to a university student by the name of Sam from Herefordshire who, studying French and Business, was coming to the end of a three-month placement at the Hôpital Corbet. He was enhancing his understanding of French healthcare business processes. I couldn't shut him up.

Sam was young and technically competent. He was able to confirm who I was, and my professional relationship to Jan Collins, via the electronic records system. I put in my request for information about Jan's medication as delivered by Nick Shafer. The hospital had his name recorded as Liam Brookes.

'Oh, I remember him, and her,' Sam said.

'You do?'

'Yes, it was my first shift here, that evening. I chatted with Mrs Collins quite a lot when she was here. The nurses said she was really psychotic when she came in but she was getting better within a day or so. Also, I met her other half when he dropped off her belongings one evening. Although I wouldn't have guessed that's who he was, he was a bit short to be her boyfriend and he didn't seem to want to see her. Then again, I s'pose that's understandable, he was really pissed off that she'd broken their laptop. When she first came in she was still carrying the mains adaptor in one hand and a flash drive in the other, but that was totalled.'

'Sorry? Totalled?'

'Yeah, smashed to bits. Useless. We tried it to see if it would work. Look, I'll see if we have a list of your patient's meds that the boyfriend delivered and I'll phone you back.'

'Are you sure that's okay? It would be great if you can. Before you go, can I just clarify a small matter with you? You said that Jan's boyfriend was shorter than her, I've never met him and we are trying to track him down. Can you describe him?'

Emma had seen something in my face that indicated trouble.

'Em, I need to swear. A lot.'

She took me into her cool, dark, thick-walled larder and watched me as I put both hands up to either side of my face and whispered, 'Fuck a doodle do, Em, Nick Shafer didn't visit Jan in hospital. It was another man. Shorter than Jan, about your height by the sounds of it, mousy, short, neat hair, grey eyes, but no obvious features apart from missing most of his little finger on his left hand. Who the fucking hell was he?'

When my blood pressure had finally returned to a normal range, we left the soundproofed larder, but stepping into the kitchen we both screamed, hugging each other, confronted by a man in full motorbike leathers removing his helmet.

'Max, you bloody idiot! You scared the life out of us.' We laughed at our own nervous response to my husband who, for once, had listened to the telephone message that I left him.

He knew that two patient deaths in as many months would threaten to break my steadfast and strong exterior, and he was right. The cracks were beginning to show, but as things stood, only Max and Emma had noticed their appearance. My forgetfulness, unusual emotional responses to situations, doubts and uncertainties about my abilities; the signs were there.

The evening descended into farce when Deefer, on hearing Max's voice, thundered down the stairs, barged the door open and ran into the kitchen dressed as Little Miss Muffet. He had a lacy bonnet on his head and a frilly blue dress covering the front half of his muscular body. The rear half was wagging madly. Max was appalled.

'What have they done to you? Who has turned my four-legged friend into "Transvestite Dog"?' A giggling Jake appeared behind Deefer and took a photo, before both Max and Jake trooped upstairs to tickle the children, as a punishment for turning our dog into a girl.

As a result of the disruption, it was some time, a cuppa and a portion of lasagne later, before we resumed our investigations into the possible reasons behind the deaths of Jan, Nick, Father Joseph, and Ben. We had originally agreed to meet to resolve our concerns over the break-ins at our homes so there were unspoken fears that matters had taken a more sinister turn.

Emma had already done a considerable amount of background research into Nick Shafer, based on the contents of his office, and she was desperate to share this.

'I have really vital info I need us to think about and we need our combined brains. Then we should split up the work depending on the questions we have at the end. Does that make sense?'

Emma had the floor. She paused to let Jake's mother take a cup of tea into the lounge. Grandma Frost had settled the girls for bed and was desperate to put her feet up and watch her favourite soaps on the telly. 'Goodnight, young people.'

'Goodnight, Grandma Frost,' we chorused like a scene from *The Waltons*.

Emma began.

'Facts: Nick Shafer was a journalist and he was being paid through Aitken, Brown and Partners with instructions coming directly from a Thomas Aitken. I have also uncovered that Nick had email correspondence with a man called Mike Rezendes, an investigative journalist and Pulitzer Prize winner, who works for the *Boston Globe* in the US. Bear with me on this. Mike Rezendes is part of a team on a magazine called *Spotlight*. They investigated and exposed systemic organisational child abuse and cover-ups within the Catholic Church. They published a couple of years ago and the earth-shattering ripples are still rolling outwards. The *Spotlight* team identified that the Catholic Church were aware of abuse and covered it up for decades. This does not relate to one wayward sick priest. It involves hundreds of them.'

There was silence for a while before I spoke.

'Is that what we have stumbled into? It's possible. We know there are connections between Father Raymond and Jan, Nick and the Tierney family. There is also a link to Father Joseph, who Ben has publicly accused of abuse. Most people believe that Father Joseph has only been in Lensham for four years, but this is his second stint as priest at St Francis' Church, I heard him say so myself.

'Em, if your proposition turns out to be correct, then Benito Tierney has not been paranoid. He was telling the truth about Father Joseph. I know other people didn't believe him, but I did. Could he have been telling the truth about the other conspiracy claptrap he came out with?' I asked, incredulous at the enormity of the suggestion.

'Let's put it as our hypothesis and work it through.' Emma reached for the Sylvanian hedgehog-people that she had labelled earlier, and placed them on the centre of the table.

'Jan and Nick here, were working together. We must assume they both reported to Thomas Aitken. There is question number one. Who is Thomas Aitken? Max and Jake, how about you follow up on that one? I'll give you the emails, letters, and anything relating to Nick's life as a journalist that we salvaged from his desk. Max, you know about the contents of the journals, but we think that these were deliberately created by Jan and Nick as some sort of trap that backfired. Here's the info on that.'

Jake, Max, and I stared at Emma in disbelief. She was behaving like a detective inspector. A woman on a personal mission, she had copied information, collated it, and placed the relevant paperwork into large envelopes. She was in charge of operations.

'Who are the goodies and who are the baddies?'

Emma was irritated by Max's flippancy. 'Look, Max, this is serious. We have four deaths. We don't know if the police can be trusted, we don't know if the likes of Father Raymond or the church groups can be trusted. We have no idea who stole the journals or why. Monica and I have strong suspicions that deliberate poisoning has been the cause of three out of the four deaths.'

Max held his hands up. 'Whoa there, Emma, I *was* being serious. Are we to assume that Thomas Aitken is someone on the right side of the law, or do we consider him to present a risk to us? If he is a goodie then who are the baddies?'

Emma gave Max a squeeze of apology. 'You lovely big bear. I'm sorry. Jake and I have been awake for hours each night puzzling over this. Is our family at risk? If so, who from and why?'

Chapter Twenty

'Can I say something?' I asked, stirring my cup of tea to help focus my thoughts. 'We have drifted miles away from our timeline plan. Can we please stick to that and work through the basics?'

We laid the Sylvanian hedgehog-people out in order of death. Next to hedgehog-Nick we placed a Sylvanian mouse-person labelled with a question mark.

'Nick was killed by carbon monoxide poisoning,' I said.

'Was he? We've been told that he was. But was he?' Emma asked. 'Write that down as a question to be answered or confirmed.' She was right, I realised. This was so complicated that we had to be sure of the facts; we couldn't afford to make assumptions, but without taking a best guess we couldn't begin to unravel the mystery.

'Yep. Good point. We think Jan escaped being killed in France at the same time as Nick and we also think she deliberately smashed their laptop. Was this to ensure that their killer could not access the contents? This would make sense. It could be the reason why the same person, the man with half a finger, broke into our homes to steal the hardcopy items relating to Jan and Nick's investigation.'

'Then your patient, Jan Collins, was followed back to England and killed by Half-finger-man, making it look like suicide. He had cleverly led everyone to believe that Liam Brookes had been alive and had visited Jan in hospital in France, when, in fact, Nick Shafer was already dead,' reminded Max. 'Or was Jan killed by Half-finger-man at all? Correct me if I'm wrong, Mon, but didn't you say that Father Raymond had access to Jan's house, had befriended her and visited her in Pargiter Ward? And it was Father Raymond who led everyone to believe that Liam Brookes aka Nick Shafer was a cunning trickster after Jan's money? That's no way for a man of God to behave, now is it?'

Jake stood. 'Right. All agreed? We identify one possible perpetrator mice-person, as Father Raymond.' Jake was impassive as he made a label and stabbed Raymond-mouse in the head with a cocktail stick. We looked at each other. I began to have grave doubts about where our guesses were taking us.

'Stop, stop. This can't be right. None of it. Father Raymond doesn't have half a pinkie and he's not shorter than me and he's easily recognisable. What's more, he seems so genuine.' I'm sure it was a nervous reaction, but I couldn't help myself. This was ludicrous. 'Look at us! Mice-people killing hedgehog-people because the Church needs to cover up abuse. We've got so carried away with ourselves.'

Max and Jake didn't laugh. They were ignoring my odd response by reading through the information that Emma had given them in an envelope earlier, looking for reference to Father Raymond. They had copies of the photos taken at the auction. 'I'm certain we are in the middle of a whole heap of trouble,' Jake piped up. He asked us who we thought would go to the lengths of photographing people at an auction, of writing a fictional account of abuse and murder and 'goodness knows what else.'

'Shit. Look who it is. There in the background.' Max was pointing to one of the photos at the auction. The Father was standing next to me in the foreground. We were smiling and relaxed. There, several rows back, was the head of Charlie Adams.

What did this mean? 'God, is Charlie a goodie or a baddie?' asked Emma looking at Max for an answer. 'If Father Raymond is a baddie, then is it safe to assume that Charlie is onto something and that he is a goodie?'

'Could be. Maybe he was there spying on behalf of Aitken, Brown and Partners to see what happened to the journals. We could ask him,' suggested Max.

Emma was beginning to flag. It was getting late and we were all tired after a day at work. We needed a plan of action. Despite her weariness Emma made a stunning proposal.

'Instead of asking Charlie why he was there, why don't we pretend that we know nothing about it? We discuss the journals and the auction with him at the weekend and see if he tells us. I think we should set him up. Make him prove himself. We don't know who to trust apart from each other and I'm not keen to disclose our investigations to him. I have the children to consider.'

My crapometer was registering significantly high readings as a result of my friend's concerns. Emma was usually stoical and not easily unnerved, so to hear her make a statement about fearing a risk to her family had me worried.

'So, we are saying this *is* serious. Father Raymond and a man with half a finger may be responsible for four deaths between them. We have what they're looking for and the police are covering up crimes.' As I said this, I began to feel stupid for being dismissive previously. This was no laughing matter. 'If Charlie turns out to be a goodie, then we should get a label ready for DI Lynch, Charlie's boss. In the meantime, can we please label a mouse-person as Half-finger-man?'

I reminded everyone again that it was DS Charlie Adams who had approached us for help, putting his career on the line, and that he had told us about Father Joseph's death by chilli con carne. 'Charlie was furious when DI Lynch pulled the charges against Ben for threats to kill. He has to be a goodie and DI Lynch has to be corrupt. He kept calling me Mrs Davis today and yet everyone at the station knows me as Monica Morris.'

'That's because he knows you as my wife, from the bike club. Don't you remember him at the barbecue and big band charity event? You must do …'

'Oh, was he the really obnoxious oaf who kept invading my personal space and breathing beer in my face?'

'Yes, that's him.'

'Most definitely a baddie then. He's already on my "needs a good slap" list. I can't stand the bloke.'

Looking at the evening's work, I saw there were scribbled notes on the flip charts, lines and arrows crisscrossing the long paper timeline, as well as swirling marks denoting the dates of deaths, disappearances and known whereabouts of suspects and victims. Green for goodies, blue for baddies and question marks for not sure. No one but the four of us would have been able to make sense of it.

We had homework to do. I had to research Jan's medication history and investigate any information on abuse in a Catholic boys' home in the 1970's and find out a bit more about the Catholic Church. Why was there a reference in the remaining journal to 'the one true Jesuit'? Why had Jan written that? Who or what was this Jesuit?

Emma was to continue in her efforts to glean clues from the information that we had gathered. She planned to send an email to Mike Rezendes in Boston. The boys were going to check out the business dealings of Aitken, Brown and Partners in an attempt to determine the goodies from the baddies.

Jake and Max carefully gathered up our HQ incident room into boxes and an old tea chest, and they secured it in the barn with Jake's vintage tractor. Some of the geese were housed in there at night from that moment on.

I was about to take Deefer back to my car when my telephone rang. It was Sam from the Corbet Unit, France. He asked for my email address and promised to attach scanned details about Jan's medication. The staff nurse in charge of the ward at the French unit had given Sam permission to hand over any information I needed. He had remembered my hilarious attempts at speaking French back in August. Great. I was famous for the wrong reason.

'The only one we were not sure about was the HRT. She had at least six patches on her body when she was admitted, but there was no information from her GP about them. Her records said she was on a coil for that, so the nurses removed the patches.

The poor woman had enough to handle. Dr Reynaud asked Mrs Collins about the patches and she seemed mystified. We assumed it had to do with her unstable mental state at the time.'

'HRT patches?'

'Yes, unless she was giving up smoking and the patches were for that instead. But she said she didn't smoke.'

'No, she didn't.' I thanked Sam for his excellent work and added HRT patches to my homework list.

Max beat me home by several minutes and was already in the shower when Deefer and I strolled through the front door. My head had been buzzing with chaotic thoughts during the short drive home from Folly Farm.

'If I hadn't gone to that bloody auction, none of this would be happening.'

'Yes, it would, Mon, we just wouldn't know about it,' said Max, rubbing himself dry with a towel as he emerged from the bathroom.

That night I was desperate for sleep, but my mind refused to rest, so instead, I rescued my copy of the BNF – the British National Formulary – from the boot of my car and looked up what I could about hormone replacement patches, but the information wasn't helpful. Changing tactics, I fired up the computer. With a handful of research databases at my disposal, courtesy of my recent studies, I searched for information on ACS – anticholinergic syndrome. Most of the research papers repeated the same information about the symptoms, the helpful mnemonic and the importance of enquiring about over-the-counter products. 'Dr Reynaud knows her stuff,' I mumbled quietly to myself.

One article in particular caught my attention. It was an investigation into the bioavailability of various anticholinergic preparations and their impact on toxicity.

I shuddered as I slowly became aware of someone else in the room, behind me. Holding my breath, I wrapped my hand around a large mug, which I had left next to the keyboard, only dregs of tea remaining. No other suitable weapon was within reach. As the floorboards creaked immediately behind me, I leapt up from my seat, turning to face the intruder, mug in my raised hand.

'Why didn't you speak, you plonker? One of these days I'll die of fright or shit myself!' For the second time in less than twelve hours my own husband had scared the pants off me.

'Sorry, I was being quiet.'

Max had given up sleeping, too. Bleary-eyed, he had wandered downstairs to find me, without a thought for the impact his nocturnal creeping might have had. It seemed we were both destined to be sleep deprived for the foreseeable future.

Nodding towards the computer screen, Max said, 'Go on then, tell me what you've got. In layman's terms if you can, please.'

'Right. Here goes. There are certain types of medication, such as travel sickness pills, anti-diarrhoea tablets, and drugs we use to counteract side effects from antipsychotics. If these types of drugs reach high levels, they can have nasty side effects of their own, and when this happens, to a serious degree, the patient will need treatment. The side effects of toxic levels can be wide-ranging but include feeling hot, urinary retention, confusion, hallucinations, and in severe cases, coma and death.'

'Thanks, simple enough.'

'Good. Here's the interesting thing. You would have to take a whacking great dose to kill yourself by using over-the-counter products or even prescribed formulations. However, what I'm reading here may shed light on why Jan was covered in HRT patches when she was found by the police in France.'

'Was she? I must have missed that bit.'

'Oh yes, sorry, love, you did miss that bit. I had a call back from young Sam at the French Corbet mental health unit after you had left this evening. Anyway, I was thinking, what if they weren't HRT?'

'Go on.'

I explained to Max that Jan was on a coil and not patches to help with menopausal symptoms. The research article in front of me was indicating that transdermal patches or gels containing anticholinergics had been shown to be more effective in providing greater amounts of the active drug than that of liquids or tablets. These types of patches were useful for seasickness.

'I'm with you so far.'

'Good. Here's my best guess. Imagine, in Nick's flat in Perpignan, a would-be murderer had devised a way to kill Jan without arousing too much suspicion that anyone, other than herself or Nick, were to blame. Jan was covered in patches by this person, the man with half a little finger, scopolamine patches for argument's sake. She was also made to drink hyoscine liquid, as if she were taking it as a prescribed medicine. However, before the patches could be removed she managed to escape, either because she went psychotic or in desperation, we'll never know. We *do* know that she managed to smash the flash drive, and possibly the laptop, before she ran into the street. Nick's killer may have done the same to him, we can't know that either, but he is dead. He probably never got out of the flat. The killer then delivered Jan's belongings to her including her medication, not expecting her to have lived. He provided enough clues to her death in the shape of the liquid hyoscine. Because of her mental illness everyone has assumed that her actions and behaviour were as a direct result of a manic episode. Do you see? If it wasn't for Dr Reynaud and the nurses at the French unit, Jan should have been dead.' I looked at Max, waiting for him to tell me that I was exaggerating, and that this was a set of assumptions too far. Max stared down at me, glanced back at the computer screen and shook his head.

'I'll update Jake tomorrow.'

Chapter Twenty-One

'Morning, Kelly, morning, Barbs, morning, Steph; how are you doing?'

'Morning, Monica. More to the point, how are *you* doing? You look exhausted. Are you sure you should be at work today? It's Friday, why on earth didn't you take the day off?' Kelly had genuine concern for my wellbeing, for once.

'I wouldn't know what to do with myself,' I answered honestly. 'Is Sue in yet? I need to run a quick question past her.'

'No, she's down at the hospital and won't be back before lunch. Can I help?' offered Barbara, a senior social worker of great experience and wisdom. Unfortunately, her skills were redundant. I needed to ask Sue what she knew about ACS. Sue was our consultant psychiatrist and she was shit-hot on side effects. 'Patients have enough to cope with in life,' she always reminded us. 'No one wants to look as if they're taking medication.'

'Monica, I'm sorry to have to pressure you today, but as you're here ... have you finished that report for the coroner yet? You're being chased by the risk department,' Kelly asked.

'Bloody hell, I thought I had a total of two weeks ...'

She took one look at my expression and swiftly added, 'Forget that I asked. I'll fob them off.'

I was grateful for her offer to be spared the pressure, and for the timely reminder, but I knew full well that a few hours had to be found to finish that report. Getting it completed early would provide some respite from the relentless pressure. I also realised that it would help to focus my mind on the details of Jan's death. The rough timeline that I'd pulled together two days previously looked innocent enough and when I wrote out the final report, any hint at foul play could not be found. I wrote the facts as I knew them to be, and gave a potted history of Jan's contact and support from mental health services. Finally, I listed her current medication. I made reference to her 'male friend, Liam Brookes' and carefully ensured that he was not painted as a predatory abuser in any way. I mentioned the reported break-in at Jan's home the week before her death, but ensured that doubt was thrown on its legitimacy.

The report for the Coroner's Office was a knotty one to write because I knew there were so many other facets to Jan's death, but could not submit them to paper. If I had written details of a man with half a finger, a suspect priest, an investigation into abuse, and an earlier poisoning in France, Eddie would have had me suspended on medical grounds, as he would assume I had finally reached burnout. In truth, I wasn't far off.

Having produced what was asked for, I reminded Kelly to ensure that Eddie scrutinised the report before sending it to the risk department, who would then forward it to the coroner. 'Not my best work, Kelly. I hope it passes muster.' She gave me an encouraging nod and assurances that the report was 'absolutely fine.' I didn't believe her for one moment.

My emails at work were few and far between as the majority of the organisation thankfully hadn't yet embraced their use for irrelevant comment, or for replacing the written referral methods of letter and fax. There was one from Sam at the French mental health unit, with an attached list of Jan's medication as documented by the admitting nurse. There were no unexpected additions to what I had known beforehand, and I was disappointed with the lack of progress. *Clever Mr Half Finger,* I thought. He had achieved the result intended. No suspicions, no evidence.

I composed an email to Sam to thank him, but debating what he had said over the phone, I decided to take advantage of his willingness to help by asking another favour.

'Hello Sam,

Many thanks once again for being so prompt in sending the information I asked for. I wonder if I could ask for your help? We have a mystery at this end. Jan's boyfriend, Liam Brookes is still missing. He hasn't returned to the UK and he missed Jan's funeral, which is most unlike him. Could you check with the local hospital whether he was admitted just after you saw him at the unit? We would hate to think that he is seriously unwell or injured and that no one has identified him. His friends have tried his mobile phone to no avail, and they don't have money to fly to France to see if they can find him. We believe he may have had a friend called Nick (Nicolas Shafer) that he stayed with in Perpignan.

Your French is so good that we are sure you can help us.

Kind regards

Monica Morris

Deliberately using my work email for correspondence with Sam was the best way I could think of to maintain privacy and to keep up the appearance that contact was on a purely professional matter. A line was being crossed. This was way beyond my usual remit, and I knew it would probably be the following week before I heard back from Sam, if at all, but it had to be worth asking.

Once I had dealt with my smattering of emails, I picked up the phone and noticed the fine tremor in my fingers as I dialled a familiar number, ready to leave a message. 'Hello, Sean, this is Monica Morris.' I wasn't expecting any answer. 'Goodness, I thought you'd still be in hospital. I hope you don't mind me phoning, but I want to offer my support to you both. Would it be helpful for me to visit you?' There was a long pause, during which I wondered if I had caused offence, until I heard the low sobs of a man with a broken heart. 'Can you come now?' he eventually asked.

I arrived outside the Tierneys' home at the same time as a solemn-looking Father Raymond. As soon as I caught sight of him, an internal deliberation began. *Should I go in anyway? Or should I sit in the car and wait for him to come out? Is he a poisoner or is he a good man?* My head and my heart had differing opinions and these were causing a great deal of indecision.

Stepping as confidently as I could up the path to the front door, I took the plunge. 'Hello, Father. I was on my way in too, Sean Tierney asked me to visit. It looks as if he forgot that you were coming to see them both. Shall we go together?' The risk was considerable. My suggestion could be viewed as insulting in the circumstances, but it did allow for the priest to back down and rearrange his visit, should he decide to. I had my fingers crossed that he would come in with me, as I was desperate to see and hear the exchanges between the Tierneys and Father Raymond. The situation felt safe enough; even so, I couldn't help but glance at Father Raymond's left hand. Fingers all present and correct.

Feeling like the agnostic outsider that I am, I sat on an unforgiving chair at the dining table watching the scene in front of me. I held the hand of Manuela Tierney who was unable to cry any more. Her expression was vacant. There, kneeling on the lounge carpet in supplication before Father Raymond, was Sean Tierney. He had been released from hospital and told to rest, but his reaction to Father Raymond demonstrated how overwhelmingly important his religion was to him in his most hopeless hours.

Father Raymond prayed over Sean as he wept uncontrollably and from the depths of his soul. He was inconsolable. I learnt nothing until Father Raymond, having seated Sean back on the sofa, pleading with him to rest, walked towards Manuela, prayer book in one hand, his right hand raised in preparation for prayer.

Manuela stood up, looked him in the eye with venom and spat in his face. 'Get out of my house. You are not welcome here. You reside in the house of the devil. Get out! Get out!' Her hatred spilled out into the room with such force that I was momentarily stunned. Father Raymond recoiled in surprise and Sean sank his head into his hands as he begged for forgiveness.

'She doesn't know what she's saying, Father. It's not true, none of it. Pray for her ...'

'Don't you pray for me, ever. I shall pray for your godless soul, you filthy animal. You knew what he did and you did nothing. I wish I *had* killed him. God forgive me.' Manuela's disgust was showing on her face as she vomited the words from her lips.

Finding my own voice at last, I politely invited Father Raymond to the front door. In the hallway, he stood head bowed and silent. When he looked up at me there was desolation in his eyes. He shook his head slowly and left. I had no idea what that gesture was supposed to convey to me. 'I'll phone you later, shall I?' I asked.

Chapter Twenty-Two

As I drove back to the office on automatic pilot, tears gradually began to roll down my cheeks and the journey didn't register. I stopped to park outside the office building, and only then did I lose self-control to weep unashamedly. Benito Tierney's death had been so very tragic and yet, until that moment in my car, I had kept the pain at bay behind a psychological wall made subconsciously to protect myself.

As large sobs wracked my entire body, I saw flashbacks to the CCTV footage of his death. Why was he undressing as he ran along the train tracks? It had been a chilly day, drizzling with fine rain.

The truth of the matter was obvious to me. *As hot as a hare*, I thought.

It was nearly an hour before I could steel myself to make the phone call to the Coroner's Office. 'Hello, this is Monica Morris, CPN. Is it possible to make an enquiry about a post mortem on the body of Benito Tierney? It's really important.' I wasn't aware of any law that prevented me from making this request, yet despite this, I felt as if I were being underhand. 'Is there a way I can ask for a particular substance to be tested for?'

'A full range of toxicology tests will be carried out, Monica. I can take some details and will pass them on to the pathology lab, but perhaps the information should go through the police if it's significant or indicative of any crime having been committed.'

I blagged my way through by insisting that as Ben's community nurse I was privy to his most recent treatment details and wanted to give direct, first-hand information, to help the post mortem process. It was the coroner's officer who took the details, a lady by the name of Carol Langford. She was a pleasant enough woman and I managed to engage her in a conversation about my unfortunate experiences of having lost two patients recently, and needing to assure myself that I had equipped the authorities with the facts in each case.

'There was something peculiar in Ben's behaviour immediately leading up to his death.'

'Were you there?'

'No, well yes, briefly, I saw him run past my car. But I was asked by the police to view the CCTV footage at the station and Ben was tearing at his clothes, pulling them off as he ran. I had a case recently involving anticholinergic syndrome, ACS, and his behaviour was strongly suggestive of the same. He was not prescribed any anti-cholinergic medicine you see, which is why I needed to call you directly. This could easily be missed and discounted as being the behaviour of a mentally ill man or a drunk. Poor Ben was seen as both.'

Had I gone too far this time? There was a brief pause from the coroner's officer.

'Yes, I do see. I'm scribbling down the main points here. Can you spell anticho- whatever for me? I'll pass this on to the pathologist, who I'm sure will appreciate the time you've taken to raise the matter. He's exceedingly thorough, so please be assured that he will take this seriously. Let me have your contact details as well, in the event that we need to call you back.'

Floundering around, lost for ideas or a sense of direction once that call had been made, I began to unravel. I sat at my desk, present but not functioning or productive, staring into space like Manuela had done an hour earlier.

Eddie and Sue stepped in to rescue me from myself and took me to the cosy confines of Sue's office, where they sat me down and closed the door. Hugging a mug, I listened as they gingerly probed into the state of my wellbeing before making a decision to send me home.

'Monica, this report for the Coroner's Office, are you quite certain that what you have written here is correct?' Eddie wafted the printed pages of my report. 'How did you conclude that Mrs Collins's man friend was supportive and generous? We were under the impression that he's still wanted for questioning in relation to a burglary, as well as a possible investigation under the Protection of Vulnerable Adults legislation for accusations of financial abuse.'

'It turns out, Eddie, that those were vicious rumours and totally untrue. Liam Brookes paid for the holiday to France, he had a flat there. He hasn't run off with Jan's money because she lent her savings to her brother, who could easily have carried out the apparent break-in at her house. Liam reportedly visited Jan when she was in the Hôpital Corbet, the unit in France. He hasn't been seen since and his friends have been unable to contact him on his mobile. I couldn't write anything other than that in the report.'

'That's reasonable enough. At least you had the good sense to check out the facts. Are the police following this up as a missing person?'

Why hadn't I thought of that? It was a simple response to the situation. A Miss Per. Report the person as missing.

'No, the police aren't doing anything, but I could contact the French police and report him as a missing person, couldn't I?' I had been a first-class dunce, sending emails asking a young man to investigate a missing person, when all I had to do was to report it to French police authorities. That way we could have a factual confirmation of Nick Shafer's death and not have to take the word of the UK police, who perhaps could not be trusted.

'His friends should be doing that, or his family …'

'Yes, I'll suggest it.' I wasn't aware if Nick Shafer had any family. It was reasonable to assume that if he had, they too would be looking for him. Aitken, Brown and Partners were likely to be trying to trace him as well. Someone must know what actually happened to him.

'Monica, I'm sending you home. Have a rest over the weekend and see how you feel on Monday. Focus on the medicine amnesty and don't worry about anything here. There'll be a request for another report from the coroner, I dare say, but it won't arrive for a week or two. Take a break. I'll refer you through to the Trust counselling services.'

'No thanks, Eddie. I appreciate your intentions but I can't stand that sitting, nodding, "tell me how you feel" shit. No psychobabble bollocks either. I'll take the dog for a walk instead. Much more therapeutic.' Eddie knew not to try to persuade me. Counselling and therapy. Really?

Grateful for the chance to return home, I gathered up my belongings and checked my message book and emails before giving in. There was a response from Sam in France.

'Hi Monica,

Happy to help. I phoned the police station here. They weren't too keen to give me details but they did have a suspicious death of an Englishman in the flat at the address we had for Liam Brookes. It made the newspapers as well. There was a fire and the body of the man they found turned out to be the resident or owner. Therefore, it probably isn't who you are seeking. Death was by carbon monoxide, probably from the fumes. Investigations indicated that the fire had been deliberately set, an accelerant used and the perpetrator had called the pompiers. *No other residents were injured or killed, which was lucky. The police had no family to contact, but had traced the victim's employers in England. Perhaps you could contact the police too for confirmation and to ask about Liam Brookes. Unless he is the man that set the fire. The police here still haven't caught anyone.*

If I find anything else I'll let you know.

Hope that helps.

All the best

Sam Wilson.

What a good chap you are, Sam, I thought as I replied with a quick gushing gratitude email, before closing the computer and leaving the office.

Half-finger-man had destroyed any further evidence. Smart man.

Strolling to my car I thought back to what DS Adams had said. He had the correct information on Liam Brookes's death, which meant that he had been telling the truth. Death by carbon monoxide poisoning. I decided to phone Max to update him with the news of my mental implosion and about the update from Sam.

'No, Mon, that's not quite right. Charlie Adams said that a flue had been deliberately blocked causing carbon monoxide poisoning. He didn't mention a fire. The French police would have told him that important fact, I'm sure. Maybe Emma was right. We should test him out.'

Chapter Twenty-Three

The facts indicated that Half-finger-man had been in France, had been at Jan's house, my house and Emma's house and yet we had no idea who he was. We didn't know exactly what he wanted either. Getting closer to the underlying factors had only served to confuse and bewilder us.

Jake and Max had been busy.

Max phoned me with the latest update. 'Jake called Aitken, Brown and Partners asking to speak to Thomas Aitken. He does exist. He declined to confirm much over the phone but is coming to the farm tomorrow to meet with us. The weirdest thing is, he was not surprised at our call. He told Jake that he had been expecting to hear from us sooner, so I think we should carefully manage our contact with Charlie Adams and arrange to meet him on Sunday.' Max was determined to throw doubt on DS Charlie Adams. Indeed all four of us, Max, Jake, Emma, and I, were becoming jumpy and distrustful of others.

'Max, I'm not clear why we would trust Thomas Aitken, who we've never met before, over a police detective sergeant who we do know.'

'Think about it, Mon. The solicitors were the ones who made use of the journals, because they were fully aware that Jan had fabricated every word. They employed Nick Shafer and Jan. They have to have the answers and we can hand over the paperwork and the rest of the stuff from Nick Shafer's desk. That way we can't be putting ourselves or the children at risk anymore. We hand it all back, and they can find someone else to expose the bloody Catholic Church.'

'What about the deaths?'

'We have no proof. Only hypotheses.'

I sighed. 'Are you coming home early by any chance? I'm knackered and befuddled. I can't see clearly, now my brain has gone.'

'Oh, I know that song. "I can't see clearly now my brain has gone, I can't see all obstacles in my way…",' Max sang down the phone line as I chuckled at his life saving humour. 'You nutcase. I think Deefer and I could do with a good long walk, so I'll take him out and see you when you get in. Pub tonight?'

'Great idea. Sod it, let's have a beer or two and a good sleep. It's a date. See you later.'

A walk through the autumn leaves, breathing in the earthiness, was on the cards, followed by a shower and beer. That was a much better idea than any crappy counselling. Deefer and I stepped out into the lane and headed in the direction of the woods. Waterproofs and wellies were the order of the day. Poo bags and dog treats in one pocket and a bottle of water in the other, I was set for a few miles. As I turned left along the tranquil village high street, a car slowly drew alongside, making me check my stride. I assumed that it would be someone asking for directions.

It was Charlie Adams.

My pulse quickened and a cold hollow feeling accompanied a creeping sense of vulnerability.

'This will save me a phone call,' he said, as he lowered the window to talk to me through the passenger side. 'When are we meeting at the weekend?' Charlie's hands were on the steering wheel and to my immense relief I could see all ten fingers and thumbs.

'Hello, Charlie, that's a coincidence, I've just spoken to Max and we thought Sunday would be best, if you can make it then? We're a bit busy on Saturday, as Max has to work. Want to come over to our house about eleven o'clock? Unless you're going to church.' I tried to sound casual but it wasn't easy since Max had sown a seed of doubt about Charlie, which I couldn't ignore.

'That's perfect for me. I've had weekend leave cancelled anyway because of the railway incident, but I can spare an hour or so. Thanks for your help on that, by the way, and sorry it was so harrowing to watch. Such a sad end for a young man with a family.'

He looked at me and must have read my expression well. 'By the way … I hear Frank Hughes made some threats. Try not to worry, although he'll probably get bail. I can't say what he's been charged with but it's serious, and he'd be an idiot not to keep his nose clean. Any trouble, phone straight away. I've put a SIG marker on your house just in case.'

'Thanks, that's really good of you,' was all I could muster as a reply.

'A good walk will help, you know. I won't keep you. See you both on Sunday. I mean you and Max, not you and the dog.' He laughed and waved briefly as he drove away. Instinctively I said cheerio and waved back. He never used to be so light-hearted. When I first met Charlie Adams he was boring and monotone and I wondered what had changed.

Every few minutes I glanced behind me as I walked the familiar footpaths, and once or twice I was startled as a bird took flight from the undergrowth. Finally exhausted by my constant state of alertness for assault, I sat on a fallen tree trunk in the middle of the woods, throwing a stick for Deefer. Patting my pocket, I took out my work phone, which I had taken with me out of habit, not intending to make use of it. I reassured myself that I had not lost it, and that I could summon help if it were needed.

There was a missed call from "Fat Ray".

The phone was placed smartly back in my pocket. I didn't want to talk to anybody, least of all Father Raymond. The evidence was mounting against him. Manuela Tierney had obviously accepted that Father Joseph had abused her son and I could still hear her bitter words as I recalled how vehemently she had launched her hatred in Father Raymond's direction. Maybe she had discovered something that implicated Father Raymond in a cover-up of Father Joseph's terrible deeds, but if that were not true then he must have been hurt by those accusations. Despite all that, or maybe because of it, I couldn't face talking to him.

'Not now. Maybe tomorrow,' I thought aloud.

Emma and Jake were expecting us at two o'clock in the afternoon of the next day, and as the girls were spending the weekend with Emma's parents, we could safely have an uninterrupted meeting with Thomas Aitken at three. With these arrangements in place, Max and I seemed to be able to relax on the Friday evening. Putting our worries aside with the aid of alcohol, we even managed much needed sleep, waking later than usual. We didn't hear next-door's cockerel that morning, so we must have been tired.

Max did go to work for a couple of hours on the Saturday morning, but was back at home in good time for us to make our way to Folly Farm after lunch. We took Deefer along for the ride and a change of scenery, without the indignity of being messed about with by Sophie and Thea. Although Sparkey was not impressed that Deefer was visiting again, and he sauntered away in disgust when we arrived.

Once settled in the farm kitchen, we prepared for our visitor by agreeing how best to handle the meeting.

'We let him speak first to see where we stand. Agreed?' Emma said.

'What if he has half a finger? I asked.

'He won't. It can't be him. Thomas Aitken was the contact for Nick Shafer and for Jan. We are the ignorant ones here. I dread to think what we don't know about.' Those words from Jake were to prove painfully accurate.

Mr Thomas Aitken parked his shiny Mercedes in the farmyard, where he was met by Jake and the collies, who were doing a fine job of alerting the whole farm to our visitor. This set the geese cackling, and as Mr Aitken walked through the door into the spacious kitchen, Jake and an orchestra of animal noises accompanied him. He seemed unflustered as he was introduced to the rest of us.

'Please, call me Tam,' he said. Not unexpectedly, a broad Scottish accent added flavour to those words, and I made an internal note to myself to avoid the usual embarrassing accent mimicking. Today was too important.

I wasn't sure what type of man to expect, or what he would look like, but was agreeably surprised by his straightforward manner and easy approach. A tall sturdy man with a strong jaw, like a retired rugby forward, Tam didn't spend unnecessary time on platitudes or pleasantries. He got down to the business in hand without mincing his words.

'Thanks for contacting me. You took your time, so I can only assume that you have had some difficulty in deciding whether Aitken, Brown and Partners are legitimate, and that we have a bona fide connection with Mrs Janet Collins and Mr Nicholas Shafer, both now sadly deceased. I'll lay out my stall, shall I? Then you can follow suit. Shall we see how many boxes I can tick for you?'

There were no arguments.

'Nick Shafer: Journalist.' Firm nods were produced from around the table, which Tam was clearly expecting to see. He glanced briefly at us after stating each fact, checking our awareness. 'Okay. Good. He lodged here of course, under that name, and you also have identified him as Liam Brookes, his cover identity. Janet Collins: well-known theological historian and writer who had worked in the Civil Service.' We nodded again as Tam confirmed Jan's part in writing the journals that had been in my possession until stolen.

'You have one journal remaining in your possession, I believe.' Without a conscious thought I checked for the little fingers on both of Tam's hands. Entire. Present.

'You also have correspondence and papers that were in Nick's cottage.' We nodded in unison. 'You could have saved yourselves a lot of trouble if you had contacted our offices sooner.'

'How?' Max asked. I was holding my breath as we waited for the answer.

'Your burglaries were carried out by a colleague of Jan's. I've never met him in person, only Jan knew his identity. He's been central to the work being carried out by Nick and Jan for months, if not years. He and Jan knew each other through their academic studies, but for protection his identity has always remained a secret. We refer to him as the Guardian. He was asked to retrieve what he could of the paperwork, but you had done such a wonderful job of hiding everything, that we couldn't lay our hands on the important stuff.'

'Oh, that explains why the dog wasn't hurt.' I paused awhile, allowing the facts to be absorbed.

'Mrs Davis, Monica, you were *not* meant to have been the purchaser that day at the auction. We hoped our target would show their hand, but we were far too late. He'd already killed Jan and Nick and, rather sadly, we didn't have that fact confirmed until after the auction.'

'He?' Jake took up asking a series of questions. 'Who is he? And as you're confirming that he killed Nick and Jan, can you say if it's possible he also killed Father Joseph Kavanagh and Benito Tierney?'

Tam opened up the leather document folder that he had with him. He took a deep breath, expanding his chest to full capacity, and let out a long releasing sigh. 'How long have you got?'

Once Tam had finished his explanation, we sat in silence. The kettle was placed on the range and biscuits were opened but left untouched.

'We weren't too far off with our hypotheses, then,' Emma concluded. 'But can I ask, if there has been this amount of work done to expose systematic child abuse and cover-ups by the Catholic Church, then why don't you report the evidence to the authorities?'

'It has been, several times. Way back in the 1980s several extensive damning documents were handed to the Home Office evidencing organisational abuse. Not solely the Catholic Church, by the way, this involves most denominations. The then Home Secretary, Leon Brittan, remember him? His office mislaid them; they disappeared. Why? Because the information contained within implicated top politicians, business organisations, high profile individuals, and the churches.'

I was puzzled. 'Does this mean that Ben was right even about the Freemasons? I looked that up and they don't sit within the Catholic Church. The Masonic connection doesn't make any sense.'

Tam laid both his palms flat on the kitchen table. 'Yes, it does. Think money, Monica, not sexual abuse. Financial abuse. The Vatican Bank holds vast sums of money. They have dealings with other banks worldwide and national debts. Where do you think the Nazis kept their fine artworks and antiques, gold, and insurance pay-outs from Holocaust victims? It can't all come from the humble congregations or charity fundraisers. The Vatican have already paid out millions in hush money in cases of alleged abuse by Catholic priests.'

I had visions of Sean and Manuela, sitting in church giving money each week at the offertory. Bread, wine, and bribery. They were supporting the very organisation that had allowed abuse of their son, and who were instrumental in his death. A sick irony.

'It's a monstrously large financial empire,' continued Tam in earnest. 'The attempts to investigate the financial misdealings and misappropriations involve the Freemasons and the Mafia, as well as European politics. No one is ever charged, and allegations are vehemently denied by the Vatican, just as they do for any whiff of scandal. Organisations trying to expose these underhand business dealings are discredited or slammed as being anti-Catholic cults. Look up the name Calvi when you get the chance, and the Trinity Foundation. You'll soon see what I mean.

'Sexual abuse is covered up, and there are cover-ups of cover-ups. The deaths in Lensham are a small part of a scandal of such incredible magnitude that it's almost impossible to comprehend. The Vatican or the Freemasons have sent in a sweeper here, to clean up a minor mess created by the exposed allegations from Ben, Jan, and Nick. In their world, this is a trifling matter, but nevertheless instructions from the Vatican are being followed.'

I sat transfixed, listening intently to every single word being said by Tam Aitken.

'There was a directive in 1962 ordering the strictest secrecy to be maintained within the Catholic Church relating to any sexual scandal. The problems, in the shape of the offending priests, were moved within the Catholic Church to different dioceses, not reported to the authorities. This effectively means that the interests of the church are put before that of justice. Father Joseph had to be disposed of as a matter of course, as he seems to have been moved back to the diocese where he previously committed acts of abuse against children. An error by the church.

'You worked out that no one is to be trusted, because otherwise you would have gone to the police. You haven't. You also delayed coming to me.

'Why? I'll tell you why, because none of us can go to the authorities with any certainty of justice. Aitken, Brown and Partners provide legal services for a large organisation representing adult survivors and the families of those abused as children. We have no connection to government. The only route left to us is to involve the IPCC where we find police mishandling, and for exposure in the press. To go the route of the *Spotlight* team. Ever heard of them?'

Emma perked up. 'Yes. I had an email back from them yesterday, otherwise we wouldn't be sitting with you today.'

I didn't know this snippet of important information and threw my friend a quizzical look.

'Sorry, Mon, I didn't tell you at the time, I thought you'd enough to contend with. Anyway, Max said to leave you alone for the day.' She turned to look back at Tam. '*Spotlight* confirmed who you were and that, as well as our local problem, you're in the middle of exposing a significant case at a school, where abuse by catholic monks has been going on for thirty years. The *Spotlight* reporter said the police in Yorkshire have taken over a year to investigate, and the repercussions could be substantial.' Emma sighed and placed her chin into her hands, elbows propped onto the table.

'What is it about the Catholic Church? Remaining celibate isn't natural, so it's asking for trouble to expect grown men to remain so, in my view. You really do have to ask yourself if all the denominations provide safe havens for the sexual deviant and then blatantly deny any wrongdoing.'

Emma's voice was getting louder and her tone more heated until Jake put his hand on her shoulder in an effort to restore calm. She shrugged it away. 'It's my soapbox and I'll stand on it!' she said, turning on him. Then she smiled, realising that her opinions were not being challenged.

Tam was nodding and drumming his fingers on the table as Emma spoke. He allowed her outburst to continue, as if accustomed to these, before he continued.

'Aye, we've taken on a number of cases as a firm, and wee cracks are beginning to show in the armour of the Vatican but we desperately need the press to enlighten the wider public. You'd be surprised at the efforts gone to and hindrances put in place to undermine justice.'

We returned to the immediate problem of our own safety. Jake is a farmer, Max an engineer, Emma and I nurses. We knew nothing about investigative journalism and exposés in the press. Out of our depth and paddling furiously, we had managed to get this far without getting ourselves killed.

'Can I straighten one thing out before we move on? What Jan wrote in those journals, was it total fiction?' I asked.

'No, far from it. She was a remarkable woman. The storyline was based around a set of true events, but the background was based on Jan's historical knowledge and hush-hush work for the Home Office after the Cold War. Names and initials were changed in the journals to protect people, but the stories were true, as is the information on poisoning.

'We think there is a sweeper out there who knows his poisons. We had hoped to catch him like a fly in a spider's web.'

I was struggling not to become emotional. 'So, the comment that two boys, now men I presume, are involved in investigating this abuse is true. They were in the boys' home in the 1970s. Who is the one true Jesuit then?'

'No idea, sorry, everyone, I'm not sure what Jan was trying to communicate. You'll have to tell me. The Jesuits are a powerful group in the Vatican. It may be a good line of enquiry.'

'We were hoping to hand everything over to you and walk away,' Jake said. 'We're clearly caught in the middle of something far larger than we realised. We have murders, not suicides, and sweeper assassins as well as an unknown guardian. Max was right. Who are the goodies and who are the baddies?'

Chapter Twenty-Four

It was our turn to inform Tam Aitken what we knew of a man with a half finger, about the methods of poisoning that we had hypothesised, and our suspicions about Father Raymond. The police were considered unreliable by default, as despite being reported to several times over the last four years, by Ben, they did nothing. The police were sure to label us as conspiracy theorist cranks. They had failed to investigate Jan's death sufficiently enough to cast doubt on her death.

Detectives had been defective.

They hadn't managed to make any connection between Jan's death and that of Liam Brookes, even when I had gone to the trouble of identifying that Nick was using a false name. Was this down to sloppy police work, disinterest, or deliberate avoidance? It was impossible to know why they had not pursued any of these matters.

Tam tried to round the facts up. 'Whoever our sweeper man is, it's possible that he believes his job to be complete. You haven't reported your suspicions to the police, and there's no way your contact with me can have been common knowledge. It's the four of you who have taken it upon yourselves to investigate further. You can walk away if you so wish.'

'We'll think about it,' I said.

It seemed wrong to cut and run.

Max asked Tam for advice on how we should handle Father Raymond and our planned meeting with DS Adams. 'Tell me about their connections with the other victims,' Tam said with a strong note of intrigue.

Meanwhile, Jake was despatched to the barn to collect our spaghetti diagram, flip charts, and Sylvanian tree people.

Despite the seriousness of the subject, we still had to smile at the incongruous sight of Nick and Jan hedgehogs, cocktail stick flags in their heads. Tam, however, was delighted at the thoroughness of our deliberations. 'Well I never did …' He shook his head in wonder. 'This is magnificent work, people.'

As I sat silently watching Emma setting up our investigation HQ materials, there was a creeping realisation that I had revealed important information to the Coroner's Office which implied that I was suspicious about the cause of death for Ben Tierney.

'It's not magnificent. I think I might have dropped us in the soft and smelly.' I had asked the pathologist to consider anticholinergic toxicity. 'What did you say exactly?' asked Max when I recounted what I could recall of my request. The disapproving looks said it all.

'I shouldn't worry too much. How is that going to cause a problem?' Jake tried to maintain order and convince Emma that their family life had not been placed in jeopardy.

'It might be a problem if the police are informed by the pathologist or if the coroner asks for you to explain yourself,' Emma confirmed.

I hadn't quite finished undermining my friends' faith in me. 'Also … I asked for help from the French police, indirectly through Sam at the Hôpital Corbet. He's a really bright lad, so I led him to believe that Liam Brookes and Nick Shafer were two different people. He was the one who told me about Half-finger-man pretending to be Liam Brookes and about the HRT patches and about the laptop being broken.' My confession was made in the spirit of contrition.

Tam interjected as an intermediary. 'There you are. Without taking that risk, we would be short on facts and information. Your biggest danger areas are the two main subjects here,' he said, pointing to Father Raymond-mouse and to Half-finger-man-mouse. 'One is unknown; the other is a suspect by virtue of his proximity to the victims. Father Raymond cannot, however, have killed Nick. His whereabouts were known. He was feeding Jan's cat and was in the UK. As far as we are aware, he has all his fingers. *Digitus intactus.*' He paused. 'Sorry, that was my effort at levity.' For once, none of us laughed.

'I think it's Half-finger-man who is our sweeper,' Tam concluded. 'However, if Father Raymond is following Vatican policy, I suppose he may be under suspicion for the poisoning of Father Joseph. But the question would be, why now? He's been in Lensham for six months, you say.' He looked me directly in the eye and fixed me with a benevolent smile.

'Monica, you're closer to Father Raymond than anyone else we have available. Can you probe for information?'

I wasn't certain that I had the energy left to be that good an actress, but my loyalty to Jan and Ben drove me to agreeing to this proposal. 'I'll try. But what about Charlie Adams? Can't we ask him to investigate and support him in reporting his superior officer to the IPCC?'

Emma shook her head, 'Mon, we don't even know if we can trust him. He hasn't been in the area long. He came to you for help, but we don't know why he had the need to do that.' Emma was right as usual.

Max, Jake, and Emma were waiting for me to say something. 'What?'

'We have no choice really, do we. Can you and Max handle Charlie Adams and Father Raymond? We need to keep the kids safe. We'll do any background work to help.'

I understood completely what Jake was asking us to do, but Max didn't even wait for my reply, and he was passive in his aggression.

'No problem. We'll be the front men on this one. See if we can get ourselves killed into the bargain, shall we? Although *I* should be all right but Monica will be most likely to be the next victim, wouldn't you say?'

'Max! They have to protect the children. We all do.' I was shocked at my husband's attitude.

Tam, without hesitation, played the advantage.

'Not just your own children, remember. If we can expose the cover-ups, we'll be preventing the abuse of many hundreds of children and be providing justice for adults who lost their own childhoods to abusers.' He said this in muted tones, but deliberately and slowly. The meaning was not lost on me, and I knew, looking at Max, that he was now regretting his hasty protest. I saw him mouth an apology to Emma and Jake, who waved their understanding.

'This is not beyond you,' continued Tam, holding my gaze. 'We only need evidence of the crimes. Evidence of one murder will be enough. Push the coroner to question the deaths, but be careful. Find Half-finger-man and we're halfway there. Pardon the pun. He might have disappeared back to wherever he comes from, but if there is a chance, then we should try. If the police are covering up then we ought to get evidence of that, too.'

'More questions than answers again,' Emma said, verbalising my thoughts.

Max spoke. 'Okay. I apologise for what I said and for being a right selfish bastard. I'm worried about Monica, that's all. She's been through an awful lot lately and we've hardly slept for days. Sorry, everyone.'

I was caught up in my own thoughts for a moment, accepting the fact that it was me that was about to place myself within poisoning range of a man with half a little finger. If I cocked up, I could place my dearest friends, their children, and my one and only soul mate, in danger. Whether I wanted to or not, I couldn't walk away. Too many cases of abuse had passed through the doors of mental health services, as if there were an abhorrent insidious virus with several mutations working its way through mankind. Changing the future for children and improving the present for adult survivors was the only way forward.

'How do you suggest we handle DS Charlie Adams tomorrow?' I asked.

'Stick to Emma's original, plan. Suss him out, set him up and play stupid.'

'The last one is easy …'

Tam Aitken left the farm, having given us his direct contact details, and advised us not to email with correspondence or put his name into our phones. He became "Big T" on my personal contacts list. It felt altogether better that we had shared our fears with Tam and helped us to realise that we had not worked ourselves up into a form of exaggerated hysteria. What Tam had confirmed was that we had stumbled upon the tip of a monstrous iceberg. We couldn't melt it but we could help to chip away at it.

Max dropped me at home with Deefer and then indulged his other love by heading for the bike club with Robbie, but not before I made him check every single window and door, put on all the outside lights, and lecture Deefer about the role of a guard dog.

Sitting down at the kitchen table, with a notepad and a pen, I began to define the subjects for discussion the next morning with Charlie Adams. I had two columns. One on the left for 'safe subjects' and the other for 'don't go there'.

I was confident that I could confirm how I had discovered by chance that my friend's missing lodger, Nicholas Shafer, was in fact Liam Brookes. I could also disclose that there had been a mysterious break-in at the Lodge House.

Discussing Jan's death as a suicide was also a safe topic, and it would even be possible for me to suggest Jan's brother as the likely culprit responsible for the apparent burglary at Jan's home before she had died. That had a high probability of being correct. However, Father Joseph's death was a mystery and Ben Tierney's was still under investigation, so, given my enquiries at the Coroner's Office, it would be better to avoid that subject if possible. The ace up my sleeve would be my own delicate mental state; I could feign memory lapses if necessary, I decided.

Confidence was returning. Charlie Adams would have to prove himself, thus giving Max and me the upper hand. He could not know what we had already discovered unless we saw fit to tell him, and he would have to be a man of the highest integrity before we entrusted him with any information.

My thoughts were interrupted when my mobile phone rang, making me jump. Max was calling me. 'Mon, are you sitting down?' Max was whispering loudly into the mouthpiece at his end.

'Yes, why? And why are you phoning me from the bike club? Are you in the toilet?'

'No, I'm outside. I don't want to be overheard. Why are you whispering?'

'Because you are.'

'Idiot. Listen, I needed to tell you this before I forget the details. Get a pen. Got one? Okay. Peter Lynch is here, rather the worse for wear.'

It took me a second or two to work out who Max was referring to.

'Detective Inspector Oaf, you mean.'

'Yes, that's the fella. He and his cronies have had a liquid lunch, which seems to have turned into a liquid afternoon tea. They're really loud and obnoxious. He's been shooting his mouth off about your boy's argument with an express train. The bloody graphic details are enough to turn your stomach, but I guess you know that. The police are assuming suicide, as we thought they would, but the important information is about who was doing the chasing that day. Father Raymond and a man called Philip George. Now who could he be?'

I knew the answer straight away. 'That's Pip, he attends the Pathways Project with Jan's friends. He's a lovely man, wouldn't say boo to a goose.'

'Well they were both at the Rectory together when your boy ran past. That's why they were chasing him. Is Pip a close friend of Father Raymond?'

'I don't really know. I suppose it would be all right to ask him that question myself, unless he has a missing finger, of course. I've never noticed one before, but then again, I wasn't looking.' Obsession with half-fingers was driving me to distraction. 'I don't think either of them knew Ben very well, so I wonder what made them run after him like that.'

'Before I go back in, you might want to hear the other news that old Foghorn Leghorn upstairs told the whole clubhouse. Frank Hughes didn't get bail. Apparently, he had a poor-quality solicitor whose arguments backfired, so he's on remand. One less thing to worry about. I'm going now. Robbie and I might have a few beers, so can you pick us up later? We'll collect the bikes tomorrow. It'll be a good excuse to get rid of cheerful Charlie once we've had enough of him. I'll ring you when we want to come home.'

Everything was right with the world. Max and Robbie were at the bike club drinking beer, just as they should be. I was at home, radio on for company, with the dog, watching the leaves fall from the trees in the garden and being irritated by state of the lawn, which needed a cut.

Chapter Twenty-Five

It was well before eleven the next morning when our doorbell sounded, heralding the arrival of DS Charlie Adams. Deefer rushed to greet him with his usual enthusiasm for any visitor. 'Bloody hell, I didn't realise he was so bouncy. He was asleep last time I was here.' Charlie brushed raindrops from his shoulders as he entered the hallway.

'So he was. I'd forgotten you hadn't met Deefer at full throttle before. Ignore him and he'll calm down if you're lucky,' Max advised Charlie as they shook hands. 'Take your coat off and come on through to the dining room, I think Monica might be able to run to tea, coffee, and biscuits. I'm a bit bleary eyed this morning, so forgive me.'

'A few beers last night?' Charlie asked with a smile on his face in appreciation of Max's hangover.

'One or two. I saw your boss as it happens, I was surprised he wasn't out detecting or inspecting somewhere, especially after the week you've had.' I looked across at Max and grinned a welcome to Charlie. Max was doing a far better job of being natural and relaxed than I could ever hope to achieve, so I focussed on the task in hand. Safe subject: 'Coffee or tea, Charlie?'

Charlie seemed distracted by Max's announcement that Peter Lynch had been seen out drinking the night before. 'Did you have a chance to speak to him then?' he asked.

'No, you must be joking, he was with his well-oiled important pals and associates, if you get my drift. I don't really know him well enough to chat to.' *Neatly done, Max,* I thought, as he tied that one up. It was dangerous ground, suggesting an acquaintance with a senior detective inspector, especially as we were expecting Charlie to make certain accusations against his senior officer.

I followed the action plan that Max and I had agreed. 'What do you think to my latest investment? Max keeps spending money on bikes, so this is my revenge.' I directed my gaze towards the Regency ship's cabinet, next to the fireplace. 'I can't believe how fortunate we were not to have it stolen. Those burglars must have been youngsters. They took the old TV set but left something much more valuable.'

'Lovely,' Charlie said as he walked up to the cabinet and stroked it. 'May I?' I gave permission for Charlie to open the cabinet door. 'It is the dose that makes the poison. Paracelsus, as it says on the front. Classy.'

'I had to look that up on the Internet. My Latin isn't up to your standard, I'm afraid.'

'I saw you at the auction, when you bought this,' Charlie said, still staring at the cabinet and touching the bottles one by one. 'You were bidding against me at one time, but I had to back away before I spent my savings.' What a relief. Charlie had openly confirmed being at the auction. Test number one passed with ease.

'Do you go to auctions like that very often?' Max asked.

'If I got the chance, I'd go far more frequently,' came the reply. Charlie switched his attention to me. 'How are you doing since Thursday's dreadful accident? You did really well not to throw up, by the way. Not many would have been so tough. We confirmed exactly who it was chasing Benito Tierney onto the tracks in the end. Although you probably already know by now.'

'No, we haven't heard anything other than the news reports. Who was it? Were they trying to stop Ben?' Max nodded almost imperceptibly, confirming that I had judged my words well. I was hoping to avoid too much focus on this subject in case it led to references about the coroner or the pathology findings.

'Yes, they were trying desperately to stop him before he got as far as the tracks, and very nearly lost their own lives in the process. It was Father Raymond from St Francis' Church, and a man who goes by the name of Pip. You might know him. He has his own mental health issues to deal with and knew Ben by sight. They weren't friends as such.'

'Yes, Philip George. He attends …' I hesitated briefly, 'one of our clinics every so often.' I passed Charlie his mug of coffee and put a plate of ginger nut and bourbon biscuits down on the table. Charlie reached for one as I looked again at Max for reassurance.

'My favourite, ginger nutters,' said Max who then unexpectedly stood up before announcing, 'Shit! Sorry. Forgot to lock up the bike shed, can't be too careful these days, not since that burglary, anyway. Back in a few minutes.'

I hesitated briefly then stumbled over my words as I tried to keep the flow of conversation going. What was Max up to?

'Have you heard anything more about Liam Brookes? I mean Nick Shafer?' I asked this, not wanting to return to the subject of Ben's tragic death. 'Did the French police shed any light on the blocked flue? How sad, especially as Jan died thinking he was a scoundrel.' Forcing myself not to ramble anymore, I stopped, waiting for Charlie to fill in some gaps with the truth.

'The French had no luck at all. By the way, they did email with confirmation eventually, and I must have misunderstood what they said over the phone in the first place. Nicholas Shafer did die of carbon monoxide poisoning but it was because of a fire in the flat, not a blocked flue. An electrical fault, apparently.'

'Oh, my God,' I exclaimed, in my worst possible theatrical voice. 'Was anyone else hurt?'

Charlie gave the same information that we had also received from Sam. No one else had been caught up in the fire. Things were looking promising for Charlie, and improved further with his next piece of information. 'It looks like Nick could not have broken into Jan Collins's house. He would have been dead at that time. So, we're beginning to suspect Jan's brother was fishing around for confirmation of how much money his sister had left to lend him to save his drowning business. But we don't think he killed his sister.'

Blimey. None of us had considered that as a possibility.

'That explains his interest in the rumours about Jan spending money on an apartment in France. I take it those rumours were not true either.' My head was swimming with which facts I could agree with or not, and I had lost my wingman Max to the bloody garage. Why did Max have to leave me to cope with these questions on my own? Sodding motorbikes.

'Jan's death was a simple suicide, then? I thought so, as soon as I saw all the tablets on her kitchen table.'

Max strolled back into the kitchen, apologising again, with a false grin plastered over his face. 'What about Father Joseph and the kidney beans, any luck with that one?' asked Max brazenly, and seemingly without thinking.

'I'm not sure how much I'm allowed to say. As Jan's death was not suspicious after all, and Nick Shafer died in an accidental fire, I think I was ridiculously hasty in suggesting any cover-up, let alone asking for your help. The matter of Father Joseph's death is still under police investigation and we have questioned Father Raymond several times.'

It was an enormous relief in that moment to conclude that DS Adams was an honest man. He had confessed to misreading the situation, leading me to feel reassured that we could trust him, but I decided to leave it to Max to ask about the abuses by Father Joseph and the possible murders of Jan and Nick.

Once that was achieved, we could walk away.

Sure enough, right on cue, Max leant forward towards Charlie. 'We quite understand. We were sleep deprived that morning anyway, but I have been wondering about something, and you may be able to help, Charlie, before you have to go again. When Ben Tierney went to report at the police station, sober for a change, that a priest at St Francis' church had sexually assaulted him as a child, why wasn't it investigated?'

Bloody hell. That was an interesting opening move, but I could see Max's thinking behind the novel approach.

'Excuse me,' I said as my phone rudely interrupted. Planning to switch it off, I picked it up, but before pressing the red button I saw Emma's name. She would know not to ring at this crucial time. Something was up. 'Hello.'

'Mon, I'm so sorry, there has been a dreadful incident. Can you come right away? It's Sophie.'

'Oh God, I'm on my way.' I didn't stop long enough to ask Emma what had happened. I looked at Max, who saw the anguish on my face and bundled me out of the door and into my car. Charlie offered to help but was ushered back to work. 'It's a family matter, but thanks for the offer, we'll call if we need you,' Max shouted as he closed the car door and we sped away down the lane towards Folly Farm.

'Christ, Max, it's little Sophie. Something is dreadfully wrong.'

'Yep. It most certainly is. Sophie has discovered the Sylvanian hedgehog people with cocktail sticks in their heads and she's very upset. She took a large pair of kitchen scissors to her mother's favourite apron in revenge.'

'What the fuck are you talking about?'

Max pulled over in a lay-by well before we had reached the farm entrance. It was lashing down with rain, and the sound on the roof of the car made a drumming noise which acted like an intense soundtrack to what Max said next.

'Sophie is fine. I had to find a way of getting you out of the house without arousing suspicion. Your acting is rubbish, so to make it realistic I called Emma.'

'But why?'

'Charlie Adams reached for the biscuits with his left hand and you missed it.'

'Missed what?'

'The little finger.'

'But, Max, it wasn't missing, he has all his fingers and thumbs, I saw them and you saw them today. He's not Mr Half-Finger. You are a berk at times.'

'Not as much of a berk as you think, madam. When your mate Charlie Adams reached for the ginger nut biscuits with his left hand, his little finger remained bent double. Holding something like a steering wheel, you wouldn't notice. But from above or from the front with his left hand hanging down it looks just as if the top half of his finger is missing. That's what Sam saw, and that's what I saw just now.'

I didn't know what to say.

'Come on, let's go to the farm and regroup. Sophie probably needs your wise words to help her understand why her parents have brutally assaulted her Sylvanian tree people.' Max took my head in his big fat hands and kissed my forehead as if to make it better. It didn't work.

Chapter Twenty-Six

I wasn't planning on doing any more than checking in at St David's Church Hall on Monday morning, pretending to carry out my duties in respect of the amnesty. If I wrote an article for the local paper and gave some feedback to DJ Danny Wakeman, I was positive that would keep the managers happy. Coping with anything more taxing was beyond me.

Resolving to keep my promise, I had also planned to contact Father Raymond.

He must hold secrets.

Dutifully, I phoned the office to update Kelly with my movements for the day, and she couldn't wait to poke at me with her annoyance stick. 'Whatever your plans were, you'll have to change them.' Curt words spoken with glee. 'The Coroner's Office want to speak to you urgently. I've made an appointment for you to go there this morning at nine-thirty. You should make it through the traffic in time.'

'Thanks a bunch.' Clearly Eddie had neglected to inform Kelly of my requirement for delicate handling. I could have cried, but I didn't have time. Rushing back upstairs, apologising to the dog for no reason, I put on a smart work suit. 'Bloody Kelly.'

Parking difficulties and pouring rain conspired to unravel my professional appearance. By the time I stumbled through the front door of the building which houses the Coroner's Office, I was bedraggled and flustered. Any confidence boosted by a veneer of competent professionalism had been wiped out, leaving me feeling like a stupid child who had lacked the common sense to use an umbrella.

'Good morning, how can I help?' asked a plastic, orange-coloured receptionist, with perfect make up and solid hair tied in a bun on top of her head. Another plastic, orange woman stood at the far end of the same desk. They weren't twins but I could only think that there is a factory somewhere that makes identical plastic receptionists for office blocks. The plastic women seem to be everywhere there's a formal reception desk and they give me shivers, like clowns do. I followed orange-woman's directions, taking a short diversion to the ladies' toilets in order to rearrange myself.

The receptionist at the Coroner's Office was human, thank God.

'Good morning, I have an appointment to see Mr Williams the coroner, at nine-thirty.' I had made it with one minute to spare.

'Yes, that's right. Thanks for coming in at such short notice. Take a seat for a moment please, Monica, he'll be with you shortly.' She took in my damp clothes and rain-soaked hair. 'There's a radiator near the window, which may help dry you off a little. Nasty weather, isn't it?'

I didn't dry off. I steamed, which can't have gone unnoticed by the coroner himself who greeted me with a firm handshake and a warm smile.

'You must be wondering why I have asked to see you.'

Stupidly, I hadn't taken the time to figure out what could be so urgent. I had simply assumed that my report had been inadequate and that I was going to be given the benefit of proper guidance, and chastised for my poor-quality writing standards.

'I can be assured of confidentiality. You are a registered nurse, so I'll take that as read. Monica, we have two cases involving patients that you have been involved with directly. The first, Mrs Janet Collins, appears to have died at her own hand. Your report ...' *Here we go. Here comes the painful criticism* '.... Is markedly different to the report filed by the investigating officer from the police.' He flicked at the paperwork in front of him and I saw DS Adams's name on the report, which brought me up short. I gasped behind my hand, and coughed to cover it up.

'You make some interesting implications in your report. You identify Mrs Collins's male friend as rather more benevolent than the police have done. Why is that?' Mr Williams asked.

When I explained the dilemma he seemed to appreciate the fact that I had taken the trouble of talking to Jan's friends and that I had contacted the Corbet Unit in France to try to trace Liam Brookes. Mr Williams was an intelligent man. 'If the rumours were untrue, as you say in your report, then where, Monica, is Liam Brookes now, and why did he not support his lady-friend when she returned to the UK, if he was the kind-hearted soul you make him out to be?'

Good grief.

I didn't know what to do at first, but then I had a miraculous moment of inspiration. 'Oh, I thought the police would have put that in their report. He's dead, too. I found out through the French authorities. He died in a fire at his flat in Perpignan, before Jan's death. She would have been in hospital there at the time. I'm sorry that information is not in my report, but I only found out on Friday after my report had been submitted.' I stopped abruptly. I had only given my report in to Eddie on Friday morning, so how did the coroner have it so soon? 'How did you get it so soon?' The words were out of my mouth before I could stop myself.

'We coroners have a fair amount of clout. I'll be straight with you. It was your call to my officer that prompted the request. You asked for a particular substance to be accounted for in the death of your other patient Benito Tierney and I want to know why. Another report from you on this matter would be appreciated. I need one regarding Benito Tierney's contact with mental health services, but I want a specific explanation about your request. Why haven't you raised this with the police? Why come direct to our office?'

I stared at Mr Williams, again not knowing what to do. I had been cornered by a coroner and was about to disclose information that could get me killed on one hand, or which could imply police corruption and a murderer within their organisation on the other. 'Are you a Catholic?'

'What?' Mr Williams was clearly taken aback at my question.

'Sorry but I have to know if you are either a Catholic or a Freemason or both.'

'No, I am neither, and I don't see why those questions have any bearing on my request,' he said, sounding offended.

'Thank God for that,' I replied, sinking, trembling into the office chair that was now damp from my sodden clothes. If he reacted in that way, then he couldn't possibly be either. Stupidly and out of sheer habit I checked his hands and counted his fingers. Looking up, I saw Mr Williams glaring at me angrily.

'Well? What is going on?'

'I can't report my concerns to the police because I think one of their officers might be responsible for the deaths, but I can't prove it.' Feeling faint, I tried to steady myself in the chair.

'Goodness me, young lady, no wonder you look so dreadfully pale. Mrs Jennings, could you come in here for a moment,' he shouted to the receptionist. 'Hot, sweet tea, Mrs Jennings, if you would. Then get me Milo Granger as a matter of urgency.'

'IPCC?'

'Yes please, Mrs Jennings, and if you can get hold of Carol for me too, I would appreciate it.' Such a polite man. 'Don't worry. You have done exactly the right thing. Drink your tea, have a biscuit, steady yourself and we will work this through.' Not for one single second did I doubt what Mr Williams said. My fear began to dissipate along with the rising steam from my tea and my damp suit.

He talked as if to keep me occupied for a while, giving reassurances. 'I'm not a Mason, although I know quite a few. You see, I couldn't possibly have any question about my impartiality as a coroner. It's not really my thing anyway, boys' clubs. I enjoy my wife's company too much to exclude her from my spare time activities. We play a little golf, very badly I'm ashamed to say, and we do both like to watch a good game of rugby.'

Ordinarily those remarks would have sealed the deal. In other circumstances, I would have considered the man to be 'a goodie' and thus to be honest and trustworthy enough to be on our team. However, I had almost credited Charlie Adams with the same qualities. My judgement about allegiances was not to be relied upon.

'Who have you contacted?' I asked with a high-pitched squeak to my voice, giving away my anxiety. Crapometer readings had hovered at maximum for several days, and they were not getting any lower sitting before the coroner. The pressure inside my head made solving complex puzzles decidedly more testing, and I could barely identify the component parts of that day's problem.

'I have a legal colleague who works in the Independent Police Complaints Commission. The IPCC. A good man, Milo Granger. Top legal mind. Rubbish golfer like myself. I don't want you to report this to me, and then the IPCC hearing it second hand. If I can get Milo here, we can take the details in one sitting. Does anyone else know about this?'

Still fearful of the potential for a major balls-up, I asked permission to contact a friend for advice. Mr Williams looked most perplexed but actually encouraged me to make the call and left me in the privacy of his office, while I phoned Tam Aitken. 'Goodness, Monica, you're a fast worker. Half-finger-man yesterday, and the coroner today. I'll check Mr Williams out for you and message you back ASAP. What's his first name and initials?' I had to scrabble about on Mr Williams's desk to get those vital details, but once done, Tam chuckled at the end of the phone. 'No need to wait for a message. Mr Howard Ivor Williams is as honourable as they get. I would willingly bet my life on it. He's your knight in shining armour, Monica. You have struck lucky. Aye, go with his advice. Well done.'

'Aye, I will,' I said. The accent-mimic-filters had failed. I had said 'aye' back to Tam, which was a good sign. Far more normal.

Chapter Twenty-Seven

Milo Granger was one of the most handsome black men I have ever had the pleasure to encounter in the flesh. A cross between Denzel Washington, Will Smith, and Mohammed Ali, he strode across the office to greet Mr Williams warmly by the hand. 'Castle, wonderful to see you.'

Mrs Jennings followed, carrying more refreshments. 'Ah, thank you, Moneypenny,' said Milo Granger with a wicked smile aimed directly at Mrs Jennings. She leant forward and whispered in my ear, loud enough for everyone to hear, 'Don't get too excited. He's married.' She winked at me and left the room, leaving me to wonder if her statement could be true or if she was joking with me to keep him to herself.

'You know why they call him Castle, don't you?' Milo Granger turned to face me. I didn't know they called him Castle at all. 'It's because, like castle walls, nothing gets past him, and once he has taken you prisoner, you can't escape. In the nicest, and most legal of ways. He's a veritable law fortress.' Wide grins and warm handshakes dispensed with, the two legal men settled down to suck my brains out. Every fine detail, every conversation, thought, supposition, assumption, and hypothesis was explored. Then I was cross-examined to within an inch of my sanity. I had been mind-raped.

'It's the four of you and Tam Aitken. That's it, no one else until this morning. Good. Monica, you have no idea how brave you are about to be,' stated Milo with a deceptive warmth to his voice.

'Pardon?' I experienced a horrible sinking feeling as the meanings of his words were eventually absorbed by my energy-depleted brain.

'You have personal contact with DS Adams and he believes you are ignorant of the fact that he has committed murder – if what we think is right. You have legitimate access to him because of your interest in Jan and Ben's deaths. Correct? You are also close to Father Raymond, working on the medicines amnesty. So, you see, we can't really do this without you.'

'Do what?' I knew the answer.

'Help us find the evidence we need to convict DS Adams of murder, and expose the deliberate concealment of child sexual abuse at St Francis' Church. You've already shown your determination and courage …'

The door opened and in stepped a stylishly dressed lady, slim and fragrant. 'Ah, Carol. This is Monica Morris who spoke to you last week. Monica, this is my deputy Carol Langford. News from pathology yet?' Mr Williams asked.

'I spoke to Patrick first thing, and we have a young man who looks to have some anticholinergics in his bloodstream, and evidence for thorn apple in what they could find of his stomach contents along with, or as part of, a ham salad sandwich.'

'Hell's Bells,' I said.

'Quite.'

'No, sorry, that's what it's called, "Hell's Bells". I can't remember the Latin name for the plant but it's deadly. I looked it up when I was researching for anticholinergic toxicity. Ben wouldn't have needed much because of the alcohol, it makes it so much worse, and he had liver problems. I didn't mean to swear.'

Mr Williams laughed.

'I think we should send Monica on her way. We can't keep her here any longer, people will get suspicious. Just tell everyone that I was extremely rude and kept you waiting for several hours. Then I criticised your report and have asked you to focus on improving your standards for the next case. How about that? Realistic enough?'

'It's fine. Before I leave, can I be certain that not a word of my disclosures gets out. Emma, Jake, and the children, might be at risk and I couldn't stand the thought of anything happening to them.'

'Is the Lodge House on the farm still available to rent?' asked Milo.

'Yes, I think so.'

'Well in that case we'll rent it, making use of Aitken, Brown and Partners as cover for the tenancy agreement, and I'll request that a couple of our officers are stationed there. They'll be an innocent looking couple who can make it a safe base for meeting with you, Max, Jake, and Emma, as well as being on hand at the farm. Will that help?'

I was grateful for the quick plan, but cautioned Carol, Milo, and Mr Williams that poisoners, on the whole, work remotely and with a delayed action. 'Poison on Tuesday, dead on Thursday with no evidence to be found at the scene.'

Fancy me having the gall to tell the coroner about death. Thank goodness he'd turned out to be a wise and tolerant man.

'Quite so, young lady. However, we will do what we can. In the meantime, I will have to open a new inquiry into the death of Mrs Janet Collins because of information coming to light. In the course of the new inquiry, if what Monica has told us is correct, then a crime is most likely to be uncovered. The DPP will have to be informed of this and I'll request further reports which, in the interest of public safety, will not be disclosed to the police. Hearings will not be public. Lots to do, Carol.' Mr Williams was sorting through papers on his desk and intermittently handing items to his deputy.

'Monica, can you find a way to fathom what it is that Father Raymond is hiding? He must know something,' said Milo, who was taking notes and about to make a call on his mobile phone. Mr Williams opened the door for me to leave, thanking me and holding a reassuring hand on my shoulder, but before he wished me goodbye Milo piped up again, 'Do you have a voice recording facility on your mobile phone? Maybe you could accidentally switch it on when you meet either of the two gentlemen we have in our sights.'

I nodded, too drained to argue against the idea.

I liked Mr Williams, despite having to collate more information for another report. Thanks to him, my phone call to the office was strangely enjoyable.

'Hello, Kelly. I've only just this minute finished at the Coroner's Office. I thought you said it was urgent. Well let me tell you, it wasn't. He kept me waiting for two hours and then informed me that my report was substandard. I told you it wouldn't pass muster. Not only that but I have another one to do, as well as corrections to the first. Who sent it off before it went to the risk department for scrutiny?' I knew damn well that Kelly had faxed it and she would have had great pleasure in sending it on Eddie's orders.

A sheepish Kelly could do nothing other than apologise.

'Game to Monica Morris, new balls, please,' I said aloud as I drove out of the congested car park.

St David's Church Hall was an example of serene organisation. Groups were being held in the main hall, and the medicine amnesty arrangement had been running smoothly without me. The deliveries had reduced to a trickle and the elderly lady volunteer on duty was resigned to reading a book and sipping tea quietly, in the corner of the entrance hall. I recognised her immediately. 'Only four more days to go, dear,' she said as she looked up at me. 'Still no raids by the druggies …' I think she had probably been reading too many gangland murder novels.

Father Raymond had noticed me through the glass in the hall doors and could be seen excusing himself to come and talk with me. His gaunt face and haunted look reflected the levels of stress he must have encountered over recent days. As I caught my own reflection in the hall mirror, I too was a picture of nervous exhaustion.

'Shall we escape to the Rectory for a warming drink and a slice of cake? Dora here made me a special Victoria sponge with homemade jam. I simply can't do it justice on my own and the curate is on a diet. I've donated most of it to the group this morning, but there are two enormous slices left for us.'

The aim of visiting the hall had been to meet my commitments to the medication amnesty and placed me in a position of control as to when I arrived and when I could leave. To meet Father Raymond on my terms. His suggestion of cake in the Rectory was unexpected.

'It's a tempting offer, Father, but I only have a few minutes. I wanted to pop in to see how you were coping, and to apologise for not phoning you back on Friday, I was in no fit state to hold a reasonable conversation. Sorry.'

He had caught me off guard, but I had taken control back. Then I doubted myself. Should I go to the Rectory with him? Would this be the opportunity to get the evidence needed to identify those responsible for four deaths? I was so unnerved I couldn't decide what to do for the best.

'Are you sure you can't spare a few minutes? A cup of tea and a slice of cake won't kill you,' he said, smiling with encouragement. I hesitated.

'No really, I can't. Can we make it another day? Tomorrow maybe. I have another report for the coroner to write and he sets high standards and short time scales.' It was far too risky to be on my own with Father Raymond. 'After all, what would the neighbours and Dora think of us disappearing to be alone together in the Rectory?' I was only too aware that I could get locked in a cellar, poisoned, and buried alive. No one other than Dora would have known I was there, and she, of all people, would have been dismissed by police as a wild fantasist.

'That's true, Monica. Very unseemly. We wouldn't want any gossip now would we? No indeed.'

'Seriously though, tomorrow would be better. Can we say after lunch, about two?' I asked. I could take someone with me, I decided, even if it was Deefer the dog. 'That'll allow me a few hours to finish my report in the morning and then I can give you my full attention. How are the gang doing, by the way? Karen, Vanessa, and Pip ... especially after Ben's death?'

Pip, it turned out, was in a poor state and had been admitted to hospital immediately after the events at the station on the previous Thursday. I pretended to be surprised by the news of Father Raymond's and Pip's involvement with Ben's dash to the railway line. 'Oh, it was you on the CCTV pictures. How incredibly lucky you weren't killed yourselves.'

Pip had apparently been transferred to Pargiter Ward.

'Shall we visit Pip tomorrow instead, and have a cuppa at the hospital?' suggested Father Raymond.

'What a great idea, I'll meet you there at two.' What a reprieve. That was a much safer option. Public places were preferential to being in the Rectory alone with Father Raymond and Father Joseph's ghost.

I phoned Max when I was safely cocooned in my car. It was drizzling with rain and the wind had picked up again, making it a day for watching a black and white film and dunking biscuits into a mug of tea. The phone rang numerous times. No answer. I left a message. 'Nothing urgent. See you at home later and I'll tell you about my day. I'll light the fire.'

There was no need to reference my patient notes in order to write the outline of a report for the coroner regarding Ben Tierney, so I drove home and wrote a sizeable chunk of it sitting in front of the fire with Deefer for company. Kelly could type it up first thing in the morning for her sins, once I had cross-referenced the dates in my diary with those in the notes. This had to be accurate and I didn't hold back on Ben's disclosures of sexual abuse or his attempts to report them to the authorities.

I hadn't quite finished when my phone beeped with a message. 'Oh shit.' It wasn't Max, it was from Charlie Adams – the word 'Dynamic' had appeared on the small screen. The message was polite and simple. *'Hope your family crisis is resolved. Thanks for your support and sorry I worried you and Max unnecessarily. Charlie.'*

There were no sinister undertones, and no double meanings to be found. An innocent enquiry and an apology. Yet receiving a text from DS Adams generated a feeling of such uncertainty and dread, that I stood up and had a sneaky peak through the curtains into the dark of the lane outside, in case he was lurking there.

'Poisoners don't lurk, Deefer. I should know that. Poisoners plan very carefully what they are going to do and how. If we are not a threat to secrecy then we are not a target.' Deefer listened intently and licked his lips. 'Was that a hint? It's your dinner time isn't it, silly me, and there I was thinking that you were interested in my knowledge about poisoners.'

Talking to myself seemed to soothe my anxieties, and so did sharing the burden with Mr Williams and reporting the facts to the IPCC, which had certainly alleviated much of my internal angst.

I fed Deefer and wanted to settle back down in front of the fire but waiting for Max to get home, and him not returning my call, prevented any sort of relaxation.

When he did eventually turn up, safe and oblivious to my frantic worry about him, I was crotchety.

'Where the hell have you been, you thoughtless great pillock?'

Chapter Twenty-Eight

Emma was enthusiastic about having officers from the IPCC stationed in the Lodge House at Folly Farm. She phoned me with confirmation. 'You've been busy. Tam o'Shanter was mightily impressed by your work with the coroner and the man from the IPCC, but I don't understand why there isn't enough evidence to arrest Dynamic,' Emma said, choosing to avoid real names.

'Well, I think the IPCC have to find evidence to place him at the scene of the fire at the flat in France. I should think they'd need to take statements from the staff at the Corbet unit, and speak to the gendarmes, and their equivalent coroner and pathologist. The coroner here is opening a new inquiry into Jan's death, which will question police evidence and their lack of a proper investigation, I should think. Now that will put Dynamic in the spotlight as the investigating officer.

'There'll be a review of the investigation into Father J's death, I would also imagine, although there's evidence that he and Ben were both poisoned, it's the evidence of who poisoned them, how and when, that's absent.'

It was helpful to précis the current situation in this way to Emma, but it was rather too simplistic.

There was a massive hole yet to be filled.

'Well, they don't hang about at the IPCC, that's for sure,' Emma said. 'Mr and Mrs Braithwaite, the nice couple who are renting from us, have phoned already to make arrangements. Someone else is coming at the crack of dawn to put CCTV cameras up at the farm and at the Lodge, covering the farm entrance. We're already feeling much more secure. What's your next move, Sherlock?'

'I'm going to Hollberry Hospital with Father Raymond to visit Pip tomorrow.' My surprise invitation to join Father Raymond for tea and cake at the Rectory had shocked Emma. She immediately warned of poisoned jam sponge, being dissected, and buried in an unmarked grave. My reassurances were dismissed as crass stupidity, but she did finally credit me with using common sense to renegotiate a plan to meet in a public place instead.

'But I didn't, Em, it was Father Raymond's suggestion.'

'Blimey, Mon, you're pushing your luck. Maybe he realised how obvious he was being. Be careful and don't forget to switch your mobile to silent tomorrow when you meet him, and turn off the vibrate function as well, that way you won't draw attention to your phone. Record everything. Phone me before you go, otherwise I'll worry. By the way, as I'm on back-up duties, what else was it you wanted me to look up for you? I've found some stuff on Freemasons and banking, but there was another task I offered to take on …'

'Yes, Watson, "the one true Jesuit". Who the hell is that? I think it's connected with the boys' home scandal in the remaining journal, can you follow that up?'

Emma and I were back in the swing of our comfortable friendship after the testing meeting with Tam Aitken, when the scale of what we had become entangled with had hit home, hard. Both of us were painfully aware that there needed to be a speedy resolution to proving that DS Adams was involved in murder.

What we didn't know was whether he was working for, or with, Father Raymond.

I had decided to explore the relationship between Father Raymond and Pip during the visit planned for the following day. It was a worrying development that Pip had been with Father Raymond at the Rectory. Why were they there together? Tea and cake perhaps? Or was it something more ominous?

Struck by another series of possibilities, I phoned Emma. 'Em, sorry to bother you again. Can I just ask whether, on our list for possible guardians, we can add any of the other vicars at the Pathways Project? The Jesuit could be among them. Also, I was thinking, does it have to be a male? If not, then we could add any number of people, even Dora. She did offer to ride shotgun to protect me from druggies, remember.' The other members of the clergy involved in the Pathways Project would have studied theology; therefore, any one of them could have met with Jan at university. Emma laughed derisively. 'Jesuits are all male, but I'll add the female clergy to the list if you like.'

After shouting at him for being late home, I did nothing to improve Max's mood when I updated him with details of my meeting with the coroner and the intervention from the IPCC.

'Can't they do this without you?' Max stormed around the kitchen opening cupboards, for no good reason other than to have a door to slam when he couldn't find what he wasn't even looking for.

Deefer padded out of the kitchen to find a safer haven elsewhere.

I tried to explain. 'The longer it takes, the more likely it is I'll be implicated, and that means you, Jake, Emma, and the kids will be back in the firing line again. So, no, Max, I don't think it can be done without my help.' Max was making me cross by behaving like a toddler.

He turned on me.

'Do you always have to be such a martyr? It's so incredibly bloody selfish.' There were tears of rage in his eyes as he shouted, and he was thumping the kitchen work surface with a fist. 'I should be protecting you. Not the other way around.'

So that was the reason for the stroppy, irritated Max. He wanted to be the caveman and kill the wild animal threatening our lives. He wanted to spear the dangerous beast through the heart and then skin him.

'Well, you can beat your chest like Tarzan for all you're worth, but it won't change the fact that it's me in a position to help here; not you. You can't be the hero arriving in the nick of time to save the bloody day, so there is little point in getting aerated about it and behaving like a spoilt child.'

'Will you at least wear an alarm of some sort?'

Milo Granger had the same idea. He contacted me early the next morning and asked me to drop into the Lodge House to meet him before work. Happy to do so, I arrived at eight o'clock to be greeted by Emma shouting through the car window as she drove past in the opposite direction, taking the children to school.

'It's open, your new boss is waiting for you, lucky girl. Such a shame we're both married …' What a lascivious expression she wore, as she gestured to where Milo was standing in the doorway of the Lodge House, waving.

'Let's go in, Monica, shall we?' Milo was extremely business-like as he explained the plan of action. His department were anxious to put as many safeguards in place as was possible within a tight time frame. They had been working through the night.

'We think you should wear a listening device, so I've brought this along.' He held out a small black fob. 'It fits neatly onto your NHS ID lanyard. All you have to do is to press the two buttons either side, simultaneously, and the device will pick up the conversation. This will then be relayed back to one of our communications team, as well as being recorded. It has GPS tracking to help us gauge where you are, but it isn't pinpoint accurate, so dropping a few hints into a conversation would be wise if you can manage that safely. We'll send a text to your phone to confirm that the device has been triggered and is working.'

I seemed to have walked onto the set of a James Bond movie. Q had forgotten to give me a Walter PPK and exploding bubble gum and there was no sign of an Aston Martin anywhere. 'How disappointing,' I said. 'Is this it? No other gizmos or weapons, not even a magnifying glass or deerstalker hat?'

'You've lost me there, I'm afraid, Monica. What were you hoping for?'

I explained to a bemused Milo about my obsession with Sir Arthur Conan Doyle and my desire for a James Bond mission. Instead of which it was me, an emotionally unstable, obsessive, idiot-woman with a listening device, two mobile phones, a pen, and a work diary.

'Two mobile phones?'

'One personal, top of the range. One work, NHS basic model, calls and texts only … when it works.' At this description Milo grinned and shook his head. A test was required to ensure the listening device or "earwig fob" was working effectively. 'What's the range of this thing? How close do I have to stand to someone to pick up the conversation?' I asked. Pressing the two buttons either side of the fob; I thrust my chest out as I spoke.

Milo was on his phone to an operator who confirmed that the device was working as required.

'Okay, I'll keep talking and you gradually take a step back, one at a time. Yep that's it, keep going. "There once was an ugly duckling, it's feathers all fluffy and brown". Yep, keep going. "Mary had a little lamb, she also had a duck, she kept them on the mantelpiece …" Right, that's far enough. That's your maximum for good, clear recording.' A text notification on my personal mobile confirmed 'device operational' as promised.

Milo continued with his instructions. 'To switch the device off, use the large red button on the base. We don't want to hear useless gossip, or worse, and you're risking a breach of patient confidentiality with this, so be cautious.' Milo was very officious, but still cheerful and positive, giving me a boost.

'I've arranged to meet with Father Raymond this afternoon at the hospital, so I'll be using it then, but probably only when we have coffee together. Before that we're visiting a patient on the ward, so I can't make use of the earwig fob,' I confirmed.

There was no more to say or do before I left for work, other than to thank Sidney Poitier's lookalike for his earwigging gift, and to arrange a debrief after work with the mysterious Mr and Mrs Braithwaite, who were due to arrive at the Lodge House later in the morning. Emma and Grandma Frost had already cleaned and scrubbed the cottage to create a most welcoming temporary home for their protectors.

Chapter Twenty-Nine

Pip managed to produce a watery smile when he saw me approach him on Pargiter Ward. He looked surprised, as if he wasn't expecting me. He wasn't. The staff had forgotten to tell him.

'It's fine. I'm pleased you came; it's really good of you. I can't seem to get over the shock. We could have been a mangled mess like Ben,' Pip stated the obvious, and the pain of the thought was showing plainly on his face.

His time on the ward had been well spent. Strings had been pulled to access psychology for him, rather than making the poor man wait for months for an available appointment. Cynically, I assumed this was purely because he and Father Raymond had been hailed as have-a-go heroes for their valiant attempts to save Ben. When giving chase, Pip had managed an ankle-tap rugby tackle, which had sent Ben sprawling, but Ben had leapt up and run off again. This moment haunted Pip. 'I nearly had him,' he said, in a voice laden with regret. 'I'm not fit enough, that's the trouble, and he ran so fast.

'He didn't want to die, Monica, he was screaming for help. He thought he was burning, Flapping at himself, he was. I can't sleep without hearing the screams.'

I didn't want to make Pip relive the nightmares but what he had to say was important, so I pushed for more detail.

'Did he say who he was running from?'

'Not really. He said the police were going to get him, but that was normal for Ben. He'd only been released from the cells the night before and had a few beers in the Green Man after that until quite late. Karen said he staggered out of there with another bloke at gone ten o'clock but I don't know what he did in the morning.'

'What was Karen doing out drinking at that time of night on a Wednesday?' This was a revelation. Karen didn't even look like much of a drinker.

'She wasn't. She was given a trial as a barmaid three or four weeks ago and they love her there. She's like a new woman.'

'Well, that's brilliant. Good for her and her self-confidence. Did she know the man Ben left the pub with?' I began to think out loud, 'I wonder if Ben stayed with him overnight? He didn't go home, you see. Don't worry, I'll ask Karen myself.' I had, at that very moment, seen Father Raymond enter the ward and he strolled sedately down the corridor towards us.

Pip leapt up to greet him.

I don't know why, but I wasn't expecting them to embrace. They held each other at arm's length at first, as if checking each other for signs of completeness. Satisfied, they held on to each other like two long-lost friends as I registered the significance of what I had seen. More than two people who had bonded through misfortune, or indeed through survival of a tragic event, these two men held deeper emotions. They loved each other. Father Raymond held one of Pip's hands within two of his own, and made a show of saying a short prayer. Pip accepted the blessing with nothing short of adoration in his eyes.

'You look so much better today, Pip.'

'I feel better, stronger in myself. It's lovely to see Monica. I don't have to pretend in front of her, she understands how I feel about Ben's death. You're easy to talk to, Monica.'

I made light of Pip's comment. 'I should hope so, Pip, it's my job. I'd like to think I was easy to talk to. Thanks for the vote of confidence.' I smiled broadly. Inside, I wondered how long Pip and Father Raymond had been in love for, and who else knew the secret. It was a remarkable testament to their discretion that their forbidden relationship hadn't been revealed, because being with the two men, I could feel the intensity of their feelings for each other, in every movement and touch they made. So much so that I felt like a gooseberry, intruding on their precious moments together.

'Shall I find us some drinks? I'll get them from the cafeteria, it's better quality from there. Who would like what?'

Making good my escape, I used the opportunity to check in with Emma. She was at the Lodge House with the Braithwaites, who had settled in and were already sifting through paperwork and setting up files. 'How's it going?' Emma asked.

'I'll tell you later, but I'm not sure if I can speak to Father Raymond on his own today. Change of plan. Can you let the team know not to expect an "earwig"? Thanks.' She knew what I meant.

On my return to the ward, another wondrous reveal was in store for me. 'I'm going into the priesthood like Father Raymond,' said Pip proudly, and again he looked at Father Raymond for assurance.

'Really? Can you do that at your age? Sorry, I don't mean to be rude, Pip, but I thought you went straight from altar boy to priesthood in the Catholic Church? You'll have to forgive my ignorance.' My powers of deduction would have had Sherlock turning in his fictional grave. For a while I couldn't tell if Father Raymond and Pip were in love, or if they were simply full of love for God.

'The Jesuits accept men at the time they find God. *Ad Majorem Dei Gloriam*. For the greater glory of God, Monica.' Good grief. My favourite Latin phrase had almost the opposite meaning. *Nil Desperandum*. Never despair.

'Pip is hoping to gain a place at a seminary to begin his training, but we're still discussing this. It's a life-changing commitment to make,' Father Raymond confirmed.

'I already have degrees in philosophy and theology and Father Raymond has been helping me with my preparations. I've moved into the Rectory to help out until a new priest is found for the diocese.'

How convenient.

Pip was as excited as a child at Christmas, and perhaps all his presents *had* come at once. No one seeing his enthusiasm and certainty would think he was in his late thirties. Or that shyness and anxiety had plagued his adult life.

'Well, good on you. If that's what you believe, then I wish you all the best with whatever adventure awaits you.' I meant it. What I had witnessed was a forbidden romance, and the story was reaching a thrilling crescendo now that the couple had found a way of being together which would look acceptable from an outsider's view. A priest, preparing his novice for priesthood, living at the Rectory together. What an opportune cover story. Chillingly, I also realised that Father Raymond could simply have groomed Pip to do his bidding.

'When will you be discharged from here, any idea?' I asked. With Pip living at the Rectory I was presented with an opportunity to track down the truth about Father Joseph's private life, and his death. If only I could secure another invitation to tea.

'In the next day or so, I hope. I'm not on a Section and I'm really only here to recover from shock. My mind seemed to depart for a while, so that I didn't have to deal with the psychological trauma, I suppose. I can't remember.'

I was feeling bolder. 'Crikey, are you sure you did philosophy at uni? Sounds like you could have studied psychology. Forgive me for prying, but you said, Father Raymond, that Pip here is going to become a Jesuit. I'm completely ignorant about what the differences are between types of priest, so what is a Jesuit and why do you want to be one of those as opposed to a Benedictine monk?'

I was deliberately showing my ignorance to both of them, but the 'please explain, I don't understand' approach had served me well over the years.

'Father Raymond is a Jesuit, aren't you?' Pip said, his eyes darting to Father Raymond and back to me. That gem of information was enough to put me on my guard and I seriously regretted not being able to use the earwig fob.

The Jesuits, I had read, were referred to as the soldiers of God, who took a fourth vow to obey the Pope. They were seen as a powerful organisation of considerable influence within the Vatican. Assassins, according to some theorists.

A cold sensation crept outwards from my stomach. It was entirely reasonable to assume the Father Joseph had died at the hands of an assassin ordered by the Pope to secure the good name of the Catholic Church. Father Raymond had been sent to befriend Jan and had uncovered Nick Shafer's intentions. He must be working with DS Charlie Adams, and had now recruited Pip, I concluded.

Three killers? Was that likely?

'There's nothing mysterious about Jesuits, Monica. We're the same as other priests really, apart from the fact that we serve the needs of the vulnerable, poor, frail, sick, and hungry and we go where we are sent. The street priest role is part of what I do, which is why I don't wear full vestments, not even a cassock.'

'Yes, why is that?' I asked, trying to sound nonchalant and interested, when in fact my mind was whirring.

'Well, we work within the community, rather like yourself, and the guidance is to wear ordinary clothes. I suppose the same reasons apply; uniform of any kind can create barriers. Some of my brothers don't even wear the dog-collar.'

'I'm finding this such a fascinating conversation. Perhaps tea and cake at the Rectory when Pip is better, would be in order,' I suggested. 'It would be lovely to hear about your hopes and ambitions, Pip. But don't get the wrong end of the stick, Father Raymond, I'm still not planning on converting.' That was without doubt my finest acting ever. I managed to sound confident and cheerful, and I had looked them both in the eye.

With the visit agreed in principle, I asked Father Raymond to phone me to let me know when I could visit to see how Pip was progressing after his discharge. Perfectly reasonable for a community mental health nurse to offer such a service, and therefore not out of the ordinary as a request.

Bubbling away in my mind was a plan, which needed careful consideration and guidance from the team behind me.

I made my way to the Lodge House.

Chapter Thirty

'How do you know they've been destroyed accidentally?' I asked. Milo Granger grabbed me by both shoulders and looked me directly in the eye in a determined effort to force the simple message through.

'Because our reliable informant assures us that the CCTV tape has been wiped. It was due to human error, a case of "erase" instead of "edit". Most likely it was deliberate. We requested the tape, pretending to be part of an undercover operation by Trading Standards, and succeeded only because the security provisions at Hollberry Police Station are slack. Or we would have done, if the tape hadn't been destroyed before it was even copied or digitalised. There is no way we should have been able to gain access that easily. Anyway, our attempts to identify the man escorting Ben Tierney from the Green Man last Wednesday evening have been scuppered, unless we question the locals, which could be risky, and too obvious.'

The idea of going to the pub for a well-earned drink was appealing, and although Max would be a token Welshman in an Irish pub, there was no reason why we couldn't go to the Green Man and ask a few questions. The landlady knew who I was, anyway. 'It would be perfectly normal for me to ask lots of questions,' I suggested to Milo. 'I could wear the earwig fob under my jumper.'

Max was offered the chance to take the male lead in the next James Bond plot. He was instructed to take me out for the evening and show me a good time, as long as we went to the Green Man, on Wednesday, had a few beers and settled for a late curry. His function was to be engaging and witty, inquisitive without arousing suspicion and to make sure we spoke to as many regulars as we could manage. I would be under his protection. He was thrilled to be asked; the alpha male, Max, felt wanted again.

Between Tuesday evening and our planned trip to the pub the next day, Emma and I were advised to maintain our usual routines as far as possible. Max and Jake seemed to have no problem in complying with this advice, however I was becoming twitchy and impatient. Not a word had been heard from DS Adams since his apologetic text, and this made me nervous. However, I did receive a short message from Father Raymond to let me know that Pip would be home from hospital before the weekend, meaning that part two of the plan could be pencilled in for Thursday.

'Here she comes, Mrs Part-Time,' I heard Kelly say as I stepped through the office front door. Assuming rather kindly that Kelly had not meant for me to overhear her waspish remark, I chose to ignore it. Barbara's scowl aimed at Kelly was still evident on her face as I said good morning to them both while retrieving my message book. There was even a message to me from Kelly herself, announcing that she had typed up my draft report on Ben Tierney, for the coroner. Evidently, she was eager to avoid talking to me.

'Thanks, Kelly, I can finish working on it today, with any luck.'

Kelly nodded, but declined to make any eye contact.

'You look less harassed this morning, Monica,' Barbara commented.

'Yes, I feel a bit better. I managed to sleep without too many dead body flashbacks for once. Also, the medicines amnesty finishes this week, thank God. I've had enough of it, to be honest. It turned into a publicity game for the Trust instead of a genuine attempt at improving suicide rates. I shan't bother next time, so kick me if I volunteer for anything that stupid again.' Barbara agreed to keep an eye on my potential for making rash decisions.

Eddie had heard my voice and appeared silently in the doorway of the main office, where Kelly presided over the comings and goings of the team. 'Can I have a chat in my office please, Monica?' He was wise enough not to hint at the reason for this request, just as I did not ask, until we were well clear of Kelly's keen sense of hearing.

'The coroner has opened a new inquiry into the death of Jan Collins. You were with him yesterday. Did he say why?' I sat staring at Eddie, not knowing which answer to give. Half a lie, or a whole lie. Denial seemed to be the safest option.

'No idea. Sorry. He scrutinised my report but asked me to make it much more comprehensive and was quite critical, actually. He kept me waiting for hours.' Eddie appeared to accept this and apologised for the interruption to my routine.

'Why? Is it important?' I asked.

'I'm not sure. I had a phone call from DS Adams a few minutes ago wanting to know if your report had been submitted to the coroner or not. He even asked for a copy.'

I froze.

'Monica, sit down, you look like you're going to faint.'

'Did you send him a copy? What did you tell him?' I felt dreadfully sick.

'No, I didn't let him have a copy, what do you take me for? Jesus, Monica. I told him the coroner had asked for the report well before it was due and that it had been sent on Friday. He wanted to know why the coroner had asked to see you, that's all.'

'You told him that I'd been to see the coroner?' I rushed out of the office, straight to the toilets and threw up. Charlie Adams would be furious. He would have worked out that I was the reason for a new inquiry. A new inquiry also meant the connection between the deaths was being looked into, that's why the CCTV tapes from the Green Man were wiped. Bloody effing Nora! Fuck, shit, and bollocks.

Sometimes there aren't enough swear words.

Eddie thought I had a nasty case of gastric flu and swiftly sent me packing. Firmly rejecting the offer of a lift home, I shakily drove to Folly Farm. Emma was at work, which I only realised when Grandma Frost answered the door. Barely stopping to pass the time of day, I did an about-face and headed to the Lodge House.

The Braithwaites were both firmly established in their new home office premises and were found beavering away, collating the streams of information coming in. They sat me down with a hot drink and reassuring words.

'He's fishing. He hasn't worked anything out yet. Monica, you're doing a brilliant job. Have you got your laptop with you? Good. We'll make your reports password protected so that nobody else can print them off and send them. Milo can update Mr Williams to instruct your managers and the police to comply with new security requirements for electronic document storage, transmission or faxed reports. We'll tie them up in knots for a while.'

'I don't think he's fishing, I think he caught a fish. Eddie told Charlie Adams that I had been asked to see the coroner urgently. Charlie will be desperate to know what the meeting was about.' The words had barely left my mouth when my work mobile rang. It was Kelly. 'Christ, what now? Hello, Kelly.'

There was no polite enquiry as to my wellbeing.

'I have a call for you from the police,' and without so much as an excuse me, she transferred the call.

'Hello, Monica.' I recognised the caller's voice immediately. I held my left hand up and bent my little finger while my eyes sought help from the Braithwaites. Both gave encouraging gestures, and without hesitation Mrs Braithwaite leant forward to press both buttons on my earwig fob, which made me pull back with uncertainty as to her intentions. I refocused.

'Is that you, Charlie?' I asked, trying to gather my thoughts.

'Yes, hi. Sorry to bother you but I've received notification that the coroner is opening a new inquiry into Mrs Janet Collins's death, and I wondered what you knew about this.'

I hesitated.

'Well, I didn't know until my manager told me. He said he'd heard it from you this morning.' There were firm nods from both

Braithwaites and Mr Braithwaite made a rolling motion with his forearms as if he was about to sing 'The wheels on the bus go round and round'.

'I'm not sure I can help you.' I made an exaggerated silent-panic face.

'That's a shame. I spoke to your manager, Edward, and he mentioned that you were ordered to see Mr Williams, the coroner, on Monday morning. Why?' Charlie wasn't mincing his words and I knew he was waiting for further hesitation, or stumbling speech to give away my lies.

'Oh, he was very rude. He demanded to see me, then kept me waiting for hours on end. When I did see him all he did was criticise my report.'

'What did he criticise exactly?'

I replied straight away. 'Said it wasn't comprehensive enough and was sub-standard. I was quite offended. Why? Have you been asked for a report as well?' I knew full well that Charlie had written the report for the police, but I was careful not to reveal this fact.

'Yes of course. I was the detective on scene just after you had left, as you know. The coroner hasn't asked to see me, though.'

I glanced up at the Braithwaites from my chair looking for guidance. 'Oh, that's lucky for you, then,' I replied while reading the piece of paper scribbled on by Mrs Braithwaite. 'Perhaps the pathologist has questioned something. Look, I don't really know, Charlie, and to be honest I've been sent home from work ill, so coroner's reports are not on my list of priorities. Being near a toilet is. Probably a bit of food poisoning. Nothing to worry about.' I was starting to ramble, and Mr Braithwaite made a "cut" gesture across his neck ordering me to stop talking.

'Okay, thanks. Sorry to bother you. I'm sure we'll get confirmation sooner or later. Get well soon.' Charlie had sounded distracted as he ended the call. Perhaps he had been just been fishing.

'You did fantastically well. No hesitation, neat and concise. Well done.' Relieved, I let out a long slow breath, making my lips flap. Mr Braithwaite aimed a finger towards my chest. 'You might want to turn that off now.' I'd forgotten about the earwig fob, even though a silent text had come through on my personal mobile to say it was working.

'Did they hear everything?'

'Loud and clear and we now have a lovely voice sample for Charles Adams. Whereabouts in the Midlands is he from? Do you know?' Shaking my head, I gave a short, snorting nasal laugh. That small fact, Charlie's accent, I had been correct on. Hurrah. My sleuthing days were not over.

Chapter Thirty-One

Max and I stepped out of the taxi, which had pulled up several yards away from the entrance to the Green Man, necessitating use of the umbrella we had taken with us. It was pouring down with relentless, fat raindrops, the gusty wind threatening to turn the brolly inside out. Determinedly we faced it into the wind and ran together towards the door of the pub, making clowns of ourselves as we manoeuvred with the umbrella through the doorway.

We fell into the warm smoky atmosphere of the pub, mocking each other. There was a decent crowd in the compact bar area. Some customers were sitting in small groups at tables, and the regulars were propping up the bar. Behind it I spotted Karen beaming at me.

'Come to check up on me, have you?' she joked. 'I spoke to Pip earlier and he said you'd been to see him. That was good of you.' I introduced Max, who began his charm offensive by chatting amicably to Karen and asking her about the types of beer on offer.

'I'll have a pint of that. Your recommendation was spot on,' Max said as he finished the small sample of an ale that Karen had poured. 'Do you work here full-time?' he asked. This could easily have sounded like a bad chat-up line, but somehow Max had the knack of relaxing people into conversations by being genuinely interested. He engaged a few of the regulars in cordial banter about what to look forward to in the coming rugby season, which predictably set the Irish against the English regulars and resulted in healthy wisecracks flying to and fro. Max took the brunt, as the only Welsh rugby supporter to be found in the building.

With my husband entertaining the crowds, I pushed the two recording buttons on my fob from the outside of my thin V-neck jumper, and managed to speak to Karen about the events of the previous week. She remembered seeing Ben Tierney. 'I can't forget. He was really drunk, but not so bad that he was ranting, like he sometimes did.' Karen remembered seeing Ben sitting with a man that none of the regulars recognised. 'He never took his baseball cap off. Ben had four or five pints while I was here. He may have had more, but they were already drinking when I started my shift, so I'm not sure. The bloke in the hat didn't look as if he'd had much to drink. They sat over there, whispering together. I think Ben started crying, which is why they left.' Karen pointed to a small round table in a corner by the entrance to the pub.

Karen turned to an elderly gentleman, sitting on a bar stool to the right-hand side of the bar where he had propped himself against the wall. 'Joey, do you remember the man who was sitting with Ben Tierney last week? On Wednesday, the night before Ben died?'

'D' fella in the baseball cap? Sullen lookin'. Don't know who d' fella was. Never seen him before.' Joey flicked the ash from his creased roll-up into the ashtray before returning the cigarette to his nicotine-stained lips. The landlady appeared from the staff entrance behind the bar, and she recognised me immediately. I didn't even know her name until Karen introduced me. 'Theresa, this is Monica, she's Ben's community nurse.' Karen then looked at me with a worried expression on her face. 'Am I allowed to say that?'

Theresa was keen to talk to me about Ben, and about his parents, and the locals tuned in, to listen to our conversation. They had already had a whip-round and sent Sean and Manuela some flowers.

'Is there anything else we can do to help them? The poor souls, they must be in purgatory,' Theresa said, wringing her hands and slowly shaking her head. 'I still don't know why he was sittin' with that copper last week …' This was almost a throwaway line.

'The man with the baseball cap?' I asked. Max had noticed the change of tone in my voice and gently slid up the bar to where I was standing.

'I can tell them a mile off; coppers. I thought it was strange. Ben had been banged up since the evenin' before, so what he was doing with a copper? I don't know. What I do know is that the copper had something over on Ben. He was still interrogating the poor boy, right here in the pub. They were doing what I call "loud whispering", so I caught what they said before they left. Plod offered to take Ben for something to eat. I could be wrong on this, but from what he said and the way he said it, I think the plan was for Ben to go back to his house with him to have a bite to eat there.'

'Did you tell the police this?' I asked.

'Of course, I did. I even told them about his missing finger.' At this I choked on my glass of cider. Incapacitated by coughing and spluttering, I couldn't speak for a while, so Max tried to rescue the situation by taking up my role. 'Who, Ben?'

'No, the copper. He had half his little finger missing. I told the police that. They'll be able to identify him from the CCTV tapes we gave them anyway. Carl followed them up the road a while, on his way home, but he didn't see Ben go into a house with anyone. We told the police that too. I s'pose they'll be investigatin',' Theresa said.

The crowd of regulars in the bar began to speculate on the possible reasons for Ben drinking with one of his sworn enemies, but I switched off the fob, satisfied that enough had been divulged to indicate that Charlie Adams had probably been the last person to see Ben alive.

Suspect number one, intent on killing Ben Tierney, had taken him home and given him a poison sandwich.

Max and I pretended to enjoy our evening in the pub and our curry afterwards, but both of us realised that we were steadily progressing towards an inevitable moment of reckoning. The unpredictable conclusion to events was coming our way and we had no clue as to how this might happen or what it would entail.

It was after lunchtime the next day before I noticed that Kelly had phoned my work mobile and had left a message. Apparently, Karen had contacted the office and asked to speak to me personally. Would I please call her on the number provided by text to follow. The message ended with a humdinger; 'I take it you made a miraculous recovery. Karen seems to think she met you and Max in a pub last night.' Bugger. I had taken the day as a continuation of my sickness and not made any effort to go into work. That morning I had filled my time with chores by the dozen and hard-core housework to loud music, which took my mind away from the tension of waiting for Father Raymond to call me.

I decided not to respond to Kelly, but I did pick up the text and speak to Karen.

'Theresa thought you may be interested to hear that the police came to the pub first thing this morning. They asked for the CCTV tapes for last night. Apparently, they have accidentally wiped the tape from last Wednesday, and they want to see if the mysterious man in the baseball cap appears again this week. Theresa told them that it would be highly unlikely but they took the tapes anyway. They won't see anything because of the rain, so it was pointless. But at least they're investigating.'

I thanked Karen for the call and took the time to say how much Max and I had enjoyed the company at the Green Man the previous evening, congratulating her on finding a job that suited her so well. The police must have been clutching at straws to bother with those tapes, I thought. The cameras were outside the building and it had been bucketing down with rain for most of the evening, making it impossible to identify customers as they made their way in and out of the pub.

I called Emma for advice. She was with the Braithwaites. Neither of us had bothered to ask either of them what their real names were, it was so much easier not to know. 'You did a brilliant job in the pub last night, you and Max. What a corking bit of evidence,' Emma said. She was trying hard to bolster my flagging confidence.

'Come off it. You know as well as I do that it's circumstantial. The say-so of a landlady who believes the man was a copper, and that he happened to be missing half a little finger. We have to get more. You do realise that if Charlie sits watching that CCTV tape from last night, he'll recognise Max and me straight away. We got stuck in the doorway trying to get in at the same time as the umbrella we were carrying. We stood there for ages laughing at each other. Then, don't you see, Charlie can make enquiries as to what we were talking about in the pub and we're blown.'

'But what can he do about it? You're allowed in a pub with your husband, and as you said yourself, it would be normal to assume you would talk about Ben and ask questions. Charlie doesn't know we were looking for a half-fingered man. He doesn't know you were recording conversations in a pub. He doesn't know that we spoke to Sam in France. He's trying to find out who knows what, but he's fumbling around in the dark not knowing what he's looking for. A new inquiry into Jan's death has set him wondering, that's all. He'll make a mistake sooner or later. At least that's what the Braithwaites think.'

Talking things through with Emma always helped me to regain perspective, and to breathe, in between my frantic questioning of events. But I had barely settled down to drink a well-deserved cup of tea when my phone rang again.

'Please don't let it be Kelly,' I said, as I picked it up. I looked at the screen. 'Fat Ray'. Butterflies arrived in my stomach. Good grief, the pair of them were homing in on me now. Him and Charlie. Deep breath.

'Hello, Father Raymond. How's Pip doing today?' I asked, trying to sound bright but with a hint of concern. It turned out that Pip was doing so well he had been discharged home that morning. Eager to share his good news with me, he invited me for a slice of cake and a pot of Lyons red label tea the next day. 'Pip says you deserve proper loose-leaf tea, and not your average teabag tea,' Father Raymond announced.

'How thoughtful of him. Three o'clock, at the Rectory will be fine. Shall I bring anything along tomorrow, biscuits or more cake?' I asked.

'No, it's our treat. Just bring yourself.'

Did I have the mental strength to be the cowardly lion entering the Christians' den? I wondered.

Chapter Thirty-Two

I had begun to wonder about Pip and whether or not he could be Jan's inside man. He fitted the profile. He had a position of trust, perhaps intimacy, within the local Catholic Church and had studied philosophy and theology. At university, he could perhaps have come across Jan Collins, maybe as a lecturer and he as a student. Pip even fitted the bill for the mystery burglar who had carefully put Deefer into the shed while he ransacked our house.

Sweet Pip was now in the hands of a master manipulator, which gave me two aims for my teatime visit. Firstly, to expose Father Raymond and Charlie Adams as being guilty of murder, and secondly to save Pip.

I met with Emma, Jake, and Max that evening at the Lodge House. We sat in a cosy huddle, Deefer in the middle of us all, and our attention was directed towards the Braithwaites.

'We are now fairly certain that Charles Adams had the opportunity to carry out the poisoning of Father Joseph Kavanagh. He had attended the Rectory in response to complaints about threats to kill. Ben Tierney was reported as being in the grounds of the Rectory last Tuesday shouting accusations and making threats against Father Joseph. We now know that it was in fact Philip George who phoned the police, and not Father Raymond as we had believed.

'Police reports make no further mention of Philip George in connection with their enquiries into events that evening. DS Adams arrived at the Rectory shortly after Sean and Manuela Tierney delivered a steaming casserole dish containing chilli con carne. He then revisited the Rectory to inform Father Joseph that Ben Tierney had been taken into custody.'

Emma was much quicker on the uptake than I was. 'Oh, I see. He had to return to carry out the poisoning because he didn't have the essentials with him at the time.'

'It's one possibility. Of course, it could be coincidence and Father Raymond could have carried out the poisoning.'

'Do we know why Father Raymond didn't make the first phone call to the police? Or whether he was at home in the Rectory when DS Adams revisited later?' I asked.

The Braithwaites looked at each other and exchanged a couple of facial queries before they revisited the timeline diagram.

'*That* is a really good question. We're basing our information on the police reports. Philip George made the first call, which we could assume was done because neither of the two priests were at home. Perhaps they were at the church building. We'll try to clarify that. The report doesn't mention Father Raymond at all. Pip wasn't reported as being present when police attended so he's likely to have left and gone home at that point. Therefore we have to assume Father Raymond is still out somewhere. How interesting.'

Father Raymond had been clear in his description to me that he had heard Father Joseph falling and called an ambulance. 'What if Pip hadn't gone home, but instead had been retrieving the journals from our house and the documentation about Nick Shafer from here?' I asked, throwing my theory into the mix.

'Could Father Raymond have been following him?' Max suggested.

Emma, as sharp as ever, noticed the flaw in that possibility.

'Father Raymond had gone out somewhere *before* Pip left the Rectory though.' She looked at the Braithwaites for an answer. They both shrugged.

Everything felt like a series of spirals, which descended to a question mark, each time. 'Can we recap? I need to be really sure what I'm trying to find out tomorrow,' I asked in desperation.

Mr Braithwaite tried to précis the main aims. 'Nick Shafer's death: possibly on description alone, Charles Adams is the most likely suspect. Jan Collins's death: Possibilities are, Father Raymond or DS Adams. Father Joseph's death: possibilities are, Father Raymond, DS Adams or Philip George.'

I interrupted.

'No, not Pip. No way. '

'Yes way,' Emma said. 'Think about it. Pip is alone in the Rectory with Father Joseph. If Father Joseph had uncovered the illicit affair between Father Raymond and Pip, then there is your motive. He might look sweet and innocent, but this is the love of his life, his redemption from a life of exclusion, anxiety, depression, and being an all-round misfit.'

'Yep, then Father Raymond returns and they hatch a plan to make it look like a fall just happened,' added Jake, who had been silent until this offering from Emma had piqued his interest.

'It wasn't the fall that killed him though, it was a heart attack brought on by food poisoning from improperly cooked kidney beans. The man who knew all about them was Charlie Adams,' Max reminded me. The Braithwaites, who were taking notes throughout our debate, now turned to their laptop.

'Yes, Max, and he was boasting,' I confirmed. 'He mentioned about pressure cooking kidney beans to increase the toxicity, but Manuela Tierney used tinned beans, in fact she was embarrassed because she only had a small tin of beans at home and would normally have used more.'

'Why is it that women have such detailed conversations about tins of beans? Men wouldn't even bother. We just eat the food put in front of us, who the hell would notice if there weren't many beans in a chilli con carne?' Max was giving the male perspective on life as per usual.

'I think that's the point,' Mrs Braithwaite helpfully acknowledged. 'If, and it's a big "if" … if DS Adams or indeed Father Raymond had returned and added pressure-cooked kidney beans to the casserole dish, then there is our means for murder. A frail old man would not tolerate that level of toxicity. He already had a heart condition.'

Our murderer was doing well. He had used medication that would be in Jan Collins's medicine cupboard. He had used kidney beans to make Father Joseph's death appear to be food poisoning causing a cardiac arrest. Goodness knows what he used on poor Nick Shafer, but he burnt him afterwards for good measure, and Ben Tierney was given a killer supper.

That was where the poisoner had become rather thoughtless and lackadaisical. The murderer would have known that the contents of a stomach would be investigated at the post mortem and the deadly sandwich had not been digested enough when Ben had met an express train. Had Ben delayed eating it for some reason? Or had he escaped before it was intended that he should be allowed his freedom? More question marks at the end of spirals.

'Let's see if we can firm up some of the probables tomorrow when you meet with Father Raymond and Pip.'

'And how the hell do you suggest that I do that?'

The Braithwaites had created a posh, high-tech version of my 'safe topic and don't go there' list, that I had used when Max and I invited DS Adams to our house. Their adaptation was also simple and effective. The first topic was Jan Collins and her work as a lecturer, to determine whether Pip was our inside man or not. 'We've sent a message to Jan's insider to let him know that you've been invited to the Rectory for tea at three. We've requested support and guidance for you. Now this may mean that if your guardian angel is Pip, things will be relatively simple, or if not, then we could expect someone to turn up on the doorstep.

'Our other suggestion would be for Emma to drop you outside the Rectory giving the impression that she is on her way to collect the children from school and you needed a lift because of a car problem. A last minute flat tyre … Emma will then park around the corner, near the school, while Jake actually collects the children in his Land Rover.'

'Why? Why is Emma waiting outside, and not Jake, or Max?'

'Because they both should be at work, not sitting in cars. It draws too much attention as being out of the ordinary. Emma's car is not well known. Yours is. She can be in direct touch with us here and we'll feed her the necessary information. She'll call at the Rectory to collect you when your job is complete and we can safely remove you without arousing suspicion or you needing an excuse to leave. Our team on the ground will be on standby for any untoward eventualities.'

'Such as?'

'They mean threats or risks to your life.' I could hear the anger rising in Max's voice, which was more about the fact that he didn't seem to have a heroic role. Fortunately the Braithwaites had anticipated this.

'This is where you come in, Max. We have a new motorbike crash helmet for you. You'll also have a direct link to hear everything that Monica is listening to, but you'll only be able to communicate verbally with us here at the Lodge. If you can park a reasonable distance away, but be available to investigate any visitors, that would be great. We want the heads up on anyone approaching the Rectory driveway from the other direction. Emma will be the town side of Bushmead, and you need to be north of that with an eye on St David's Road, please. No one will recognise you in your motorbike gear.'

Max was visibly swelling with pride at being given such a vital task. I suspected that he would be superfluous to requirements, and that the IPCC team would already be watching the premises carefully from a van or a car nearby. Nevertheless, it made him feel like my protector, which was helpful to me in many ways.

I was beginning to suffer from palpitations at the enormity of the task ahead and the repercussions if we were wrong, or worse, if we were right and I failed. There was no backing out. The coroner and the IPCC were relying on me to succeed, and quickly. So were Emma, Jake, and the children 'You make sure that if it all goes tits-up, you and Jake take the children and Grandma Frost out of harm's way. Promise me,' I said to Emma with a quavering voice. 'We don't know who we are dealing with.'

The Braithwaites must have been reading my mind. They had been collating information about DS Adams who, it appeared, was due to be moved to another force in Humberside because of a successful promotion to Detective Inspector. His posting to Hollberry Police Station had apparently been a temporary arrangement to cover vacancies, and he was due for transfer within the next few weeks. Charles Adams's police career was peppered with moves, and yet he managed promotion without a hitch, it seemed. The records were scant but the ones screened by the Braithwaites indicated that he was used as a trouble-shooter for underperforming police departments.

Personnel records showed his true age to be thirty-four and that he had an aptitude for forensics. Nothing was known in depth about his private life and family connections, but his employment record had six years unaccounted for after his PhD in organic chemistry. His thesis had been on the subject of medical applications within organic toxicology.

'That's of no surprise,' I commented unnecessarily.

'We could hazard a guess that he may have been recruited by the spooks but we have nothing to confirm that … and we don't know if Charles Adams is a member of the trouser leg and funny handshake brigade or not. Our nearest guess would be that he's a hired gun. Or in this case, a paid poisoner. We're running checks on deaths, suspicious or otherwise, in the areas where he had previous postings.'

'Are you trying to suggest that he could work for a government organisation?' Emma looked horrified at the possibility. She was gesturing to Jake by placing her right palm to her heart.

'That's exactly what we're suggesting. We've also been delving into historical records concerning Father Joseph Kavanagh to determine why this particular set of events has occurred. The key seems to lie with who he invited to watch as the children were being abused; the paedophiles in the audience. We are certain that this is the reason for the extreme response.

'So far, we have strong possibilities for a Member of Parliament at the time, a high-up council official in charge of county planning, a manager from an investment bank in London, a CEO from a well-known arms manufacturer, and a scientist who may have links with security services. We can't disclose any more to you than that, but we wanted you to know just how incendiary this case is. If any one of these people are exposed as being involved in an abuse scandal then not only does it implicate them, but threatens the security of the country.'

'This could be shit or bust then,' I said without thinking. It had occurred to my flagging brain that without evidence, the coroner would be ineffective and there would be nothing to plaster across the media. The IPCC may continue the long, slow, grinding way towards proof of wrongdoing, but there was a clock ticking to prevent yet another cover-up of murder and abuse. I recalled Tam Aitken's description of the monstrous scale of the scandal being of 'such incredible magnitude that it is almost impossible to comprehend'.

He was right.

Chapter Thirty-Three

E mma looked me in the eyes, holding my hands in hers, as we sat in her car minutes before three o'clock. 'Right. Do what you can, if it's not safe, run and hide until we come to get you out. Are both your mobiles on silent and vibrate off?'

I nodded. My mouth was so dry that I didn't dare speak.

'Okay. Press those buttons on your earwig fob and let's make sure the bloody thing is working.' We waited and sighed with relief when the confirmation text message arrived. Emma double-checked her communications with the Braithwaites, who confirmed that they also had contact with Max.

'Here we go, Watson,' I said, hugging my best friend and not wanting to let go.

'Here we go, Holmes,' Emma replied. 'No, hang on, don't get out. A woman is walking up to the Rectory. Max says she's elderly and carrying a cake tin.' It was Dora delivering the Victoria sponge for tea. I decided to walk and meet her in case, by some ridiculous chance, she was Jan's inside man. Cutting a corner by forcing my way through a gap in the hedge at the boundary of the Rectory garden, I emerged at the front entrance at the same time as Dora.

'Are you invited to tea with the vicar?' I asked her, trying to sound normal.

'Hello, dear, where did you come from? No, I'm only the delivery woman. I'm running dreadfully late. I promised Father Raymond to have the cake here by half past two, but I waylaid myself trying to find my house keys. I'm becoming so forgetful these days. By the way, he's not a vicar, dear, he's a priest.' I thanked Dora for correcting me in time.

The large, oak door was opened by a smiling Pip who took charge of the cake and thanked Dora profusely for her generous offering. She would not be persuaded to stay. 'No, my dears, I have an appointment with the chiropodist and my feet would never forgive me if I missed it. Enjoy the cake.' Pip and I watched as she toddled down the garden path back towards the road.

'I wonder why she's wearing a cowboy hat?' Pip asked. A rhetorical question. We both smiled as we saw her step into the light from between the dark yew trees that lined the entrance to the Rectory.

Pip had taken my coat and was hanging it alongside a collection of dark robes, overcoats, and jackets when Father Raymond emerged from a doorway at the far end of the dimly lit, wood panelled entrance hall. There was a musty smell about the place, reminding me of my old school.

'Come on through, Monica, welcome to the Rectory kitchen, which is by far the warmest room in the place.' The Rectory was a substantial Edwardian building with high ceilings and spacious rooms. I stepped into a kitchen of farmhouse proportions. In the centre was a long refectory table that could easily have served to seat a dozen monks. Several tablecloths had been placed over its length in an effort to introduce a homely touch to the afternoon tea. Plates, cups saucers, and cutlery were laid at the end nearest to an ancient coal-fired Rayburn, which was pumping out a welcome, warming heat. On top of the hotplate stood a giant kettle with steam wisps falling from its spout. Next to it, a brown teapot was warming.

'Sit near the range, Monica,' instructed Father Raymond. 'You look cold and shivery. Winter's on its way, isn't it?' He strolled across to the range and poured the water from the kettle into the pot. 'Proper loose-leaf tea, as promised. We've even remembered the tea strainer, haven't we, Pip?' Pip was dexterously removing the magnificent sponge cake from its tin and placing it on a cake stand.

'Well, I am privileged,' I said. 'What a lot of trouble you've both gone to. I'm sure I don't deserve this sort of treatment.' I allowed my hosts to sit, and for Pip to start cutting slices of cake before making my opening gambit. 'So, Pip, how are you feeling since being out of hospital?' A gentle start, a normal, mental health nurse question. Pip gave a polite and informative answer about his relief at being able to leave hospital and his trouble sleeping. 'But, at least I'm getting psychotherapy. Once a week for the next ten weeks. I think I was lucky.'

'You are. There's usually a waiting list. And aren't you fortunate to be moving in here, as well? You'll be good company for each other, I should imagine.' The conversation was stilted, but I persevered. 'Was it just you and Father Joseph who lived here before?' I asked Father Raymond. He nodded. 'Do you have a housekeeper like Mrs Doyle in *Father Ted*?'

I smiled as I asked this.

'Yes, and no. We have a housekeeper, but she's not like Mrs Doyle.' He then made an excellent joke by asking, 'Will you have a cup of tea? Ah, go on.' All three of us laughed, and it seemed to remove the awkward edge from proceedings. I was finding my stride.

'I expect you miss having Father Joseph around and having Pip here for company has been a godsend, I dare say ... oh, excuse me. I didn't mean to be rude.' In the most difficult of situations I had managed to choose the wrong words. The smiles indicated that I had been forgiven.

'Father Joseph and I lived very separate lives, Monica. We had our own ministries, although occasionally we met for a meal out of courtesy. It was a terrible shame that he died before he could enjoy his retirement.'

'What sort of things does a retired priest do, if you don't mind me asking? What were his hobbies and pastimes?' I was struggling to steer the conversation in the right direction, so I sipped at my tea appreciatively and aimed my fork towards a large slice of moist sponge cake filled with jam, to buy thinking time.

'That's an interesting question. Many priests don't ever retire, they stay in post until they're too frail to continue, then the church cares for them. Father Joseph was asked to retire because his health was failing.'

'He was getting on a bit,' I conceded. 'I understand he was priest here about twenty years ago. Is it usual for priests to be moved around? I know you said you move quite a lot,' I said between mouthfuls. Pip was listening intently.

'Monica, you asked about Father Joseph's hobbies and now you ask about why he was moved from here twenty years ago. The answer to those two questions is the same. His hobby was molesting children and inviting influential friends to watch or take part.'

Standing up, I spat out my mouthful of cake into my hand and yet neither Pip nor Father Raymond reacted to my extreme response. They both sat silently, calmly waiting for me to finish spitting into my hand.

Father Raymond continued. 'But you already know this information. You also know that the deaths of Jan Collins and the man we knew as Liam Brookes were connected to the deaths of Father Joseph and Ben Tierney.' Despite my proximity to the warming range cooker, I was cold to the bone.

How much cake had I eaten?

How long had I got before the poison took hold?

Where could I run to and hide?

Could I run? My legs were leaden.

'Monica, look at me,' instructed Father Raymond. 'Pip is not the man you're looking for who worked with Jan Collins and studied with her. Pip works with me. He will have the same training I had.'

There was not a scale large enough on any crapometer to represent the fear that I felt at that moment. There had been no confession to murder and so I could not leave, but I had been exposed for what I knew and without doubt I would have to die.

'What poison did you use?' I asked, desperate for an admission of guilt. 'In the cake, what have you used to poison me?'

The silence was unbearable. Father Raymond and Pip stared at each other as if I had surprised them by my astute deduction.

'Goodness me, relax. We haven't poisoned you. Pip is not the guardian you are looking for, because I am,' Father Raymond said, standing up and clearing away my spit-splattered plate. I was shaking so much that I spilt my tea when I tried to take a calming sip. Father Raymond took that away from me too.

'Let's start again, shall we?' he said, sitting down next to me and taking my hand. 'Monica, you've been incredibly persistent and determined, and I'm here to help you, not to poison you. I've worked with Jan Collins for more years than I care to remember. She was a remarkable individual and Pip here will follow in her footsteps and mine. I am a Jesuit but not one who follows the orders of an organisation, I follow the truth of God himself, which is why I can never take the fourth vow of the Jesuit brotherhood, which is to obey the orders of the Pope.

'The church has veered dangerously away from God. No man should abuse children in His name, and no church should ever deny wrongdoing or the love of one man for another. God is love, Monica.'

I wasn't feeling the love. Nausea yes, love no. Pip was wiping the tablecloth and laying my place again, with clean cutlery and crockery. 'I don't think I can manage any more cake,' I confessed. 'In fact I need a few minutes to get myself together.' Pip gave me a hug as the tears of relief sprung from the corners of my eyes. 'I'm so sorry, we thought you were working with Charlie Adams,' I said to Father Raymond, 'and that you had killed Father Joseph and Jan. I can't believe we got it so wrong.'

'I hope by "we" that you mean Aitken, Brown and Partners. Only you and Pip know who I am and I'd like to keep it that way.' His face fell as he saw my reaction. 'Who else is involved?'

I was about to answer him when the doorbell rang. 'Probably Emma coming to collect me,' I said, feeling ashamed, guilty and generally wretched. Pip went to answer the door.

It wasn't Emma, but I heard a familiar voice echoing from the hallway. 'Shit,' I muttered, looking desperately at Father Raymond. 'That's Charlie Adams,' I whispered with my eyes wide in abject fear. *Run and hide.* I slid underneath the refectory table as Pip was being directed by Charles Adams to lead him to the delicious afternoon tea he'd heard about from Karen and Vanessa at St David's Church Hall.

'They were so helpful. I needed to talk to Monica Morris and they said she would be here. Her car isn't outside, oh, and I see she hasn't arrived yet. Never mind, I'll wait.' Charles Adams pulled out a chair at the end of the table. The opposite end from where I was hiding.

I couldn't see what was going on.

'No, I think we might have been stood up,' Father Raymond said. His confident lie was impressive.

My handbag remained next to the chair where I had been sitting and I reached out very cautiously to slide it beneath the table without being noticed. I was trembling through every limb in my body. Never mind flight or fight reactions, I was struggling not to lose control of my bowels. Crapometer readings were off the scale.

'I've brought along my own contribution. As you can see I've gone to a lot of trouble and cut off the crusts. A little bird tells me that you are vegetarian, Father, so for you I have prepared a special salad sandwich. For Philip there is a selection.' Charlie's voice was mocking and distant.

'While we wait for the charming nurse we shall play a game of sandwich roulette.

'Ever heard of coniine, gentlemen?

'No?

'But you will have heard of hemlock.

'Yes, I thought so.

'Pip, you go first.'

Chapter Thirty-Four

Managing to slip my mobile phone out of my bag, I sent a shaky text.

'I'm OK I'm under the table. WAIT.'

The rapid reply gave no encouragement.

'Too quiet, can't hear him.'

I couldn't risk crawling under the table. If I was a slim, tiny, dainty thing it might have been a different matter, but a woman of my Amazonian proportions would have sent chairs crashing. Tablecloths would have moved, exposing me as I dragged them off the table in my clumsy efforts to be closer to the enemy. The only choice I had was to remove the earwig fob from the lanyard and skim it along the floor towards the far end of the table.

'Tea?' I heard Pip ask in a high-pitched nervous squeak.

'Good idea, we'll need tea to wash the sandwiches down. I'll have cake,' I heard Charlie say with a cutting edge to his tone of voice.

There was a rattling of cups being placed on the table at the far end, giving me the opportunity to slide the fob along the wooden floor towards Charlie Adams's legs. My aim was wildly inaccurate and the fob hit the leg of a chair, ricocheting to the far right. It now lay outside the protective shelter of the table above it. I winced and held my breath, hoping that the noise had not been heard.

'What sort of tea is this, it looks a bit stewed? A fresh pot please, Philip, then you must have a sandwich of your choice.'

'Which ones should he look out for?' asked Father Raymond.

I needed paper and a pen. Trying not to make a sound, I found, in my handbag, my personal diary in which I wrote in large letters, *'any that smell like mouse'* and pushed the tiny diary between Father Raymond's knees.

'The ones with coniine in should be avoided, Father. I have manufactured a superbly intense alkaloid so we shan't have to wait long to see the effects. It should make for a much more interesting game, don't you think?

'When they find you, it will look just as if you've poisoned your secret lover, and killed yourself in a bizarre suicide pact. Not a last supper, a last afternoon tea. How quaint.

'Oh yes, I know about you two. Too obvious. Gay priests frolicking together by the railway tracks.' A bitter snigger added to the insulting way in which Charlie Adams addressed Father Raymond each time he spoke to him.

A silent text came through to my personal mobile. *'Loud and clear. Prepare to be evacuated. One confession needed.'*

What did they mean, one confession needed? Pip was risking death in the next few minutes. 'Is that the same sort of sandwich you gave to Ben Tierney?' Father Raymond was playing for more time, but it was a beautiful choice of question, if only he knew it. A confession should be imminent, I thought.

'No, that was my speciality for mental health patients, Datura Stramonium, a member of the deadly nightshade family, and it contains all sorts of lovely anticholinergic alkaloids. It always fools the ignorant. This one is different, remember, I said so. Eat up, Pip.'

'It smells a bit funny,' Pip said. From my position on all fours under the table, I saw Father Raymond stand suddenly. There was a scuffling of chairs and the whole table moved above me making a dreadful scraping noise on the floor.

'No, Pip, don't eat it! I'll eat it,' I heard Father Raymond say in despair. Then Pip shouted, 'No, Ray, please don't.'

Charlie Adams was applauding loudly. 'Bravo, bravo. A bloody excellent game.'

I sent a text with tremulous fingers. *'Get an ambulance and get here now'.*

Father Raymond slumped back down onto his chair and my eyes were then level with his knees. So I reached out and touched him to let him know I was there.

'Pip, you might as well have a sandwich now, because lover boy Ray has had a big bite of his. Finish up now, Ray, there's a good man. I can't leave until they're all gone, or you are.' Charlie let out a sigh as if he was being kept waiting for an appointment. Pip had moved to kneel next to Father Raymond. 'Come on now, Philip, you might as well eat yours now; life's not going to be worth living without him. Think … you can be together forever.'

The doorbell rang.

'Oh, how lovely, that will be Nurse Monica, better late than ever. I'll let her in, shall I?'

As Charlie got up from the table, I stuck my head out from under the overhanging tablecloth and mouthed for Pip to run. He didn't move.

Instead, we listened, spellbound, to the commotion from the entrance hall.

Emma's voice. 'Sorry she can't come, she sends her apologies.' Then the most astounding, thunderous, crashing noise of body hitting floor I'd heard in all my years as a psychiatric nurse.

'*I* don't apologise, you bastard!'

Max.

There was more thudding and groaning before I could hear the voices of the IPCC's officers arriving to take over from my husband. 'Well done, sir, I think we'd better take it from here in case you overstep the mark.'

Charlie could be heard groaning, 'What the fuck?'

As Emma raced into the kitchen, with Max not far behind her in his full biker gear, Father Raymond collapsed onto the floor with Pip holding him.

Father Raymond's body was limp, but in his eyes the terror showed, as his breathing became fearfully shallow.

'The ambulance won't get here in time,' Emma said, as she rushed over to us.

'He'll be okay if we breathe for him. Wipe his mouth,' I barked as I grabbed my handbag from beneath the refectory table to find a small bottle of alcohol hand rub that I kept for no-soap situations. I passed it to Emma who used a tissue to wipe Father Raymond's lips and chin.

Emma and I took it in turns to give mouth to mouth, as we had been trained to do, every year, on a dummy. The nursing instinct had taken over.

Pip was as calm as he could manage.

'Keep talking to him. He can hear us, he's not dead. We just have to keep breathing for him until the ambulance arrives, the poison wears off eventually,' I said to Pip, trying to explain before taking my turn again. Emma was still in phone contact with the ambulance control centre. 'Speak to Guy's Poisons Unit. Tell them it's coniine, like hemlock. Same thing, apparently. We're doing mouth to mouth, please hurry.'

Emma and I sat in A&E for what seemed like an eternity of tension and uncertainty. Playing eye-spy and engaging in some less than complimentary people-watching, we made valiant efforts to distract ourselves. This failed to keep our attention for long, so Emma had then taken to wandering across the room to stare out of the window towards the psychiatric admissions wards in the block opposite. It did at least break up the strain of endless waiting.

Although it was getting dark outside, the car park was well lit.

'Here come the police with another one of ours, by the look of things. Yep. That's our friend Harvey and his wailing, German mother, causing havoc as usual. She's being comforted by Toni who's utterly drained, poor woman.' Taking my cue from Emma's running commentary, I made my way to her side. We watched together as a screeching Mrs Fields remonstrated with the police and tried to block the doorway to prevent her son from being admitted. 'That's not going to help,' I confirmed. 'Look, the police are having none of it.'

When the brief drama was over, we plodded slowly back to where we had set up camp in the waiting room on unyielding plastic seats. A&E was an uninspiring department, lit by unflattering fluorescent lights, some of which were flickering enough to set off epilepsy.

Seeing the police had set me thinking. 'I hope they lock Charlie Adams up securely; I wouldn't want him coming after me again. What with him and Frank Hughes both being on my 'should be put down list' and me on theirs, I'm going to be in a precarious position when they see freedom again. In fact, my life expectancy has shortened dramatically in the past few weeks.'

'It's been a bit of a weird one, hasn't it?' Emma commented, ever the mistress of understatement.

When we'd arrived at A&E, shortly after the ambulance, it was obvious that the staff were not hopeful that Father Raymond would make it through the next few hours. So we lied and told the staff that Pip was Father Raymond's brother, enabling him to stay by his side. 'Who cares,' Emma had said, 'It's close enough to the truth, and sometimes a lie fits better anyway. God won't mind.'

'Yeah, well, God is love and all that bollocks. Want a cardboard coffee from the machine?'

'No thanks. It'll keep me awake tonight and I was rather hoping to be able to switch off my head. Ah … I spy with my little eye, something beginning with P.' As she said this, Pip appeared and we both sat up from our slumped positions on the uncomfortable seats. His facial expression was difficult to read.

'Well?'

'He's alive.'

'Thank God for that,' I sighed, slumping again with relief.

'No. Thank you two for that. I don't know what to say.' Pip sat next to me and burst into tears, released from hours of nerves and facing the possibility that Father Raymond could have died. 'Twice in a matter of days … we nearly got killed by a train, then we're both nearly poisoned to death by a policeman. Our friend Jan is dead, Liam is dead, and Ben is dead, which will probably kill his parents. I don't want to talk about Father Joseph, but he's the reason behind all this death and devastation.'

'Exactly how much do you know?' Emma asked.

'Not much. You'll have to ask Ray when he recovers a bit more. He knew everything. But I *do* know that I can't become a priest in the Catholic Church. Not now I know about the abuse and the denials, the subterfuge, the politicians, and the government figures. I can't.'

'Ben was right all along, how bloody sad,' I said. 'Everyone thought he was deluded. You know, I still feel guilty for thinking that Father Raymond had poisoned Father Joseph and killed Jan. We thought he was hiding something because of the rumours he spread about Liam Brookes.'

Pip managed a watered-down version of a smile. 'I asked him about that myself. He did it to protect his oldest and dearest friend, Jan, from her own brother. Stepbrother, drug dealer, horrible piece of work, Frank Hughes. Ray and Jan decided between them that if Frank thought all her money had already been spent, then he would leave her alone, and that if they named Liam, the police would take his disappearance seriously enough to bother looking for him and uncover what happened to Nick Shafer, but they didn't.

'Ray changed the lock on the back door at her house, because Frank had broken in and stolen a load of cash while his sister was in hospital. What a despicable thing to do.' Pip shook his head.

'At least it explains who I saw at Jan's house the day I found her. It was Frank, looking to sneak back in. No wonder he hated me so much, I turned up at Jan's house twice when he was there, and at the Heights, at the funeral and the police station. He must have thought I was watching his every move.'

'What about you and Father Raymond?' Emma asked Pip, not one to shy away from an awkward question.

Pip did not side-step the answer. 'We discussed this before you came for tea, Monica, and we had hoped to break the news to you today over a slice of sponge cake, but some nasty individual ruined our big moment. We guessed you knew about our relationship, from how you were at the hospital, when you came in to see me. You were so thoughtful and accepting.

'The news is that Ray is leaving the priesthood for the same reasons that I can't join it and because we can't deny who we are. We'd like to work with the abuse survivors and try to see that justice is done, so we plan to get in touch with Tam Aitken.

'Imagine how powerful the message will be to the churches and the politicians when they hear the story *we* have to tell.'

'Danny Wakeman's listeners are in for a treat when he gets hold of this little beauty,' I said to Emma in a stage whisper, looking at Pip.

'Bring it on,' he said, grinning.

Chapter Thirty-Five

The Daily Albion:
Ex-Priest and his lover die in suicide pact:
Or is it something more sinister?

*T*he *small town of Lensham has been the subject of media attention for the past twelve months.*

First there was a series of unexplained deaths which all related to each other and to allegations of historical sexual abuse, a paedophile ring, and the Catholic Church.

A spokesperson from the offices of the Roman Catholic Archbishop of Westminster has emphatically denied any wrongdoing and insists "The Church takes seriously any such allegations and will take steps to commence an internal review of the evidence once this has been presented. However, at this time, no complaint has been received which relates in any way to abuses within the Catholic Church in Lensham".

Janet Collins, aged 54, divorced, was the first of the suspicious deaths in Lensham. Suicide was considered to be the most likely cause because of her history of mental health difficulties. But suicide was never proven and her brother, well-known local businessman, Frank Hughes, 47yrs, divorced, was arrested on suspicion of her murder but released with no charge 48 hours later. He is currently serving a sentence for serious drug offences.

Detective Sergeant Charles Adams, aged 34yrs and originally from Nuneaton, is on trial suspected of killing Mrs Collins. Coroner Mr Howard Williams is awaiting completion of the court hearings in the trial of Detective Sergeant Adams before he is able to announce a verdict regarding her death.

Jan Collins's journalist colleague, Nicholas Shafer, 47yrs old, was found dead in his flat in the South of France under suspicious circumstances, several weeks before the death of Jan Collins. He and Mrs Collins worked together to investigate and expose systemic abuse within the Catholic Church and their findings have formed evidence presented in the trial of Charles Adams, as have the statements from several adults who claim to have been abused as children in the 1980's by the local priest.

Back in Lensham, shortly after the death of Jan Collins, Father Joseph Kavanagh of St Francis' Catholic Church, 78yrs old, died of a heart attack brought on by food poisoning, we are told. His death is also being considered in the murder trial of Charles Adams, as is the death of Benito Tierney, 32yrs old. Ben Tierney was married with two children, and was a mental patient who spent years making allegations of abuse against Father Joseph Kavanagh.

No one listened to him, no one believed him.

Until now.

Two days ago the bodies of ex-Jesuit priest, Raymond Lovell, aged 52, and his companion Philip George aged 39, known as Pip, were found in the remains of a disused church in Swandale, near Lensham. The two men had been missing for a fortnight and had been due to give evidence in the trial of Charles Adams, who also stands accused of the attempted murder of these two men, six months ago.

It remains to be seen if the statements they made to the police will be admissible as evidence. The official statement from the police would have us believe that Raymond and Pip died in a suicide pact as a result of media attention and exposure of their homosexual relationship. However, their friend Monica Davis, who found the two men, has made an exclusive statement to The Daily Albion in response to these assumptions by police.

"I received a message from Father Ray's phone. Asking me to meet with him and Pip at the old St Mary's Church in Swandale, but I knew from the smell as I approached the altar, that they were dead. They were holding each other, hidden, lying on the ivy. There is no way they decided to take their own lives, and neither of them owned

a gun, so how did they die of shotgun wounds to the head and still manage to hold on to each other? It smacks of suspicious circumstances and a message being sent by whoever killed them. There's not a chance it was suicide. They were happy, didn't worry about being outed as gay, and were doing amazing work investigating and exposing historical child sexual abuse. They didn't want to die, besides which, dead men don't send text messages. When I found Ray and Pip dead, I ran for my life through the back of the ruins. I just left my car where it was and went to the nearest house."

Monica and her husband are now in hiding under the witness protection programme and due to give evidence in the trial of Charles Adams next week.

Questions remain: who killed Raymond Lovell and Philip George?

Who is desperate enough to cover up the abuse of children and why?

How many more cases of child abuse have there been that have been disregarded or ignored?

The Daily Albion will be investigating.

THE END

Acknowledgement

In the UK, the Independent Inquiry into Child Sexual Abuse (IICSA) was set up in 2014 following the investigations of 2012 and 2013 into the Jimmy Savile sex scandal, which brought to light serious allegations involving a number of public figures and institutions. To date the inquiry has had four different chairpersons.

Decisions taken to withdraw were made with 'deep regret' and cited a 'legacy of failure' or perceptions that the chair was in a conflicted position in terms of the individuals or establishments being investigated.

At one point twelve separate investigations were announced as part of the inquiry.

As follows:

- Children in the care of Lambeth Council
- Children in the care of Nottinghamshire Councils
- Cambridge House, Knowl View and Rochdale Council
- Child sexual abuse in the Anglican Church
- Child sexual abuse in the Roman Catholic Church
- The sexual abuse of children in custodial institutions
- Child sexual abuse in residential schools
- The internet and child sexual abuse
- Child exploitation by organised networks
- The protection of children outside the United Kingdom
- Accountability and reparations for victims and survivors
- Allegations of child sexual abuse linked to Westminster

In June 2017 the group *Survivors of Organised and Institutional Abuse* (SOIA) announced that it was formally withdrawing from the inquiry. They stated that survivors had been "totally marginalised" and that the inquiry had descended into nothing more than a costly academic report writing and literature review exercise. An IICSA spokesperson said that they regretted the withdrawal, but the inquiry would continue.

Cover-up of cover-ups...?

Lightning Source UK Ltd.
Milton Keynes UK
UKHW012231050119
334976UK00001B/63/P